THE NURSE

Lucy Agnes Hancock

WILDSIDE PRESS

CHAPTER ONE

As a general rule, Susan Trent had little patience with people who indulged in self-pity. Yet this afternoon as she left home and walked the short mile to the Whittle Tool and Implement Plant where she was employed as nurse, she was feeling very sorry for herself. She wondered gloomily if anyone in the whole world had as much to contend with as she had. And it was all so unnecessary—or so it seemed to her.

The morning at the plant had been hectic. Some eighteen new employees had reported to the First Aid for their physical. Doctor Marshall was a stickler for detail and there were all those S-47 forms to fill out and file besides attending to the needs of the usual stray employees who straggled in at all hours suffering from headaches, stomach upset, cuts, burns or bruises. This morning had been just one of those days—they came every so often—and doctor and nurse had learned to take them in stride. That had been hard enough and then to go home to lunch to find friction—dissension. It was really too much.

A frown marred the smoothness of her forehead as she entered the building. Doctor Marshall wasn't in the big outer room—in fact, the place appeared deserted. This was against rules. Either she or the doctor was supposed to be on duty from eight until five every working day. Something must have happened. She hurried to her tiny private room and changed quickly into uniform. Whistles blew for one o'clock and she returned to the receiving room just as the doctor entered from the hall. He was obviously disturbed. He was wearing office whites under his overcoat and tossed the latter with his hat into a chair, then strode to a window. Susan didn't ask questions. She knew he would talk in a minute.

"I've been over to the foundry—an accident. They're bringing the injured here, Susan."

"Was it serious, Doctor? I mean——"

"Those I saw didn't look too bad but of course one never knows. I fixed up two or three and sent one—Jake Forsetti—to City. Here they come."

The factory carryall appeared and disgorged its passengers. Two cars trailed behind and from one a man was helped and practically carried up the short walk to the open door where Doctor Marshall waited to usher them inside. They were a sorry looking lot. Blackened and bloody, they staggered into the big room and as many as could sat down to await their turn. Doctor Marshall got busy. Several of those only slightly hurt he turned over to Susan who bathed and bandaged minor cuts and applied soothing medications to burns while listening to detailed accounts of what had happened. As she worked she made mental notes on each case to later record on the employee's S-47 and in between she assisted the doctor when he needed her.

The afternoon passed quickly. The last patient departed. The pungent smell of iodoform and formaldehyde together with numerous less penetrating odors hung like a pall over the room. Susan opened windows wide to the crisp October breeze. It felt heavenly against her flushed cheeks. Doctor Marshall lighted a cigarette and relaxed, his white-shod feet on his desk, his head resting against the wall behind him.

Susan drew a chair to the filing cabinet where she riffled through the hundreds of active S-47 forms, removing those she wanted. The factory carryall left the curb in front. Doctor Marshall stubbed out his cigarette and sighed in relief as he got to his feet. Sitting before the cabinet, Susan's thoughts were busy with matters quite outside the realm of first aid work. She had been at Whittle's now for nearly three years and found herself liking it better each day. It seemed unbelievable that she had ever hesitated about accepting the job when it was first offered her. Perhaps it was because she hated leaving the hospital where she was a favorite with the staff; but Cyrus Whittle, who had known her father and whose nurse was about to leave to return to private work, urged her to accept the position soon to be vacant. Susan had often told herself that she was not in the least mercenary; but when she heard what her salary was to be she accepted with alacrity. Why, she could quite easily take care of the family now! What did it matter if it wasn't as interesting or as exciting work as confronted her each day at City Hospital—what if it was

4

often monotonous and confining and largely routine—she could get used to it, couldn't she? Others had and she could too. And now look at her. She loved it! A tiny smile touched for a moment the tender lips and she sighed for no particular reason.

It hadn't taken her long to realize that her decision had been wise. She saw with relief the lines of worry fade from her mother's face—heard her again sing as she went about her household tasks. That part was fine, but, she told herself anxiously, she had watched Barbara change almost overnight from an innocent, rather shy, pretty high school girl to a raving beauty, her head filled with a lot of false values, flattered and sought after by Ashton's youth—its wild youth, Susan mourned. That's what better, more becoming clothes and a generous allowance that permitted of taking part in heretofore prohibitive social affairs had done to her lovely young sister. And now it seemed as if she had completely lost touch with her. Barbara no longer confided in her and Susan worried because of it.

Just this noon Barbara and Dick had staged another of their heated arguments, each apparently trying to outdo the other in the smart and, so often, pointed bitterness of their charges. It had been sickening and she had held her head in despair. Barbara had immediately jeered at her sensitiveness and Dick let fly another barrage in her defense. Susan, who had watched her mother's look of bewildered unhappiness, rose from the table and left the room—her mother following. Instant silence fell on the other two and Susan patted her mother's cheek and murmured with a confidence she was far from feeling:

"Just showing off, darling," she whispered. "Better not take it to heart. It would please them too much if they thought we were really annoyed. But oh, I wish they wouldn't!" The last was said more to herself than to her mother and she donned coat and hat and slipped from the house before her mother could answer.

Dick caught up with her before she reached the corner. He was grinning shamefacedly. His manner was so often contradictory—his seventeen-year-old manhood on the defensive, his blue eyes so like Barbara's pleading with her to understand.

"Don't be mad at me, Sue," he begged, dismounting from his bicycle and laying a cajoling arm about her shoulders. "As man of the house it behooves me to keep Barb in her place—someone has to do it and neither you nor Mom seem to know how to handle her. She needs taking down a peg and——"

"Granted; but I wish you wouldn't do it at mealtime, Dick," Susan said. "Anyway, I don't think it does a bit of good. Barbara will do as she pleases no matter what you or anyone says. I worry about her, Dick."

"Well, you needn't," her brother assured her stanchly. "Barb's cute. She'll probably get into some tight spots before she comes the cropper for which she's headed; but she'll always manage to wriggle out—somehow. Why don't you make her get a job, Sue? You remember how Mom used to preach to us about idle hands? Make her go to work, Sue, and I bet a dollar she'll come to her senses."

Her brother had ridden off and Susan still wondered how he thought she could *make* his sister do anything she didn't want to. She had tried every way she knew to accomplish that very thing—a job that would please Barbara —but without success. This time her sigh was one of discouragement and she firmly put the unpleasant thought from her mind. She carried the pile of S-47 forms to her desk and sat down. Her shining brown head in its snowy cap bent over her work. Her gray eyes were serious—her face grave. In the adjoining room the doctor turned from washing up to call to her.

"Don't spend too much time on records tonight, Susan," he said. "It's nearly five and we're closing promptly—for once. I have an important dinner engagement and it's going to be such a fine evening you probably are looking forward to a heavy date yourself." He laughed, the towel with which he was wiping his face muffling the sound.

Susan made a little grimace as she shoved the forms into a drawer and locked it. She sat for a moment, one white shod foot tapping the floor. She really should work for a while tonight. She disliked leaving things half done. Each day brought its own work—its own problems. She had no date for tonight. In fact she seldom had dates. She told

6

herself she hadn't time for them—that she wasn't the type. There was no necessity for her to hurry away.

The big First Aid room with the smaller surgery adjoining was her joy and pride. She loved every sterile inch of them. The wide windows facing the very center of town where Win Brighton so ably directed traffic from ten until six and the long stretch of shops even at this distance intrigued the eye; the porcelain-topped tables and snowy enameled cabinets with their glass shelves filled with shining instruments; the immaculate walls and tiled floors—everything the last word in up-to-the-minute hygienic equipment. Her gray eyes traveled around the room, found a scrap of lint clinging to an emesis basin and frowned as she removed it. Doctor Marshall often teased her about her fussiness, but she knew he approved of it. Now she turned as the doctor entered the room, topcoat over one arm, his gray felt hat in his hand.

"You're not to stay one minute after I leave, Susan," he admonished. "I know you're the best nurse we have ever had here but there's no sense in trying to top that record, my girl. You're good—that's all I require. You suit me—and Whittle. Now get your hat and coat and I'll run you home. Or are you shedding your uniform first? I know how you feel about that, Susan. Rather foolish, don't you think? No?" as the girl shook her head. "Okay, you're the boss. Don't just stand there. Change and let's be on our way."

"Oh, don't bother, Doctor," Susan told him. "I don't mind walking. In fact, I prefer to walk. It's such a lovely afternoon and after being inside"—she puckered her straight little nose and sniffed—"I think I need some fresh, unscented air for a change. Thanks, just the same, Doctor Marshall. I hope your dinner engagement proves delightful." She said the last demurely, making no move to leave.

Doctor Marshall's blue eyes twinkled. "Listen, Susan Trent," he said whimsically, "don't try to tell me you have no special heart interest—no boy friend—a pretty, clever girl like you. I simply won't believe it."

Susan blushed, her chin lifted and her gray eyes grew suddenly dark with annoyance. This was no place—no time to discuss personalities.

"Just the same, Doctor Marshall," she said coldly, "the

7

fact remains that I am entirely heart-whole and fancy free, believe it or not." A tiny nerve throbbed in one temple and she went on less pugnaciously: "I'm not the type, I guess, and then, too—oh, don't let's talk about it. I'm not interested in men—I have far too many other—more important things on my mind. There, are you satisfied? Better hurry, Doctor," she said somewhat pointedly. "You don't want to be late for that important date."

"It's not that important," the man said, wondering why he hadn't before noticed how very pretty his nurse was. She was sweet—intelligent, too, and somehow very appealing. He enjoyed working with Susan. There was something stimulating and satisfying in their daily companionship. "She wears well," he told himself. "One could never grow tired of Susan." He tore his suddenly aware gaze from the face of the girl standing quietly before him and said almost brusquely: "Good night!"

Susan's startled eyes followed him. What ailed him, she wondered. What had she said or done to annoy him? He had never before appeared curious about her private life. She shrugged and went into her tiny dressing room where she changed quickly into street clothes. And almost she wished she were a girl with a past—an intriguing past. She smiled wryly at her own foolishness and gave a last look about the big room, closed the windows she had opened and locked the door. She turned to meet the smiling gaze of Jennifer Burton, Cyrus Whittle's attractive secretary. Mr. Whittle was coming down the stairs behind her and greeted Susan jovially. "Doc left, Susan?" he asked.

"Just a minute ago. Did you want him?"

"Oh, not especially. It can wait until morning. I just wanted him to read a letter. It's from a firm in Illinois. They're sending a young feller east to look into that housing project we've been discussing. Doc has his own ideas on the subject and I want to tip him off to do a little soft pedaling for a change. After all, it's a bit out of Doc's line, seems to me. We might as well hear what the youngster has to offer. Doc's a stubborn cuss—didn't approve of my letting this architect come east at all. Seems he's a friend of Judge Martin—or his dad is or was. Small world, this."

The "old gentleman" was a great visitor and often rattled on without waiting for, or expecting, replies. He appeared quite old and yet Susan knew he was still in his fifties—fifty-four, she understood. She liked him. He was kind. Now his deeply shadowed eyes became alert for a moment. "Had a busy day, haven't you? That foundry accident was pure carelessness. Malfa got the brunt of it—seems like. The others got off easy. Something will have to be done over there. Can't have this sort of thing recurring too often. Spoils our record. Going home, Susan?"

The three had left the building together. The Whittle limousine with its liveried chauffeur stood at the curb and Mr. Whittle offered to drive Susan home but the girl shook her head.

"I've got to stop at Harvey's, Mr. Whittle," she told him, "and anyway, I like to walk. I need it after being inside all day. Thank you."

Jennifer Burton and Cyrus Whittle were driving away and Susan, with heart somehow miraculously lightened, stepped out briskly in the late afternoon sunshine.

As she prepared for bed that night her thoughts reverted to her work at the First Aid room and the events of the afternoon. She was always fascinated at the way in which Doctor Marshall worked. So quiet yet competent—so gentle yet firm. She stood beside him, his "third hand," he called her, anticipating his needs and ready to assist at all times. She adored working with him. There was such a deep satisfaction in it. Idly she wondered why he wasn't married. Oh, for a time he had been attentive to Jennifer Burton but that somehow petered out. Just now the Howard girl—Lorraine Howard, young, lovely, wealthy—appeared to hold the spotlight. And Susan wasn't pleased. What if Lorraine Howard did have an extravagantly beautiful face? That didn't mean she had a beautiful soul—that she was lovely inside, and somehow Susan had a feeling she wasn't. She had met her only once—the time she came to the office and with a perfectly shameless proprietary air announced she was taking the doctor to a very special affair. At that very moment Susan had—she acknowledged to herself—formed an intense and unreasonable dislike of her. Jennifer Burton was worth a dozen of the Howard girl. Why couldn't he see it?

She yawned sleepily. Oh, well, there must be lots of people—men as well as women—who missed matrimony for reasons known only to themselves. There was nothing especially tragic about it. Life held many far more important things than mere marriage—or did it? She sighed and sank down more deeply beneath the blankets.

CHAPTER TWO

SUSAN CONSULTED THE RECORD of Philip Newton, age 47, married, etc. His weight when last examined ten months before was one hundred sixty pounds. At that time he was ruddy and strong. This morning he was down to one hundred thirty. He looked flabby. His eyes were dull and he stooped like an old man. She saw that Doctor Marshall was concerned.

"Why haven't you been in before, Newton?" he demanded. "Or is it you have seen a doctor? Man, what have you been doing to yourself? Come on inside and let me go over you." He turned to the nurse. "Put these two girls through the preliminaries, Susan," he said softly. "One looks husky enough for anything. I don't know about the other; however, one can never tell."

Susan reached for a blank form and prepared to set up a record on Ann Holcomb who was applying for a job in the mailing department. She had qualified as to ability and it remained to find out if she was physically fit. Ann was seventeen and her weight while below normal was partially explained by the fact that her bones were small. Her father was dead and she and her mother had two rooms over in the west end of town. Susan saw that her clothes while cheap were scrupulously clean and her general appearance was neat in the extreme. There was a tenseness in her manner and something like fear in her eyes as the nurse filled in the record.

"Is this your first job, Ann?" Susan asked, trying to put her at ease.

"My first real job. I'm really very strong, Miss Trent," she said earnestly. "I'm never sick."

Susan smiled and the girl's eyes brightened. "I don't believe they will overwork you in the mailing department, Ann," she told her.

"What will the doctor do to me?" the girl asked tremulously.

"Oh, he'll test your heart and lungs, your reflexes and so on. It won't be too bad. Why?"

"Nothing—only I'm sort of scared, I guess."

Susan looked more closely and read the story of poverty

11

in the colorless cheeks, thin, nervous hands and threadbare clothing.

"There's nothing to be scared of," she assured her kindly. "I'll be right here—to give you courage," she smiled. "Now, Dora Brown, how old are you? Nineteen. And *you're* overweight by some fifteen pounds!" as she recorded the amount. "Better get rid of it while you're still young, my dear. Cut out the sodas and sweets for a while and watch your skin clear up and your weight go down."

"Oh, I don't mind being plump, Miss Trent," Dora laughed good-naturedly. "My mother and dad are both stout —we're a healthy family." She said it proudly and Susan shook her head, but said nothing more. She wrote busily for a moment and looked up as the door opened and a young man slipped inside and sank into the nearest chair. His face was drained of color and his lips had been bitten until they bled.

"Anything I can do?" she asked, trying to remember the newcomer's name.

"Isn't Doc here?" he asked huskily.

"He's busy just this minute. What's the matter? Is it your hand?" as she saw that he kept it in the pocket of his Mackinaw. "Let me see. Perhaps I can take care of it."

The girl Dora Brown let out a squeal of dismay as the injured man withdrew his hand which, though wrapped in a towel, was bleeding profusely. Susan brought a basin and antiseptic solution and bathed the injured member while Dora hurried to the window and remained with her back to the room. Ann, however, watched and asked if she could help. Susan shook her head—then suggested she bring a glass of water. The girl hastened to comply and held it while the young man sipped it.

"I think there will have to be several stitches taken— the doctor will know," Susan told him. "How did it happen?"

"It was entirely my own fault," he said. "I was just too smart—I guess. I was busy—well, sort of preoccupied—and used my left hand to loosen a nut on a sprocket and it slipped. I've done the same thing a thousand times and nothing happened. I've always prided myself on being ambidextrous—but never again. Do you think I will be laid up for long, Miss Trent?" he asked anxiously.

"I can't tell you that," she said. "I'll bandage it lightly until the doctor sees it and—if you will—I can't remember your name, although you look familiar."

"Morse—Henry Morse, Miss Trent," he told her. "I work in the testing room."

Susan found his card and laid it on her desk as Doctor Marshall came out of the surgery. Philip Newton looked somehow relieved. He stood straighter and walked with a firmer step. Doctor Marshall accompanied him to the door and Susan heard him say as he pressed his hand on the man's thin shoulder:

"Go home and pack what you need and I'll have Pete there at five-thirty to pick you up. Tell your wife it's doctor's orders and she's not to worry. Everything will be taken care of. Two weeks will soon pass and I'll guarantee you'll come home a new man. S'long, Phil. Be good!"

He stood for a moment watching the departing patient as he went down the short walk to the street, and turned as Susan said:

"Here's a job for you, Doctor. Henry Morse needs some of your expert stitching on his hand. The girls won't mind waiting a few minutes longer, I'm sure."

"Of course not," Ann Holcomb said but Dora Brown pouted a bit and shrugged plump shoulders. Susan removed the bandage and Doctor Marshall went to work. Susan explained the accident and the doctor shook his head.

"You're lucky, son," he said. "You might easily have lost your hand—a few fingers at least. Carelessness is one of the things we can't overlook, you know."

"I know," the young man muttered through white lips. "I thought I was being smart—saving time."

"And you'll probably be laid up for a couple of weeks. What does Stewart say to that? They're shorthanded over there anyway, aren't they?"

"The boss was kind of tough at first but—well, I'm a good man, Doctor." He said it frankly—not boastfully—and the doctor smiled.

"I see," he said. He arranged a sling around the young man's shoulders and draped his coat and Mackinaw over them, buttoning both snugly before he opened the door and preceded him into the hall. Susan listened as he ushered him out into the raw late October afternoon. "Goodbye, son. Drop in day after tomorrow and let me look at that hand. If it's so you can't come in have someone telephone and I'll drive over to see you. But come in if you can— we're pretty busy, you know."

"Thanks, Doctor," the young man said and Doctor Marshall returned to the room where Dora Brown rose quickly and said:

"Won't you see me first, Doctor? I'm in a dreadful rush. I have an appointment at four and it's nearly that right now."

Ann Holcomb sighed and settled back in her chair. Susan said nothing and Doctor Marshall adjusted his stethoscope and tested heart and lungs while the girl watched him through her lashes, a little smile on her full, red lips.

As he let the instrument drop, his eyes swept her from fluffy head to high-heeled, open-toed pumps. "You seem to be okay now," he told her; "but offhand I'd say you ate too many sweets. However, I doubt if that will make you any the less efficient—for the time you will remain with us." He smiled and the girl dimpled and held up her left hand. The doctor nodded. Susan frowned. If they weren't so short-handed in the stenographic department she knew Dora Brown would never have been accepted. She would probably leave in a few months.

Ann Holcomb stood up as Doctor Marshall dismissed Dora and Susan felt a wave of sympathy for her. The doctor adjusted his stethoscope and listened intently; then dropped it and smiled.

"Not afraid of me, are you?" he asked teasingly. "I haven't eaten a little girl in years. Reformed, you know. Is something worrying you? You can tell me, you know." He laid his hand on the girl's thin shoulder and said to the lingering Dora: "That's all, young lady. You're accepted. Goodbye." He glanced at his watch. "You'll have to hurry if you're to keep that appointment. It's four now."

Susan's eyes glowed. How thoughtful he was! The door closed after the smiling Dora Brown and the stethoscope was again put into use. But Ann had had time to quiet down and the examination went forward without delay.

"Heart and lungs sound, no thyroid disturbance but you're too thin, my girl. I suppose that fact doesn't bother you in the least? No, I thought not," as the girl shook her head. "However, you would be better for a few extra pounds. Who's your family doctor?"

Again the girl shook her head. Her eyes were bright with unshed tears and she choked as she answered: "We just moved here—after my father——"

"That's all right," the doctor said appearing unaware of her agitation. "Then I'll prescribe something—a tonic to build you up. Can't be losing you so soon, you know. Mailing, did you say, Susan?" and at the nurse's nod he went on: "You won't find the work too hard for you; but I'd like you to drop in here every week for a month or so. However, you're quite fit, you know. You youngsters don't give yourself enough rest to allow an ounce of fat to stick to your bones." He was talking just to give the girl a chance to compose herself, then went into the surgery where most of the medicine was kept and after a few minutes returned with a bottle which he handed her.

"I don't suppose you're going to like taking this," he told her; "but it contains all the vitamins you need and I want you to take it religiously—not miss a single dose. Will you do that—for me?" he smiled and the girl smiled in return, her eyes very bright. He patted her shoulder and turned to Susan. "I've got to run over to City for a while and may not be back this afternoon. Got a tonsillectomy. Yes," he went on, "you've guessed it. Newton's the patient. Terrible shape. I'm sending him to Hilltop for two weeks when he gets out of City. He'll need rest and plenty of the right food. Too good a man to take chances with."

"Goodbye and thank you—both," came softly from Ann Holcomb who had her hand on the door knob. "You have been very kind." The door opened and closed quietly and Susan looked up at the doctor, her eyes warmly approving.

"You were sweet to that girl, Doctor. I'm going to find out something about her and her mother. They need help—neighborly help, I mean. She wants this job pretty badly. I hope Miles doesn't impose on her. She's quite capable of it, you know."

"Don't you worry about Miles, Susan Trent," the doctor muttered. "I'll put a bee in her bonnet. If she thinks this—this child—what did you say her name is?"

"Ann Holcomb—aged seventeen," Susan replied.

"Well, if Miles thinks Ann is a protégée of mine she will watch her step. The old gal's got a righteous awe of me, you know."

Susan laughed. "No, I didn't know; but it might be worth utilizing in this case."

Doctor Marshall left the office and Susan went to work on the pile of records before her. She made a list of convalescents that should be visited within the next few days and was surprised at its length. It appeared that Ashton wasn't as healthy as usual this fall. Or perhaps, some of these people were prolonging their convalescence because of the fine fall weather. She couldn't blame them altogether and yet with the increased demand for Whittle products they couldn't afford malingering among the employees. She put question marks against several names and determined to telephone them in the morning if they weren't back at work. Many of these men had simply stayed at home—telephoning they were ill and unable to work. No doubt they had their own doctors—if they were really ill. She intended finding out.

The door opened and a girl from Accounting entered, looked anxiously toward the surgery, then put her hand to her head.

"Gosh, Miss Trent," she moaned, "I've got a beastly headache and have a date for the basketball game over in Weston. My boy friend is meeting me at five and we're driving over. His cousin plays on the Weston team. Can you give me something—aspirin or phenobarbital?"

"I'm sorry Doctor Marshall is not here, Miss Thompson," Susan told her getting out of her chair and opening a small cabinet. "Here is something the doctor gives for headaches. Take one in water now and another in two hours if not relieved. They're perfectly harmless but better lie down for a half-hour if you can."

"Fat chance!" the girl muttered, swallowing a tablet and

16

drinking the rest of the water Susan gave her. "Do you realize what day this is? Monthly statements and I'm swamped. Thanks. I'll have to fly but I'm not staying one minute after five—believe me!" The door slammed and Susan returned to her files.

It couldn't have been more than five minutes later when the telephone summoned her to the rest room upstairs. One of the stenographers was violently ill. Of course this would have to happen while the doctor was out, Susan told herself hurrying to the elevator. The girl was lying on a couch, white and spent, while several frightened co-workers stood around trying to help. The nurse did what she could for her and sent someone to ask a car-owner to drive her home. She returned to the First Aid room to find two men waiting. One had a cut over his right eye which she bathed with antiseptic solution and covered with a prepared bandage.

"What, no sewing?" he asked.

"Oh, it's not very deep and will probably heal in a day or two with no trace of a scar," Susan assured him.

"Well," he laughed, "that's good news. You see I'm going to be married in four days now and———"

"It won't spoil your beauty," Susan smiled. "Of course it will show for a few days but—why, it might even provide a touch of———"

"Mystery? I can stand that, Miss Trent," he grinned. "Mary knows me like she knows her own self. Why not come to the wedding—to the church at least?"

"I'd love to," the girl said.

"Fine. Plymouth Methodist—Saturday evening at seven."

He went out and she turned to the other patient who had been holding a handkerchief to his mouth for some time. She thought his lips were cut or bruised; but when he tapped his chest and tried to talk she knew he was probably in for a bout with pneumonia. She suggested his going to the hospital at once but he shook his head violently. He wanted no one but Doctor Marshall. Susan promised to get in touch with him as quickly as possible and asked:

"Have you a car handy? With that fever you should not be out."

He shook his head again; his face was flushed, his eyes glassy. She wondered why he had waited so long—why he hadn't come in earlier when the doctor was almost sure to be here. Some of these people were so stupid. She couldn't understand it.

"I'll have someone take you home," she said, reaching for the telephone.

He croaked one word. "Taxi," and she asked Ida to summon·one at once. It was quarter of five when he left the office and Susan relaxed in her chair. It had been a busy time since the doctor left and, suddenly, depression like a pall settled on her spirits. It was Barbara who went to all the games—baseball, football and basketball. Lately it had been tennis and golf that interested her most. She kept unearthly hours and never rose in the morning before ten or eleven. Susan knew her mother worried about it and that Dick jeered at what he called Barb's "gate-crashing," and while Susan had tried to talk to her younger sister—to advise and warn—she found it entirely wasted effort. Barbara laughed at her old-fashioned, stodgy ideas and dubbed her a Martha—wasting her youth at a job when there was so much fun to be had in the world.

It was quite useless to point out that she enjoyed her work—loved nursing—and thought herself fortunate in having her job in the Whittle plant. She forebode mentioning the fact that the salary was what kept them going —paid the bills and gave Barbara a few of the luxuries she was wont to hold in contempt as picayunish. Susan had hoped against hope that Barbara would go to work—find a position that would interest her and wean her away from the crowd of young people who were giving the girl such inflated ideas of her own worth.

It did no good to talk. She had found that out and had made up her mind to let things rest for a time. But it was too bad to let the girl go on until she was hurt, for Susan was convinced it was inevitable. None of the men in that crowd was serious in his intentions. She had seen it happen before. When they married it was within their own circle and Barbara's vaunted pride was due for a fall. There were not many King Cophetuas—in Ashton, anyway.

Now as the shadows lengthened and the hands of the clock crept to five, these thoughts brought a frown to Susan's smooth forehead. The play at the Country Club in which Barbara had a small part and over which she had worked so hard and with such enthusiasm, had been a huge success. The local papers gave it plenty of space in the morning and evening editions; but Barbara Trent was not mentioned as being one of the actors. If the girl felt either anger or hurt pride, Susan didn't know. She said nothing—laughed and hurried away on another date. It was all pretty sickening to Susan; but her hands were tied. She felt she could do nothing. After all Barbara was nineteen—old enough to know what she was doing.

Bells rang, whistles blew and sirens sounded five o'clock. Susan put away her work, locked her desk and went about seeing that everything was in order before she changed to street clothes and left for the day. The Whittle limousine stood at the curb and George touched his chauffeur's cap to her as she passed. She knew a feeling of warmth and satisfaction that she belonged to the Whittle organization; of pleasure that she was deemed competent to be associated with Joel Marshall—the company doctor. Susan knew his reputation—knew that older, better known medical men often consulted him—accepted his decisions and liked and admired him for the splendid physician and surgeon they knew him to be.

Cyrus Whittle had certainly succeeded in obtaining the services of a miracle man when he found Doctor Marshall. That seemed to be the consensus of opinion of the entire Whittle organization. "The old gentleman," as the owner of the Whittle plant was affectionately called, was obsessed with the idea that good health and well-being were essential to efficiency. The services of the company doctor were, therefore, available to the employees at all times without cost to them. This service was by no means obligatory. Each employee was privileged to call his own physician, but few did. Doctor Marshall was liked and trusted. Each of the six hundred and more employees was given an annual check up and each newcomer had to submit to this same rigid physical before being accepted for any position, whether office or factory.

Three generations of Whittles had owned and operated the Tool and Implement Plant and labor trouble was practically unknown. Cyrus Whittle was by no means a millionaire. He appeared satisfied with the modest wealth he had and seemed more interested in having contented workmen than in amassing a huge fortune. People called him an idealist, a dreamer, a philanthropist, while less charitable folk dubbed him a fool. None of this affected "the old gentleman," however. His factory was his family. He was a confirmed bachelor and designing women had long since given him up as good husband material. He cared nothing for society and little for women and if he was lonely at times no one suspected it. His huge house was staffed entirely by men and he spent all his free time in the book-lined library where his friends came to talk business or politics or have a friendly game of poker. He was called a man's man. Men invariably liked him—boys considered him their ideal—dogs followed him on the street and women wondered why he never married.

Cyrus Whittle wasn't a handsome man by any stretch of the imagination. His nose was too big, his eyes too deep-set, his large frame too loose and his graying hair always on end. But his smile was sweet and his heart as big as the world in which he lived. He was never too busy to listen to a hard luck story or to hold out a helping hand to an unfortunate. People said he was too easy; but Cyrus Whittle was shrewd. Not many imposed upon him and he contended he would rather err on the side of generosity than neglect to give help where it was actually needed.

Lend-Lease had upped production in the small tool department considerably. When the new building was erected Washington awarded a sizeable contract for airplane parts and the Precision Department was born. Only "specialists" worked there and everything was very hush-hush. More and more Susan had come to feel herself a part of it all. She was proud to know that Mr Whittle liked her and that he went out of his way to be pleasant to her, because after all she was just the company nurse. Her chin lifted and her step quickened.

The wind was raw. There were heavy clouds in the west and she felt sure the spell of fine weather was about to be broken and there would be rain followed by colder temperature and snow. But the fresh air felt good and she breathed deeply as she walked briskly along Main Street, not stopping to window shop as was her usual custom. She passed the four corners and lifted a hand in answer to the traffic cop's salute. It was a good world and she was glad to be a part of it.

CHAPTER THREE

SUSAN RAN INTO LILY THOMAS two blocks from home and the two stopped to chat. Lily was looking exceptionally pretty. Her cheeks were pink and her eyes sparkled with excitement. She caught Susan by her two arms and swung her about.

"Walk back a ways with me, Sue, while I tell you my big news." As they fell into step she gurgled: "I'm going to be married—in less than a month! Jim is being transferred to Denver and insists that I go with him. Isn't it thrilling, Sue? Honestly, I don't know if I'm afoot or on horseback."

"I'm so glad for you both!" Susan said enthusiastically, her errant thoughts registering the knowledge that if Lily was leaving the bank then there might be a chance that Barbara could get her place. Lily was urging her to come over and see her things.

"It's going to be just a simple home wedding, Sue. No one but Jim's people and mine. Not even a bridesmaid or best man and we're hopping a train right after the ceremony for Denver. It will be honeymoon enough for both of us."

"Of course it will. Who is taking your place at the bank, Lil?" Susan asked, wondering if she was being too precipitate and, for once, not caring. "I wonder if Barbara could get it. Do you suppose she could?"

"I don't know," the other said somewhat vaguely. "I heard Mr. Dunbar talking about a Margaret Wellman. Know her? I don't either. I tell you what I'll do. I'll mention Barbara to him—sort of get him to hold the place for her—say, until nine-thirty tomorrow. You see, they want this new girl to come in and work with me for a while so I can show her the ropes. There's really not much to it. Of course you have to keep your mind on it and— I wonder if —— But I'll do that for you, Sue. Have Barb there at nine, will you? Dunbar's a stickler for promptness. You'll come over, won't you? I've got some lovely things and I'm dying to show them to you. 'Bye!"

Susan broached the subject to her sister soon after she reached home. "I'm sure you can have it if you apply the

22

first thing in the morning, Barbara. Lily isn't leaving for two weeks and can show you just what there is to it. You already know some of the people in the bank and wouldn't feel at all strange." She tried to make it sound attractive to her sister; but Barbara turned up her nose at the idea.

"The bank!" she jeered. "Stuffy old place with stuffy people working there. What ever gave you the idea I would accept a position in a bank, Sue?"

"Well, it might be a good thing if you considered it," her sister told her somewhat sharply. "You've got to get a job some day and this seems to be made to order. You're without training and not many places are open to you."

"Now isn't that just too bad?" Barbara scoffed. "Why don't you tend to your own knitting, Susan Trent? When I want your advice or assistance I'll ask for it. I'm not taking any bank job. That's definite. Understand?"

"But, my dear," mild Mrs. Trent said, "don't you think you should? After all, good positions aren't too plentiful and this bank place seems the perfect answer. I'm sure you would be happy there and——"

"Oh, for heaven's sake let me alone. All right. I'll apply for it. There, are you satisfied? But I bet I won't get it. I'm just not the type." And Susan heard her mutter as she turned away: "Anything to make you quit hounding me."

But Barbara didn't get the bank job and somehow Susan wasn't at all surprised. It would have been almost too good to be true. It would have solved so many problems—taken her away from the crowd whose influence was so harmful. Weaned her away from Mrs. Halsey—at least during the day. Perhaps in time given her a love of work—a feeling of being independent—of paying her own way. Susan had hoped for it and yet wasn't surprised when it didn't materialize. She was, however, horrified at the unforeseen obstacle that had prevented it.

She was awake when Barbara came unsteadily upstairs at a little after three in the morning. She heard her go into the bathroom and went in after her. Barbara was wretchedly ill and Susan knew she had been drinking. Why did she persist in doing it when she knew it always made her sick? The elder girl held her sister's head and when the paroxysm had passed, helped her back to her room and applied the simple home remedies she had used on the previous occasions of Barbara's indiscretions. Barbara lay back on her pillow, whitefaced and blue-lipped.

"Feel better?" Susan asked gently.

"No. I wish I were dead." Tears slipped through the closed eyelids and ran down her cheeks. "They—they laughed at me—I couldn't take it—I never can really belong until I—I do. He—he—tried to make them stop pestering me. He did—I know he did—he—he———" She gulped. "He pitied me—ME———" The last was a wail. "Oh, I wish I were dead!"

"Hush!" Susan cautioned. "You'll wake Mother." She longed to know who "he" might be but didn't ask. She was sure Barbara had not the least idea of what she was revealing by her disjointed mutterings. "There, there," she soothed as a mother might. "Forget it, darling. Just try to sleep. You'll feel better in the morning. You know you're going to see about that bank job and you want to look your best. I'll put out your light and you try to sleep. If you want me just call, dear."

But if the girl heard, she made no answer. Her once lovely mouth was slack and a faint snore showed that she was already dead to the world. Susan put out the light and went slowly from the room. She was heartsick. Her beautiful little sister the associate of such people! Yet she knew that most of that crowd were decent, well-bred folk. It was a few of the younger ones—a dozen or so wild youngsters—who drank to excess and did the rowdy things that gave a bad name to the Country Club crowd. Mrs. Halsey was their leader. She had been twice divorced though still in her twenties and had leased the lovely Remington mansion where—so gossip had it—disgusting and scandalous orgies went on night after night. With what appeared to be an inexhaustible supply of money, Eve Halsey spent lavishly and the young people adored her. It was considered a mark of popularity to be invited to her parties and for some reason she had taken ·Barbara under her wing. The girl worshiped her and the older woman treated her with a mixture of affection and patronage that annoyed Susan and worried her mother.

Being beautiful herself, Eve Halsey had no reason to be jealous of the younger girl's fresh loveliness and Barbara was at the Remington mansion almost every day.

Susan lay awake for the rest of the night wondering what she could do to remedy the situation. It wouldn't work to forbid Barbara having anything more to do with Mrs. Halsey or the Country Club crowd. That would only serve to drive her to them. The bank job seemed out of the question now. Barbara would be in no condition to apply for it in the morning and without doubt it would be filled by noon. Perhaps she could inquire about it. She would telephone Mr. Dunbar as soon as she reached the office—no, better make it nine o'clock. He was usually there at nine. But would Barbara qualify? She was an excellent penman when it suited her purpose but she was so unpredictable. Well, she could but try.

Six o'clock found her still wide-eyed and she got up, took a cold shower and dressed quickly. She went downstairs and started breakfast. Another day had begun. She wondered if the time would ever return when she could meet the day with courage—even excitement. She used to. "Every day is a fresh beginning—Every morn is a world made new." That was all right; but the old problems, the same worries plus a few new ones, stalked like ghostly shadows beside her, darkening the morning and taking the joy out of life for her. She shook her head resolutely. Mother must not know of Barbara's condition. It would break her heart. Mrs. Trent was a member of the Frances Willard Society and wore her white ribbon proudly. She had read a paper at the last meeting. Susan had helped her prepare it. It had brought forth applause and commendations and had been printed in the local newspapers. How could she endure knowing that her youngest daughter, the darling of her heart, had come home at three in the morning sadly under the influence of liquor? No, Mother must never know.

Susan put a cup of black coffee on a tray and went up the black stairs to Barbara's room. The girl lay in a heavy slumber—one arm covering her eyes, the other thrown wide across the blanket. Susan brushed back the

25

bright hair but the girl didn't waken. She shook her gently, whispering:

"Wake up, Barbara. Drink this coffee and you'll feel better."

"Go 'way!" Barbara muttered, turning her face to the wall. "I'm sick. Get out! I don't want any coffee. Leave me alone."

"You've got to wake up," Susan said firmly. "You've got to drink this before Mother gets up. You don't want her to know, do you?"

"Shut up!" the girl said but she sat up abruptly, brushing back her hair and opening her eyes with difficulty. "Here, then, give it to me."

She gulped it distastefully, her eyes glazed with sleep. After a moment her gaze steadied and she stared at her sister's grave face.

"Well, say it, why don't you? Say I was drunk and sick as a dog and that you're ashamed of me." Tears of self-pity filled her eyes and rolled down her cheeks flushed with sleep. "Go on. Tell me I'm a bum—see if I care."

"For heaven's sake shut up, Barbara," Susan said shortly. "I'm not going to say anything. You punish yourself when you do things like this. You're not a bum, Barbara Trent. You're just a foolish young idiot. Now finish your coffee and lie down for half an hour. Then take a cold shower and come down to breakfast. If you don't, Mother will be up to look at you and as you are right now you're not in the least a pretty sight."

"I suppose I look dissipated!" the girl challenged sulkily.

"Well, not that exactly, but slightly wacky if you know what I mean. Come on, darling, forget what happened last night and start over. That bunch isn't worth remembering much less spoiling one's life for."

Barbara stared warily at her sister's serious face. "Sa-ay, I *must* have been high!" She grinned wryly. "What did I say? Did I name names even? Go on. Spill all the dirt, Sue. What did I tell while in my cups, as the saying is?" Her tone was flippant.

Susan's face was sad and she turned away.

"Oh, come back here, goon," Barbara entreated a little

frightened. "Nothing very terrible happened. A crowd of us were doing stunts and a couple of lads insisted we try their own special brand of cocktails. They dared me into drinking two and like a simpleton I went cuckoo. Gee, am I ashamed! Just a simple, middle-class, small-town maiden—that's me, I guess." The soft lips hardened and the wide blue eyes took on a steely glare. "But I'll show 'em yet," she warned, huskily. "It was probably because I hadn't eaten my dinner—because Mom had lamb stew. It's really her fault—all your fault——" The ready tears flooded her eyes again and Susan turned away, this time in disgust.

"Honestly, Barbara," she said sharply, her distaste apparent in her voice and face. "I really think you *are* an idiot. You're certainly not quite bright. Blaming Mother for your foolishness—your wickedness, for you are a wicked, wicked girl. There, that's straight from the shoulder and you can like it or lump it. I'm ashamed of you. What do you expect to get out of it? That crowd doesn't really care for you. You amuse them by making a monkey of yourself, that's all. I should think your pride would prevent your acting the fool just for their entertainment. But I guess you haven't any pride."

"You get out of here, Susan Trent!" the girl blazed. "I've got more pride than any one in this family, I can tell you that. And I refuse to take any grubby job just because you're all too stubborn to ask Aunt Charity to give us some of the money that's rightfully ours, anyway."

"How do you figure that out?" Susan asked curiously. "Aunt Charity made her money by saving and grubbing and investing—by going without everything but the barest necessities until she amassed a fortune. Now let her enjoy it. We certainly don't want any of it."

"Speak for yourself, you drudge—you money-grubber! When she wanted to adopt one of us Mother did me a great wrong by refusing to let me go with her. I wasn't born for this sort of life. Sneer if you like, Susan Trent; but I'm going to get out just as soon as I can."

"Not by way of Aunt Charity you're not," Susan answered and instantly regretted it.

"Not right away, perhaps," Barbara conceded cunningly, "but I have my plans and you'll know them all in good time. Now get out and let me alone."

"Are you coming down to breakfast?" Susan demanded.

"Later. I don't want anything except more coffee. If anyone telephones before you leave tell them I'm okay —never better." As her sister didn't answer immediately, she went on: "Well, will you?"

"I'll hardly announce the fact that you came home last night in a beastly state," Susan said coldly. "I, too have my pride, you see."

"Good gal!" Barbara murmured and yawned widely.

"Mother planned waffles for breakfast because you're so fond of them," Susan offered as she opened the door.

"Ugh!" the girl shuddered in distaste. "Not for me. S'long, Martha," she said derisively. "See you in church—sometime."

Susan went out and closed the door. She could hear her mother moving about in her room down the hall. She opened her brother's door and looked in. Dick lay rolled up like a cocoon, his fair hair standing on end. His windows were wide to the crisp October air and Susan crossed to close them. She stood for a moment looking out. There wasn't much to see for it wasn't yet light although the sky was growing gray in the east and trees were leaving their concealing shadows and beginning to stand out as maples, elms and even apples—bare mostly but each retaining its own individuality, for so Susan thought of trees. For a brief space her gloom lifted and she breathed deeply of the autumn air before she pulled both windows shut and turned as Dick's alarm whirred.

Dick reached a groping hand to turn it off, his eyes still closed, and Susan laughed aloud. Her brother sat up with a jerk.

"What's up?" he demanded. "Anything the matter? What are you doing in my room?"

"Oh, I was up and in passing I thought of your open windows and decided to shut them for you. I didn't know you had set your alarm. We're having waffles for breakfast so don't be long, Dick."

"Gosh, I'm tired, Sue!" he yawned, stretching his arms

high above his head. "What sort of a day is it going to be? I thought it might snow."

"It's just beginning to get light. After all, it's still October."

"Beat it!" the young man advised swinging his legs to the floor and feeling around for slippers. "See that breakfast is ready when I come down, woman. I'm hungry as a bear. Is the bathroom clear?"

"I guess so. Mother's getting up but Barbara probably won't for an hour or more." She closed the door and went on downstairs.

When her mother appeared a little later, Susan was pouring batter into the hot waffle iron. She apologized for usurping her mother's place; but explained that she had wakened early and thought she might as well get breakfast.

Dick came in and sat down at the table. He didn't look especially amiable. In one of his moods no doubt. Susan sighed. It seemed to her they came oftener as time went on. After his second plate of waffles he laid down his fork and looked warily at his mother across the table.

"What's the use of leaving all that money in the bank, Mom?" he demanded. "I'll never make a lawyer in a thousand years. Don't you know that lawyers have to be born? I'm no talker and I couldn't argue a man out of a difficulty if my soul depended on it."

"In that case, why waste your time trying to change my mind?" his mother asked with unaccustomed logic. "You know your father wanted you to follow in his footsteps. He started the fund for it when you were born and we have added to it as we could all these years. You are young, my son. You will find that you love your father's profession just as he did—when you really get into it. Judge Martin hasn't found fault with you, has he?"

"No, but he hasn't shown any particular enthusiasm either. It's just a waste of money, Mom, and of my time as well. I bet Dad would have listened to reason if he had lived," the boy went on. "They need men to work on planes and war material. I could be earning a darned good living while I'm waiting for us to get into it." Seeing the set look on his mother's face he shrugged and subsided.

Later, he went into his father's study, there to remain until he left for Judge Martin's office.

"I wonder if we are doing the right thing, Mother," Susan murmured as she folded her napkin and laid it beside her plate. "You know the world is full of square pegs in round holes. Perhaps Dick won't make a lawyer. Maybe he should be allowed to choose his own job."

Her mother shook her head. "Dick is very young," she said. "He doesn't know his own mind. It was, of course, unfortunate that he failed his entrance examinations but better men than he have done that. He'll settle down after he gets to college. I'm sure of it." She smiled and eyed her daughter for a moment. "Did you hear Barbara come in last night, Susan? Was it terribly late? I slept soundly —I always do when I take one of the tablets Doctor Ingram left for me."

"I stopped in her room this morning and she said she would be down a little later," Susan explained.

"And that position at the bank?"

Susan shook her head. "I think she was spoofing, Mother," she said. "I doubt if she ever had any intention of taking it. But just the same I'm going to ask about it this morning. Maybe if she knows she can have it she won't mind taking it. You know some people dislike asking for a job. I don't know why, but they do."

"I don't like Eve Halsey, Susan," Mrs. Trent said suddenly, putting down her cup. "She exerts a bad influence over Barbara."

"Barbara is nineteen, Mother," Susan reminded her parent. "She is surely old enough to know right from wrong. She had the same bringing up that Dick and I have had."

"But she is so pretty and——"

"The trouble is we have all spoiled her. We have catered to her whims, given in to her moods and among the lot of us we have succeeded in making a conceited, selfish, completely undisciplined brat of her." Susan spoke quietly and coldly and her mother's eyes widened in consternation. "I'm making no excuses for our part in her ruination, Mother," Susan went on slowly with deadly calm. "It's our fault she is as she is; but just the same she owes something to us—some loyalty and affection to her family—not to mention duty. That's a word she dislikes; but just the same Barbara needs a lesson—something that will shock her into an awareness of what she is doing not only to us but to herself as well. She doesn't have to do everything Eve Halsey suggests, does she?"

Her mother shook her head. Susan went on.

"Sometimes I wish Aunt Charity would come forward and take her—for a visit at least. It would get her away from Eve Halsey and that crowd."

"It was you Charity wanted to adopt, Susan," her mother pointed out. "But perhaps if she saw Barbara now——"

"There would be no question as to her choice, I'm sure," Susan said and if there was a slight edge to her voice her mother failed to notice. "Well, it isn't at all likely to happen, Mother," she added as she rose from the table. "It's twenty to eight and I must rush. Probably Barbara will be down in a little while. Why not leave the dishes for her to do?" She made the suggestion ironically, knowing full well her mother would do no such thing. Barbara never did anything at home.

She was putting on her hat before the hall mirror when the thought struck her. Why not write Aunt Charity and suggest an invitation for Barbara? She might hint at the girl's needing a change and could enclose a snapshot of her—the one taken a year or so ago when she was standing by the front porch in a white dress, looking sweet and unsophisticated. She ran upstairs and removed it from the frame that stood on her dressing table, then opened Barbara's door a crack to see if she was still asleep. She wasn't. Her eyes were wide and she said:

"Run along, Martha. I'll be down in a few minutes. I'm thinking."

Susan closed the door and hurried down the stairs and joined her brother in the lower hall. They usually walked to the corner together.

CHAPTER FOUR

SUSAN USUALLY ENJOYED THE WALK to the office each morning. She seldom rode except when she couldn't refuse a lift without danger of offending the owner of the car. Maple Avenue was only six blocks from the beginning of the shopping district and she liked to window shop before the stores opened for business. But this morning she was late and her distress over Barbara rode her like some evil spirit. She scarcely noticed Doctor Marshall as he stood on the sidewalk leading to the new wing of the Whittle Plant. He was undoubtedly waiting for her. He smiled and when she failed to respond, frowned at her preoccupation.

"What's become of the shining morning face, Susan?" he asked as he fell into step with her. "You're worried about something. Would it help to tell me? You know, it's part of a doctor's job—that of being a father confessor."

"Do you know Eve Halsey—Mrs. Halsey, Doctor Marshall?" Susan asked impulsively, pausing as they reached the door.

"Only by sight and reputation—not at all professionally," he answered. "Why? Is it the beautiful grass widow who is worrying you? And just where does she come into the picture? What has she been doing, Susan?"

The girl already regretted her outburst and hesitated to explain. She looked into the kind eyes above her and said slowly: "She seems to have completely hypnotized my sister, Doctor Marshall, and we don't like it. Barbara is flattered by her attention and—well—it isn't good for her."

"I see," the doctor murmured. "Your sister's a very pretty girl, Susan. Spoiled, no doubt?"

"Yes, and we are all guilty. As a child she was so sweet and so pretty it was easy to give in to her and very hard to refuse her anything. I can see now that it wasn't kindness to her —— Oh, why can't people be granted a little foresight, Doctor? If we had only known what we were doing to her——"

"Bad as that, Susan?" the man asked, his eyes on the

32

girl's worried face. "Listen, my dear, I shall be only too glad to help if I can. You can trust me, you know."

For a moment Susan was silent. How could she tell this man that last night her little sister came home intoxicated?" I know it, Doctor Marshall," she said, at last. "It's only that she is so dissatisfied with her home—with her surroundings—with us, her family."

"Just what does she do? Is she working? Perhaps——"

"That's just it," Susan cried. "She never seems to be able to get a job—not——"

The doctor laughed ruefully. "A lily of the field, she toils not neither does she spin and yet Solomon in all his glory,' etc. And her devoted sister keeps her robed like a princess? Ah, Susan, can't you see you have the remedy right in your own hands? Take away her luxuries and watch her come to time."

But Susan shook her head as they went inside. "It's not as easy as that. Let's forget it, Doctor Marshall," she said, shrugging out of her coat. "It isn't your problem and I don't intend saddling you with it." She went into her dressing room and closed the door. "This is one difficulty it won't help to discuss," she told herself firmly, "and during working hours see that you put it completely out of your mind, Susan Trent."

When she returned to the consulting room three patients from the factory were already seated there. Betty Barber from the bookkeeping department opened the door and begged for aspirin or something to ease the pain in her side. Doctor Marshall eyed the girl through half-closed lids and shook his head. He went into the dispensary and returned with a small phial which he handed her.

"Better go home for a day or two, young lady," he told her. "I'll have Pete drive you and you go straight to bed. Follow directions on that bottle and don't let me hear of any more dancing—for a while, at least. I'll see you this afternoon."

The girl's eyes widened in amazement. "How—how did you know, Doctor?" she asked.

"It's my business to know," he told her, shaking his head. "Won't you ever learn?" he demanded.

"But—but—it wasn't a late party——"

"Run along and do as ordered," was his only reply. He turned to Susan. "Call Barnes and explain that I sent Miss Barber home for a few days. Now, young fellow, what's your difficulty?" he asked, dismissing Miss Barber and turning to a thin-faced youngster in his late teens. "O-oh, I see. When did this happen?" He examined a lacerated hand that had been hastily wrapped in a towel.

Susan had a card before her and prepared to bring his case history up to date. His name was Walter Phipps. He was eighteen and worked in the assembly department. Someone had blundered and his hand happened to get in the way of an avalanche of falling parts. He clenched his teeth as the doctor probed for bits of steel and examined for broken bones in the long slender hand. Sweat ran down his face as the doctor worked and Susan marveled that no sound issued from his white lips. The doctor was gentle but thorough and as he bathed the torn hand he smiled in sympathy at the boy.

"Pretty painful, isn't it? I know; but you may be thankful there are no bones broken. We'll have that hand good as new in a few weeks." Again he turned to Susan. "Call Winters and inform him Walter Phipps will be on sick leave for two weeks, at least, and accept no arguments." He grinned at her and finished bandaging the torn hand. "Better keep it in a sling for a while and drop over in a couple of days to let me look at it," he advised. "Anything else?" he asked as the boy lingered.

"They told me there might be danger of blood poisoning—I guess you call it tetanus, don't you? Lockjaw? You see. I'm thinking of going into the army——"

"Don't worry," the doctor said. "You're lucky to be living at a time when sulfaminol is no longer a dream but an actuality. You'll be all right if you don't get fresh and try to use that hand. Better get used to obeying instructions if you're going into Uncle Sam's army. I'll probably be going myself if things continue to get worse. Goodbye—er—Phipps. Be seeing you in a day or two. Now, sir, what's on your mind?" as he turned to the young man slumped over in one of the office chairs. Susan reached for another card. "Let's see. Your name is——?"

The answer was glib. "I'm Karl Weiman. I work in the foundry and I think it's too hard—too heavy."

Susan found his card. He was twenty-eight, single, American born of Austrian parents. Whittle's was growing more particular about the men they hired these past weeks. He had come to work in August of this year.

"I have a pain here most of the time." He placed his hand over his heart and gasped.

Doctor Marshall eyed him closely for a moment, then motioned him into the small surgery beyond. Here the man stripped and the doctor gave him a thorough examination. As he replaced the stethoscope on his desk, his eyes were inscrutable; but his lips were grim. In the outer room Susan wondered just what he had discovered. To her this Karl Weiman appeared to be in excellent shape. Perhaps he had some obscure disease. She looked more closely as he and the doctor returned.

"What is it you want me to tell you, Weiman?" the doctor asked at last.

"I want to know what's wrong with me, of course," he answered somewhat truculently. "There must be something or I wouldn't——"

"Physically you're in excellent shape," the doctor told him shortly. "Is it the job you don't like? Why not tell your boss about it? Perhaps he can arrange for you to work in some other department. How long did you say you had been with us?"

"Three months, Doctor."

"All the time in the foundry?"

"Yes. That's why——"

"What department or work do you think you prefer?"

"Well—I thought perhaps in the assembly or even the inspection department. It would be lighter work. And after all I am something of a technician—trained in precision work. Are you sure my heart——" he began and the doctor cut him short.

"Your heart is sound as an American dollar, man. You're husky enough for almost anything, even a foundry job. You've got muscles a prize fighter might envy."

The young man muttered as he fastened his short

gray reefer. "Then why this pain at times?" he asked. "Just the same——"

"Okay," the doctor said shortly. "It's your privilege to consult someone else. Good morning."

As the door closed behind him the doctor turned to his nurse. "I wonder just what that chap's game is, Susan. He's strong as a bull and sound as a dollar. Just what do you suppose he's trying to pull off? It's a cinch he won't get transferred to either inspection or precision—unless they check on him darned closely. Have you any ideas about him —his outside interests for instance?"

Susan shook her head. "I wouldn't know," she answered, writing the doctor's findings on Karl Weiman's case sheet. "He's never been here before—that is, because of illness. Good looking, isn't he?"

"H'm'm," the doctor murmured, his eyes troubled. The hall door opened and closed and as they turned to the newcomer an old man who had been sitting unobtrusively in a corner stood up with difficulty, keeping firm hold of the back of his chair. "Oh, hello, Tim!" the doctor greeted. "Why didn't you speak up? You made yourself so small we didn't notice you. Just a minute," he said to the impatient newcomer. "Mr. Appleton has been waiting some time. What's troubling you, Tim?"

"It's this knee, Doctor," the old man told him.

"Let's see it," the doctor suggested rolling up the trouser leg and exposing a swollen and badly discolored leg. Susan flinched for a moment. "Call the ambulance, Susan," he said softly. "Tell them to get here in a hurry. Tim, I'm going to send you to the hospital for a while. You've got to stay off that leg and I know you never will if you remain at home."

"But what is it, Doctor?" the old man demanded nervously. "I ain't done nothin' to it that I recall. It just give out on me an' I went down like a log. I won't have to have it off, will I? I'd rather die."

"Of course not," Doctor Marshall said crisply. "It's an embolism and complete rest in bed and continued applications of hot saline compresses are indicated. Don't

36

worry about your wife, Tim. We'll get word to your daughter to come home for a while."

"The ambulance will be here immediately, Doctor," Susan said quietly and smiled at the troubled old man. As the doctor turned to the last patient she whispered: "You'll love it up there, Mr. Appleton. The nurses are sweet and the food—oh, but it's good!"

The last patient had a carbuncle that wasn't yet ready for lancing and after his departure, Doctor Marshall examined his appointment calendar while Susan went over the active case histories, jotting down notes as she went along.

"I'm making a number of calls this morning, Susan," the doctor said, looking at his watch. "In case anything comes up that's urgent you can reach me at these places at somewhere near the time I've designated. You take my car this afternoon for your calls. No, I'll not be needing it," he told her as she demurred. "If you go by bus or on foot it will take too much of your time and you should be back here at about four. I'll get lunch somewhere along the way and return in time for you to leave around noon. Right?" And at Susan's nod, he said: "Good girl!"

After the doctor had left the building Susan sat back for a brief moment and let her gaze wander to the windows facing busy Main Street. The sun was shining brilliantly. The sky was an intense blue. Big fleecy white clouds floated lazily across her line of vision. Beyond and above the brick and stone buildings the spire of Saint Stephen's Episcopal Church glistened in the morning sun. It would be wonderful getting away from everything for a little while this afternoon. She wished the doctor hadn't insisted she drive. Why, today was just the day for a walk. Perhaps she could talk him out of his determination to have her use his car. Anyway, she was always afraid something would happen to it and it was such an expensive car. Suddenly she remembered that she had promised herself to telephone Mr. Dunbar about that job for Barbara. It was nearly ten o'clock—time for the bank to open. She reached for the telephone on her desk and the operator put through her call. Just as she had feared. The place was already filled.

"Well, I never really expected to get it for her, anyway," she told herself as she replaced the instrument. "I wonder if she's up and if Mother suspected anything wrong. It seemed so very obvious to me; but then, Barbara knows how to bamboozle Mother. She always could." She sighed and went on with the list she was compiling. It was going to be longer than she had thought and she knew some of these home calls would have to wait until next time. Even using the doctor's car she couldn't get to more than six or eight people by four.

Mr. Whittle came in for a strip of gauze. He had cut a gash in his finger and it was still bleeding. Susan took care of him and ꞏhe stayed for a while discussing the proposed housing project.

"If we keep on expanding," he told her, "we shall have to put in a First Aid room down at the Prospect Street plant. We may have to build down there—more room—greater production. I keep telling them I'm just a little guy with a small plant; but nobody listens. All they want is production—more production."

"But that's fine, Mr. Whittle," Susan said with enthusiasm.

"I don't think Doc thinks so, Susan," he countered. "Doc insists he won't be changed. He likes it here. How about you? Would you like to be moved over there? No," as Susan's face clouded, "I can see you wouldn't. Well, it's all in the air right now. Perhaps nothing will come of it. I hope not. We're large enough. I never had a yen to be a tool and implement magnate. I guess at heart I'm just a little fellow content to plug along making a living for myself and letting the other chap do the same."

Susan said nothing. She knew she wasn't expected to, and after a few minutes he left, thanking her for taking care of him and complimenting her on the neatness of the rooms. Susan felt better after he went. How a few pleasant words of commendation brightened one's day! Too bad more people didn't go in for that sort of philanthropy.

Doctor Mashall returned a few minutes before noon

and Susan prepared to go home to lunch. At least she could walk that far. He didn't insist she ride to save time. She frankly dawdled—enjoying the gay shop windows and stopping at the florist's for a bunch of rusty button chrysanthemums. Her mother would love them. They were still buds. She saw a hat she thought she might like and hesitated whether to try it on or not and decided it would be better to wait. After all, an hour passed quickly and she always had prided herself on getting to work on time each day. She gave a last admiring look at the hat and quickened her pace. Perhaps she could stop in on her way back. She wanted that hat.

CHAPTER FIVE

SUSAN OPENED THE FRONT DOOR some fifteen minutes later and stood for a moment listening to the laughing conversation going on in the kitchen down the hall. She detected Barbara's lilting voice and her mother's subdued but adoring tones. It looked as if Barbara had the situation well in hand as Susan had somehow felt sure she would. She slipped out of her coat and called a gay hello. Barbara's head appeared through the half open door.

"You may be seated, Miss Trent," she said ironically. "Your lunch will be on the table at once. We can't let the busy little worker waste precious minutes waiting for food when every moment counts."

"How does it happen you're in the kitchen, Barbara?" Susan asked, refusing to take offense and pausing at the sink to fill a blue jar with water. "Are we having one of your favorite luncheons?" She handed the flowers to her mother who exclaimed over their beauty.

"Lovely, my dear! Ours come out so much later."

"What struck you, Sue?" Barbara asked. "Did you get a raise or did someone give them to you?"

"Oh, I thought Mother would enjoy them," Susan answered, evenly.

"Always the thoughtful daughter," the other jeered.

Susan went into the dining room and sat down at the table. Mrs. Trent bustled in with a napkin covered plate of hot rolls.

"Barbara has been telling me about the party last night," she explained. "I didn't know it was to be a party. It must have been very gay and pretty. Dear me, it seems as if these days everything is done to give young people pleasure. We are having creamed fish on hot rolls for lunch today, Susan. Thank you, my dear," she said as Barbara placed a salad bowl beside her place. "I declare I don't know where the time goes. I had intended making an upside down cake for lunch but we got to talking and first thing I knew it was nearly noon so we'll just have grapes and cookies for dessert. You don't really mind, do you, dear?"

"Of course not. Dick not home yet?"

At the window Barbara waved. "Here he comes now—pedaling along as if he thought Old Father Time was chasing him. How you two do count the minutes! I wonder just what would happen if you were late for work just once."

"Probably nothing," Susan said equably. "Hello, Dicky. How goes it?" as her brother entered.

"Hello, people!" the boy answered, sliding into his seat. "Yes, Mom, my hands are clean. I washed them before I left the office and I assure you my handlebars are entirely aseptic. How's that, Sue? Gosh, Mom, is this all there is for lunch? Ladies' food. But," he went on amiably, "I guess I can make out." Suddenly he sensed his younger sister still standing at the window. "Her ladyship not lunching with us today?"

Susan shook her head at him and his mother explained that Barbara had eaten a late breakfast and was not hungry.

"Won't you have a cup of coffee, dear?" she asked. "It's good and strong and if you drink it clear it will help wake you up."

"I'm awake, thank you," the girl answered and turned to meet her sister's level gaze.

Susan felt a sudden lump in her throat. The thought of Barbara's being used by Eve Halsey frightened her. Oh, why couldn't the girl see what was happening to her? Well, one thing was certain. She would write that letter to Aunt Charity before she left the office tonight and she hoped against hope that help would come from that quarter.

After all, she didn't stop to try on the hat. In fact she forgot all about it. When she reached the office she put aside all personal thoughts and worries and listened as Doctor Marshall recounted his experiences of the morning. The notes he had taken were as usual almost illegible. Once she had asked him why professionel men were notoriously such poor penmen and he had laughed and told her it was necessary in order to impress the public just as using long unpronounceable medical terms did. At first Susan had found it difficult to decode his notes but now she was used to them.

41

"I'd much rather walk today, Doctor," she said as she prepared to leave. "Honestly, I'm always afraid something will happen to your car when I use it. It's such a beauty!"

"Nonsense! Run along and don't pick up anyone. It's a dangerous practice. Try to be back by four. I've got to leave soon after. Due at City at four-thirty. 'Bye. Good luck!"

Susan picked up her bag and left the building. Her first call happened to be on a girl from the office who was recovering from a severe attack of tonsilitis. Both the company nurse and doctor had urged her to have her tonsils out; but after each attack she appeared to recover completely and her family physician didn't consider it at all necessary so Ruth didn't have them out. This time the girl lay flushed and uncomfortable on a couch in the small living room. Her mother hovered about like a worried hen. Susan examined the patient and said frankly:

"You are taking chances—grave chances—in putting off that tonsillectomy, Ruth. These persistent attacks can affect the heart, you know, and while you are young and in normally good health you should have them removed. When you get back on your feet again you'd better see about it."

"Doctor James doesn't approve of taking tonsils out unless they are definitely bad, Miss Trent," Ruth told her. "He says it's all nonsense and that my tonsils aren't diseased and, anyway, they are very small."

Susan shook her head. "Just the same, you listen to me, Ruth. These attacks aren't good for you and you know it. As you get older they will no doubt get worse—they sap your strength and any septic infection is a danger to the heart and apt to cause lasting trouble. She has a little fever, Mrs. Atwood. Better keep her quiet and on a very light diet for a while—I'll be in to see her again in a day or two." She turned to the girl on the couch. "Not fretting about anything, are you, Ruth? Not the job, I hope. They want you back, of course, but not until you are quite well."

She left the Atwoods and drove on to her next case. This was a man who had been in the hospital for a ruptured appendix and was convalescing at home. His wife smiled with pleasure as Susan entered.

"I know he's better, Miss Trent," the woman said. "He's

ugly as a bear today and nothing we do for him seems to suit."

"He's not in any pain?"

"Oh, no. Just cross. You know what men are. They don't know what real pain is; that is, most of them don't. If they had to suffer as we women do they'd be less ornery. Come into the sitting room, Miss Trent. He and little Jo are playing checkers—at least that's what they call it."

Susan followed her into the sunny room and Mr. Lane attempted to get up while the small boy on the other side of the checkerboard yelled when the pieces slipped from their places.

"Aw, gee, Grampa, look what you went an' done. Now we'll never know who beat an' I bet I did."

The old man smiled and patted the youngster's head. "I reckon I'm going to be all right, Miss Trent," he said as they both sat down. Mrs. Lane helped the small boy put the checkerboard to rights and drew him close to her side.

"You look much better," Susan said. "I'm sorry I spoiled your game. I just stopped in for a minute to make sure everything was all right and you weren't raking leaves or chopping wood yet. We'll be looking for you back in the Plant in a week or two now, I hope. Before you return, however, be sure to come to the office and let Doctor Marshall look you over. You ambitious people have to be watched." She smiled at him and the man flushed with pleasure. He liked being told he was ambitious. After all, he wasn't much over sixty and now that that pesky appendix was gone he felt he was good for another twenty years of hard work. Unconsciously his shoulders squared and his eyes brightened.

"Oh, I hope to go back next week—if Ma, here, don't kick up a fuss. She coddles me and I hate coddling. Now that the children are all gone I suppose she feels she has to baby someone and when Luke isn't here she picks on me."

Mrs. Lane and the nurse exchanged glances and Susan teased: "Don't tell me you dislike it, Mr. Lane." She laughed. "I know all men like to be babied when they are sick. They swear they don't, but we women know better. But as long as it helps them well, we are all for it. It has been so nice knowing you, Mrs. Lane. You have a lovely place here. I don't wonder your husband recovered so quickly."

"Can't I give you something to drink—tea, ginger ale— beer, maybe? We have it on the ice and it won't be a bit of trouble."

Susan assured her she couldn't take a thing. "I have six more calls to make and must be back at the factory by four so I'll have to run. See that your husband takes it easy for another week or so and then have him drop in at the office. Goodbye."

Now for the hard one—the one she usually put off until the last. This afternoon, however, she decided to see Alec Davis early and to spend as much time as possible with him. Poor fellow, so young to be laid on the shelf and so impatient to be up and about again. The attack of rheumatic fever he suffered in the spring a year ago had damaged his heart and it was feared doubtful if he would ever work again. His young wife worked in the office of the Plant and their two children, little more than babies, were cared for by the next door neighbor, a widow who conducted a nursery school. The expense was almost more than they could handle, but there was never a word of complaint from either one. The comfortable home was nearly paid for but aside from that there was little else.

Susan carried several of his favorite magazines with her when she went up the short brick walk to the front door. It was unlocked and she went in, calling a cheery hello. Alec was lying on the cretonne covered davenport in the living room, a gay rug across his knees. He made an effort to rise as Susan came in but she motioned him to lie still.

"Were you asleep, Alec?" she asked as she piled the magazines on the low stand beside the couch. "I'm sorry if I disturbed you. You need all the sleep and rest you can get. How are things today?"

The young man tried desperately to smile optimistically; but it was hard work. He bit his lip and asked abruptly: "Tell me the truth, Susan. Am I getting better or is there a certainty that I shall be like this indefinitely? I want to know. It isn't right that Lila should slave like she does while I lie here useless—worse than useless. I might better be dead. That way she—"

Susan felt a lump in her throat and she prayed for guidance. "Is marriage such a one-sided affair as all that, Alec?" she asked. "As I recall it the early years of your marriage—say the first five or six—were ecstatically—almost unbelievably—happy. Everything came your way. You worked hard at a job you enjoyed, bought this place, had two lovely children, saved a little and found life very good indeed. Lila had a maid, belonged to a few clubs and took life by the smooth handle. Now that the tables are turned and she must shoulder the burden while you take things easy, you rebel. Does that make sense to you? It doesn't to me. Life isn't all plain sailing—that is, the average life isn't. It seems to me it goes in cycles—ups and downs—good times and bad—happiness and misery—joy and sorrow. The one sort of compensates for the other. I don't mean to preach, Alec; but I doubt if Lila is doing any grousing. She appears to be a normal young woman. She enjoys her work and except that she, no doubt, worries about you, I doubt if she considers herself in the least put upon or unfortunate. It's just that now it is her turn to do a bit of cherishing, as the marriage vow has it, instead of you. Snap out of it. It isn't good for you to be depressed. Never take the defeatist's attitude. Try a bit of mental therapy, Alec, and *will* yourself to health. It can do no harm and will certainly raise the old morale as well as give a lift to Lila.

"Now I've talked all I'm going to. Doctor Marshall wants a complete report on you, my friend. How's the medicine holding out? How's the appetite and how do you sleep? Wait a minute until I get my notebook. I should be able to remember all these things but somehow I prefer to have them down in black and white. Memory can be very tricky and I'm accurate if nothing else."

She reached for his pulse and noted carefully the occasional skip. His temperature was near normal and while his appetite seemed rather poor she put that down to lack of exercise. It bothered her to hear of his sleeplessness. She knew Doctor Marshall had prescribed certain sedatives and asked if he still had plenty on hand. He evaded her questioning and at last she insisted on knowing if he had taken them as prescribed. He shook his head.

"I don't approve of dope," he told her bluntly. "I don't

45

sleep because I don't do enough to earn a night's repose."
He tried to grin but Susan knew he was on edge. "Very
likely you scoff at that. Lila does—says I'm foolish about
such things; but just the same it's the way I feel and you
might as well take all that stuff back to Doc and tell him
to use it on people who need it more than I do. When I
can get out and get to work again, I'll sleep alright."

"But don't you see that's what's retarding your recovery?
Sleep is Nature's restorative. We need it to rebuild our
resources used up in the day's living. Don't be arbitrary,
Alec. Just follow the doctor's instructions tonight and see
how much better you will feel in the morning. Why, last
night I had what I call one of my 'white nights' and when I
came down to breakfast—which, by the way, I prepared because I happened to be down early—I felt the weight of all
the world's cares on my shoulders. I was depressed and
miserable. Even a cold shower and two cups of black coffee
failed to lift the gloom. Even now I don't feel up to much
in the way of actual work and I'm supposed to be in perfect
health and vigor. If *I* need my sleep, how much more do
you who have suffered intense pain and agony for weeks
on end? Listen to me, Alec Davis. You take one of those
tablets at eight o'clock tonight. Get into bed and relax. If
sleep doesn't come repeat the dose in two hours; but I think
it will. I'll guarantee you'll feel a lot better tomorrow. If
you don't—well, have Lila report to me when she comes
to work and I'll—I'll see about it. Promise?" She smiled
into his haggard face and not many people could resist Susan's smile. In a moment he smiled in return and the girl's
spirits lifted. She repacked her bag and got to her feet.

"The quickest way you can get back on your two feet
again is to follow Doctor Marshall's instructions to the letter. He's a wonderful physician. You can trust him to know
what is best for you. That's half the cure, you know—having faith in your doctor. I'll watch for Lila in the morning, Alec, and don't you dare disappoint me. Goodbye and
be good."

She shook hands warmly and let herself out of the house.
She wondered what the doctor would say when she told him
Alec hadn't taken any of the sedative he left. He wouldn't

like it, she knew. He prided himself on never prescribing dope and Susan felt sure this was entirely true.

She was quite unprepared for the next patient's condition. She had thought they were all to be just routine follow-ups with the exception of Alec Davis; but Frances Clark had quite suddenly—or so it appeared to Susan who hadn't seen her in two weeks—developed into a psychoneurotic. Her sister and brother with whom she lived were devoted to her and had watched her closely, fearing she might attempt to harm herself. She had become morose and imaginative. She complained of something in her stomach that snatched up everything she ate. She breathed in gasps, declaring the air leaked out of her lungs before she could exhale. She was sure her brain was swelling—her head hurt, but she coudn't explain just where. It felt heavy—she felt heavy. Maybe her bones were changing to stone. She was tired of life. Her sister tearfully told of only that morning preventing Frances from committing suicide by leaping from her bedroom window.

"Your family doctor? What does he say, Miss Mary?" the nurse asked.

"We didn't call him," the woman said. "We were afraid he would insist upon sending her away and—Oh, Miss Trent, we couldn't bear it!"

"Frances is gravely ill, Miss Mary," Susan told her. "She should be under constant supervision. Let me call—Doctor Blaine, isn't it? Let me call him now. Perhaps he can come while I am here. It is really important, my dear."

Miss Clark stood rigid for a moment then nodded. "Perhaps it is best—the only way. Clif and I have been at our wit's end. We want to do what is best for her but—" Her hands went to her face and she shook as with a chill. Susan laid a comforting arm across her shoulders.

"It may be just temporary, Miss Mary," she soothed. "She was a pretty sick girl for a while there and no doubt her nerves are out of order. Don't let her see that you are upset or have been crying. I will call Doctor Blaine."

She dialed his number and talked with the old man who had retired twice now but still treated some of his former patients. He promised to come immediately and he was there in ten minutes. He agreed with Susan that the patient should be in the hospital. He didn't say the psychopathic ward and Susan didn't mention it either. As she was leaving, Miss Clark followed her to the porch.

"There is something I feel I should tell you, Miss Trent," she said a shade belligerently. "Frances has been upset about her position. She has felt for some time that too much was expected of her—that she has been discriminated against—that partiality has been shown to some of the other girls in her department. She told me that a Mrs. Davis—Lila, I think she called her—was given the position that should rightfully have been hers. Do you know anything about it? Do you think that might be the cause of her nerve upset?"

"Could be, Miss Mary," Susan said slowly. "She was probably run down and ill and has allowed the thought of unfairness to grow until it became an obsession. About Lila Davis. She worked at the Plant before she married and you know her husband is still an invalid unable to get about much. They have two little children and Lila, the wife, had to go to work to take care of them all. If Frances understood this, I'm sure she couldn't begrudge Lila her job. Is there anything else troubling her? No love affair?"

The older woman shook her head for a moment then said: "No, I'm sure all that was over sometime ago. She was engaged—or tentatively engaged—to a young man who without warning married another girl. Of course Frances was upset for a time; but I'm sure she is completely cured of any affection she may have entertained for him."

"How long ago was that, Miss Mary?" Susan asked, feeling sure she was reaching the root of the trouble.

"Let me see—more than a year ago. The thing that has been worrying me is that recently he has been bothering Frances—sending her cards and telephoning her, demanding that she see him—"

"I think we have the cause pretty well defined, Miss Mary," Susan said. "Why not have your brother get in touch with this man and—I almost said—give him a sound beating; but I suppose that wouldn't do. However, he could scare him so that he will quit being such a cad. How about his wife?"

"Oh, she has a child so she is sticking to him. It's a terribly sordid affair, Miss Trent, and I am sorry Frances ever had anything to do with him. Clif doesn't know he has been bothering her. If he did, I'm afraid of what might happen and it seems as if I have enough to bear without that. Please don't say anything about it, Miss Trent."

"If you tell me this fellow's name I'll see him myself," Susan said grimly. "I'll tell him a thing or two—"

"Oh, no. Just let it die a natural death. It must—in time. Here comes the doctor."

It was almost four when Susan left the Clark home. Doctor Blaine was still there. Frances was to be moved to the hospital for treatment and Susan hurried back to the Plant to make her report and to deliver Doctor Marshall's car. She was exhausted and looked white and tired when she entered the First Aid room. Doctor Marshall exclaimed when he saw her.

She sank into a chair and gave her report. She had made only four calls—two of them visits. She smiled wryly. "Alec Davis was in the doldrums, Doctor, and about ready to do something drastic. I think, however, we straightened him out for the time being. Do you know, Doctor Marshall, I feel so sorry for that fellow I could bawl. Is there any chance for him at all?"

"Of course there is," he said shortly. "There's always a chance as long as life lasts. With care and complete rest and freedom from worry he'll probably live out his allotted span. I doubt if he will ever be robust again but he should be able to do light work and have a lot of fun into the bargain. You like that young couple, don't you Susan?"

"Yes, I think they're pretty special."

"Anything else?"

"Yes. Frances Clark is—she'll have to be moved to a psychopathic ward in the hospital, Doctor."

"What? What's that you say, Susan? What happened? I thought she was recovering—"

"So did I. The last time I saw her she was eager to get back to work but she's certainly in a bad way right now. Doctor Blaine is with her or was when I left. He's the family doctor."

"But Blaine has retired. He's an old man, Susan, and— Suppose you tell me the whole story."

So Susan related what she knew of the condition of Fran-

49

ces Clark and the decision Doctor Blaine had made which coincided with her own ideas. Doctor Marshall shook his head.

"I'll get in touch with Blaine," he said, looking at his watch. "If I hurry perhaps I can catch him at the Clark home. If not I'll drive over to the hospital. How old is she, Susan?"

"Twenty-two or three," the nurse replied. "Her older sister and brother have been worried about her but wouldn't do anything for fear she would be sent away and Miss Mary told me they couldn't bear that. I'm terribly sorry for them. Frances—so much younger—is their idol. It looks to me like involutional melancholia."

Doctor Marshall nodded approvingly, then smiled. "How do you know so much about it, Miss Trent?" he asked, then answering his own question, "I suppose you learned that while affiliated with the State Institution. How long were you there, Susan?"

"Three months," she replied. "Too long. When I returned to my own hospital I could see where everyone, even the Superintendent, was a bit wacky. It took me quite a while to get back to normal. I'm glad I took that course, though, because it gave me a better understanding—more patience and consideration—of nervous conditions that so often accompany severe illness. But I doubt if I could stand it as a steady thing. It takes too much out of me."

She pressed her hand to her eyes for a moment as if to shut out the picture of the blank, staring eyes and twitching body of pretty Frances Clark. She would like to get her hands on that man—just for a few minutes. Her lips were suddenly grim and her eyes dark with anger as she reached for the bag containing her notebook.

"Better shut up shop early tonight, Susan," the doctor said as he prepared to leave. "Let those records wait until morning. You look just about at the end of your rope, my girl." His hand rested for a moment on her shoulder. "Just relax and let the cares of the world go—for tonight, at least. See you in the morning, Susan."

The door closed after him and Susan picked up her fountain pen. She would write to Aunt Charity right now and mail the letter on her way home.

CHAPTER SIX

FIVE. WITH THE BOOMING of the town clock came the long shrill siren of the Whittle Tool and Implement Factory whistles and the shops and offices emptied quickly. Susan Trent ushered the last patient from the First Aid room and locked the door. For a moment she stared with somber eyes at the streaming windows. It was queer that it so often rained just at twelve and at five when most people were quitting work. She wondered why this should be so. Her glance swept the big hospital room. Ten minutes would see the place ship-shape again. She worked fast. Doctor Marshall had left early again. She wondered if it was another dinner date—if his engagement to Lorraine Howard would be announced soon. In the back of her mind there lurked a conviction that Jennifer Burton was still in love with him. Susan sighed. She closed a cupboard door on its shining row of instruments and turned toward the windows overlooking Main Street.

Already she could hear the thumping of the janitor's mop as he went over the floor of the president's office upstairs. Even Cyrus Whittle had quit early. Were they all so eager to get home or did they have dates—interesting things to do? She sighed again and started toward the dressing room only to pause and return to stand before one of the big front windows.

There were times when traffic in Ashton (population twenty thousand) was congested almost beyond belief; when the traffic cop at the four corners became an animated semaphore; when his whistle shrilled almost continuously and one wondered how on earth normal travel could ever possibly be resumed. But Win Brighton managed it, somehow. He had been traffic cop at those busy corners for years. Even as Susan watched, the crazy, honking, hurrying maze of cars became orderly lines—two abreast eastbound— two headed west, each within its own lane of travel. Lights flashed red; brakes squealed protestingly and pedestrians scurried across the wet street, umbrellas bobbing grotesquely as their owners dodged between cars and fellow humans. Orange, and the cars seemed poised ready to spring forward. In fact, there was a movement all along the line.

51

Green, and they were away. The sight always fascinated Susan. She admired Win Brighton's patience and ingenuity. She had stood beside him one busy afternoon and watched his expert handling of traffic. He did it all so easily, so good-naturedly, that the girl exclaimed in wonder.

He dismissed it with a negligent wave of the hand. "It's my job, Miss. Just as taking pulses and temperatures is yours. I'd be no earthly good doing your job and I doubt if you'd be much of a success in mine, though," he added gallantly, "I have a notion that many's the driver'd be only too happy to stop when you signaled him—provided that driver was a man."

Susan wondered how he knew she was a nurse but after that he always saluted her when she passed. Now she watched him as he stood in the midst of traffic, his black rubber coat and hat shining with rain, a hand raised in salute or caution as the long line of cars passed him. And she wished with all her heart she could regulate the events in her troubled life as easily and efficiently as did Win Brighton. Things were always in a mess at home these days. She wondered why she was so different from Barbara. Why should she feel so responsible—had always felt responsible? To be sure she was older—almost four years older; but it seemed to her that a girl of nineteen should be able to shoulder part of the burden of the household. Neither Barbara nor Dick remembered their father at all clearly, but she did—the gentle, quiet man whom the neighbors called the best lawyer in town and his associates dubbed an easy mark for every down-and-outer who got into the clutches of the law—and he was still an active force in her life. He had died when Dick was still a baby and left his family with barely enough money to keep them together. In fact, his sister, Miss Charity Trent, had offered to take one of the girls into her home and bring her up in the luxury to which she herself, through wise investments and careful spending, had become accustomed. She had looked at Susan as she made the offer and the little girl had promptly and firmly refused to leave her mother. Of course Barbara was far too young for the transfer and Miss Charity didn't care for boys. So their sole surviving relative had washed her hands of her brother's family and returned to her spacious

52

home on the Hudson. It was only at Christmas that any message came from her. Then it was in the form of a check —small but welcome. As Susan grew older she came to resent those meager offerings and begged her mother to return them. But Mrs. Trent refused and the checks went into the bank toward Dick's college expenses.

Susan smiled wryly. "Dick's college expenses," she jeered. Why, Dick hated the thought of college! He wanted to go to work in a garage or machine shop. He wanted to earn money. Susan wondered if that was the reason he had flunked his examinations. Dick wasn't lazy. He bought a second-hand bicycle while he was still in school and delivered parcels for three or four stores as well as the Sunday papers—he had done it for years. Even now when he was spending part of each day in Judge Martin's law office studying or acting as errand boy, he still retained his paper route. The judge had loved Dick's father and was determined to see his wishes for his son realized if it were at all possible. He became the boy's self-appointed tutor and friend. Sometimes it seemed to Susan that his efforts were unappreciated. How could Dick be so stubborn? How could he hurt and disappoint his mother the way he persisted in doing? He knew her heart was set on his becoming a lawyer like his father and yet he acted like a martyr. After all, life wasn't particularly easy for anyone—at least not for the Trents. It hadn't been easy for their father and certainly Dick and Barbara ought to be willing to try to make it easier for their mother. They were thoughtless—spoiled—allowed to have their own way far too long.

Her eyes were bleak as she turned away and slipped into raincoat and rubbers, gave a swift glance around the room, turned out the lights and left the room. Tommy and his mop had reached the stairs and she called good night to him as she walked down the hall.

"No, it ain't no good night, Miss Trent," Tommy said. "It's rainin' cats an' dogs an' if it keeps up much longer we will be goin' 'round in hip boots or rowboats. Ain't you got no umbrell', Miss Trent? Say, you just wait a minute. I know where they's one. A salesman or whatever he was left it when he was here this mornin'. You wait an' I'll fetch it fer you."

53

Rain slashed at the windows in long, vicious, slanting jabs and the trees reeled dizzily before the wind. What a night! Barely five o'clock and already it was dusk. The street lights were actually on. She leaned aside to see if Win Brighton was still at his post. He was; but traffic was much lighter now.

"Here you are, Miss," Tommy said, offering her a slim rolled umbrella.

"Thanks a lot, Tommy," she said as she unfurled it. "If the owner comes after it what are you going to tell him?"

"That I ain't seen no umbrell' a-tall," the man grinned. "Oh-oh, if here he don't come—the blasted so-an'-so!"

The front door burst open and a tall dripping young man entered and shook himself on the rubber mat in front of the entrance.

He stepped aside as he saw Susan and murmured a word of apology.

"I left an umbrella in Mr. Whittle's office—" he began as he started for the stairs.

"Ain't no umbrell' there now," Tommy said firmly. "I ain't seen no umbrell' an' I been a-cleanin' this half hour. Mebbe the boss took it—"

He paused. The young man was staring at the umbrella in Susan's hand. The handle was unique. Of course he recognized it. She held it out to him.

"Perhaps this is yours," she said tentatively. "I didn't have one here and borrowed it."

Tommy stared in open-mouthed admiration. She hadn't given him away. He'd always thought she was the real thing. He cleared his throat preparatory to confessing his part in the incident when the young man spoke.

"It isn't mine at all," he said. "It belongs to Judge Martin who almost grudgingly loaned it to me. It seems he has a fondness for this particular implement and warned me to return it to him intact. I'm sorry; but can't I share it with you or accompany you and retrieve it when it has served its purpose?"

"That isn't at all necessary," Susan told him. "A little rain won't hurt me. My hat is fool proof and I'm well protected otherwise."

"Let me call a cab—"

"A what?" Tommy asked curiously. "Ain't no sech contraption in this town, Mister. We got taxis but they's never one to be had when quittin' time rolls 'round, is they, Miss Trent? I guess she'll jest have to hop a bus." He shook his head sadly. " 'S too bad!"

"I'll be all right, Tommy," Susan assured him.

"Of course you'll be all right," the young man insisted. "I intend seeing to that."

Tommy nodded his approval. Nice young feller.

"Come on, young lady—Miss Trent. I'm Alan Mac-Dowell, here on business which I hope will keep me in Ashton for life—now that I have met—er—Mr. Whittle and found him all his brother promised." His brown eyes twinkled into hers and Susan was convinced the ending of that sentence had been altered to fit the occasion. Perhaps he sensed her preoccupation and unhappiness and so felt it safer to go more slowly. She walked beside him down the short distance to the street aware that Tommy's inquisitive eyes followed their progress.

"Better take my arm," Alan MacDowell suggested. "It will make the going easier and I can perhaps keep us both dry—or drier," he qualified.

Susan slipped her hand through his bent arm and he pressed it close to his side.

"That's better. Now we can really hike along."

"I love to walk in the rain," the girl said, her spirits unaccountably lifting.

"You and me both," the young man laughed. "Listen to it—a veritable cloudburst. Don't let's take a bus. Let's walk. How far do you have to go? I hope it's a couple of miles, at least."

"Not quite. Six blocks down Main Street after we pass the business section, then half a block on Maple Avenue. I walk it four times a day—usually. I enjoy walking."

"So do I. Let's do some walking while I'm here in town—shall we? I mean, will you go walking with me some day—any day or night—soon?"

Susan laughed softly.

The umbrella bobbed frantically as a gust of wind threatened to turn it inside out, then thinking better of it allowed it to settle again to become once more a protecting canopy beneath which the two walked as one.

"I really don't know you, Mr.—Mr.——What did you say your name is? Alan something—Mac——"

"Alan will do nicely. Forget the rest of it for a while. And I hope you will tell me your first name."

"Susan—just plain Susan," she told him and bit her lip, amazed that she could feel so friendly toward a complete stranger.

He repeated it after her. "Susan—I like it," he said softly, "and I like you, and your name may be plain but I assure you——"

He felt her stiffen for a moment but he went on more firmly:

"You are anything but plain."

Susan said nothing. How was it possible that she could like anyone so quickly? But she did. He had appeared at an opportune moment—when she felt lost. Her hand on his arm seemed perfectly at home. He was a fast worker and yet he wasn't in the least fresh.

"Do you mind?" the soft voice persisted and she felt his dark eyes peering down at her in the semi-gloom of Judge Martin's big silk umbrella. Raindrops drummed above their heads and made little geysers in the puddles on sidewalk and road. Tires swished on the wet pavement and pedestrians hurried along holding onto hats with one hand and swaying umbrellas with the other. People greeted each other briefly with "Nasty night" or "Terrible weather!" but it all seemed thrilling and romantic to Susan.

"We turn here," she said almost regretfully as they reached her corner. "I can't thank you enough for sheltering me like this. I'm dry as toast."

"Don't thank me," the young man said. "Will you have dinner with me—tonight—the movies—dancing some place?"

"Oh, please—not tonight!" Susan gasped. She felt everything was moving too fast for her. It was exciting but rather frightening, too.

"When?"

"Ask me again—later." She smiled up at him as they paused in front of the broad shallow steps of the big porch on the square white house that had been the home of the Trents for three generations. "Won't you come in?"

He guided her up the steps and paused. The umbrella was now a shield. "Not right now, but I should like to come later, if I may," he said. "That is, if——"

"I shall like having you," she interrupted. "My brother is is Judge Martin's office," she told him. "We want him to become a lawyer like my father——"

"And he—your brother? What does he want to be? A policeman?"

"Oh, he's outgrown that dream. He wants to go into a shop—be a mechanic—perhaps work in a garage on cars or planes. Sometimes I think he doesn't know what he wants to do."

"He's young?"

"Past seventeen. Mother and I——"

"He'll be going into the Army or Navy in a few months," the man told her starkly. "We will all be joining up before long."

Susan stared at him with startled eyes. "Do you think so? Oh, it will kill Mother!"

"No, it won't. Our mothers will get used to the idea and be proud of us when the time comes," he assured her. "My father fought in the last upheaval. I was two when he went into it—before the United States declared war on Germany. He saw it all. I'm going just as soon as I'm needed. Just now I'm designing houses and doing pretty well at it. I'm hoping to get the job of handling the Whittle Plant's project. Whittle seems to approve my ideas. Maybe I'll decide to settle here permanently—if war doesn't come."

"It's all horrible!" Susan declared vehemently. "How can anyone possibly want war?"

"Who's this Marshall Whittle talks about? Just where does he come into the picture? What gives him the right to dictate——"

A car slid to a stop beside them and a glowing, vibrant Barbara stepped from it, laughing back at the man behind the wheel. "See you later, darling," she called in her high sweet voice and made a dash for the steps. Then, seeing her sister for the first time, she gurgled: "Fancy meeting you here, Sue! Don't you realize it's pouring—o-oh, I'm sorry. Here, let me under while I catch me breath. Who's your friend, darling?"

The young man laughed and moved the dripping umbrella a bit.

"This is my sister Barbara, Mr.—Alan," Susan said a little stiffly.

"Why does he stand out here? Why doesn't he come inside? Or haven't you invited him?" Barbara asked pertly.

"I did and he wouldn't," her sister explained, oddly annoyed. Barbara had a way of making her feel old and settled and out of things, yet why should she? After all, she was scant four years older and while she lacked the younger girl's amazing beauty, she wasn't exactly hard on the eyes. "I was just going in. Goodbye, er—Alan, and thank you." She turned away and went into the house without a backward glance, while Barbara lingered, her wide blue eyes examining the tall young man holding the black umbrella. She thought him very good looking— attractive and somehow appealing.

"You're new here, aren't you?" she asked. "Are you a Tool and Implement man by any chance?" She wrinkled her nose in distaste as she asked and Alan MacDowell knew she had small use for her sister's place of employment.

"No. I'm an architect. I'm staying at Judge Martin's just now. He happens to be a fraternity brother of my dad's."

"A-oh, I see," Barbara purred approvingly. "Has that big sister of mine asked you to come and see us sometime?"

Alan MacDowell laughed again. This younger girl was a cute little trick. "She has been very kind and I shall avail myself of your hospitality very soon, if I may."

"Good! Come any time. If Sue is otherwise engaged or the family is cluttering up the place, there's always me, you know. 'Bye. Be seeing you." She stood on the porch and waved as the young man turned to leave. He was grinning broadly as he returned her salute. Susan had gone inside and closed the door.

CHAPTER SEVEN

SUSAN WAS IN THE KITCHEN when Barbara came downstairs a few minutes later. Dick entered and tossed his wet raincoat toward the hatrack in the hall and took the curving stairs two at a time. He answered his sister's blithe hail with a sullen "Hello!" and Barbara laughed.

"Who's been treading on your sensitive tail, my fine bucko?" she jibed. Dick didn't deign to answer. Mrs. Trent, small and slender and still pretty in spite of her worries, looked into the hall where Barbara was preening before the long mirror.

"Was that Dick, Barby?" she asked, smiling at the girl's absorption. "Did you change into dry things, darling? This storm is terrible."

"Oh, I wasn't out in it, Mom," Barbara replied. "And it isn't so bad as it sounds, either. Sue walked home from Whittle's in it and I doubt if she even noticed it." She laughed impishly and slipped one scarlet-tipped finger through a curl on top of her charming head. "Did she change?"

"Of course she did," her mother answered. "Susan is sensible and realizes how easily damp feet can bring on a cold at this time of the year. A cold in the fall can quite often last all winter unless checked at the start."

"I never take cold, Mom," Barbara boasted. "You know that. I'm tough as an—an—as an old goat. But as it happens I didn't walk more than a dozen steps in the rain—just from the car to our porch. You see, I had a lift home, darling, and I have a date for tonight—quite a heavy date," she finished, a wary eye on her mother.

"Oh, Barby!" Mrs. Trent wailed. "You were out last night until almost morning. I know it was probably all right; but these late hours aren't good for you. I worry—"

"You would!" the girl pouted. "Well, I'm going just the same, my dear parent. I promised and I mean to keep it. I should think one old maid in the family was enough for you. I can't entertain my friends here so I have to go out with them. I have to get the most I can out of life, Mom, and you shouldn't begrudge me some small pleasure

59

once in a while. Lord knows I get precious little of it here in this house."

"Shut up!" Dick stood leaning over the railing upstairs. His eyes sparkled angrily and his face was old for his seventeen years. "Who do you think you are, anyway?" he demanded. "You're darned lucky to have a home and if you don't enjoy living here it's mighty little pleasure you give any of your family."

"Dick! Dick!" his mother implored.

"It's true," the boy reiterated. "She's so high and mighty lately, associating with the Nelsons and the Halseys and that Ruoff—all that snazzy bunch—she's ashamed of her own family and her home. Who provides you with your clothes, I'd like to know, if it isn't Sue—the poor sap! You ought to get a job and if you had an ounce of pride you'd get one, too, instead of living off your sister. You're a parasite, Barbara Trent—that's what you are."

"You shut up, Dick Trent!" Barbara shouted, her voice husky with passion. "You're no shining example of filial devotion yourself or you never would have flunked your college exams. What have *you* ever done that gives you the right to criticize me, pray? An errand boy—at seventeen! You make me sick!" Tears blurred her voice and she gulped angrily. Dick disappeared from the railing and Mrs. Trent patted her daughter's back. Susan came into the hall.

"What's all the shouting about?" she asked coldly.

"This place stifles me!" Barbara sobbed, her head burrowing into her mother's soft shoulder.

"In that case it might help if you got yourself a job," her sister said.

"All right. I will," Barbara said to the amazement of both mother and sister. "I'll get a job—and you can like it or lump it. You're a lot of money-grubbers and—and——"

"You think so?" Susan asked ironically. "Your earnings might lift the tone of things around here. Ever consider that?"

There was no answer and Susan expected none. Dick came slowly down the stairs. He looked scrubbed. His blue eyes were still stormy but his face was that of a small boy eager to be restored to the family's good graces. Susan breathed a sigh of relief. Dick was himself again.

"What's for dinner, Mom," he asked, joining the group at the foot of the stairs.

"Lamb stew and dumplings," his mother replied. "It's such a miserable night I thought it would taste good."

"Everything's ready," Susan said. "Let's eat. I'm so hungry I could eat the whole lamb myself." She sniffed appreciatively. "Smell that!"

Barbara shuddered. "I'm not very hungry, Mom," she murmured, rubbing a puff over her nose. "I'll just have some toast and a cup of coffee."

Susan saw her mother's concern and said hastily: "Okay, Duchess. I'm a working gal and need my food. How about you, Dicky? Hungry?"

"Starved!" the boy replied with enthusiasm and drew out his mother's chair with a flourish.

"You needn't show off before me, Dick Trent," Barbara snapped.

"Oh, for heaven's sake let us have one meal——" began Susan and stopped as her mother bowed her .head for grace. Never yet had the brief mealtime prayer failed to calm troubled waters and this night was no exception. Susan told one or two incidents of the day and Dick related a funny story at which even Barbara laughed though somewhat reluctantly. Mrs. Trent remarked that the butcher had called to apologize for the chicken he had sent last week and which she had returned.

"He was really quite upset about it," she told them.

"He should be upset," Susan asserted. "We are good customers even if not large ones. We pay our bills promptly and he ought to appreciate it."

"How very middle class!" jeered Barbara. "It's only the *bourgeois* who pay bills—promptly."

"That's all right," Dick said stoutly. "So we're *bourgeois* and proud of it. Try getting out of paying your bills and see where it lands you, my smart sister. In jail—that's where."

"Phooey!" Barbara wrinkled her lovely nose in disgust. "Who's this Mr. Alan who walked you home in the rain this afternoon, Sue?" she wanted to know, choosing to ignore her brother's comments. "He looks as if he might be interesting. Know him, Dick? He said he's staying with Judge Martin."

"I'm merely in Judge Martin's office, darling," her brother pointed out. "I never meet any of the Judge's house guests."

"You wouldn't," his sister retorted. "You lack ambition——"

"Oh, please!" Susan interrupted wearily. "Don't start that again. Alan had an umbrella and I hadn't, so he walked me home."

"Alan!" Barbara exclaimed. "Is that his first name? What's his other one?"

"Mac something. I didn't catch it."

"So you call him Alan?" Barbara laughed. "You're improving. Fast work—if, as I think, you just met. So you've actually come to picking up strange men, Sue? Allow me to congratulate you on waking up before it's too late."

Susan bit her lip determined to control her temper which was fast reaching the breaking point. "Don't be vulgar," she said coldly.

"Well, I'll say this, my dear." Barbara mocked, "I believe this time you've landed on your feet. Your pick-up——"

"As it happens I didn't pick Alan up as you insist," Susan interrupted. "He came to the Plant this afternoon to see Mr. Whittle. Don't try to make anything out of a simple act of courtesy."

"H'm'm," Barbara mused. "He said he was coming to call—and if——"

"Oh, for Pete's sake shut up!" Dick cried angrily. "You make me sick! To hear you talk anyone'd think you had a monopoly on men. Gosh, Barb, you're not the only good looking female in this family. Sue's perhaps prettier than you ever thought of being and she's got brains, too. They were left out of the assembly line when you were made."

"But you've got to hand it to me, brother," Barbara snapped. "I do get around—brains or no brains."

"It's nothing to boast about, you nitwit," Dick reminded her and Mrs. Trent looked troubled again. Susan passed her plate for more stew.

"You never made a better one, Mother," she complimented. "Just the right amount of each ingredient—not too much meat. Have some more, Dick—Barbara?"

"I hate stew!" Barbara complained. "Mom knows it and I don't see why she makes it so often."

"You're not the only one to consider in this family," Dick said sharply. "Sue and I like it and so does Mom. You don't have to eat it if you don't want to. No doubt your swell pals feed you larks' tongues and humming-birds' breasts."

Susan looked from one to the other in exasperation. "What ails you two?" she asked curiously. "What's gotten into you? You didn't use to be like this—quarreling and wrangling every time you get together. It certainly isn't particularly pleasant for Mother or for me either."

"There speaks the saintly big sister," jeered Barbara, eying Susan through long golden lashes, her full red lips curled in scorn. "Doesn't your halo get tiresome occasionally? Let me tell you something, darling," she went on her eyes narrowing as she saw that her sister intended ignoring her jibes, "it doesn't pay to be too sanctimonious —too domestic either. Men aren't interested in the quiet, stay-at-home Marthas any more. We have to show 'em. We have to have pep—be smart—lead 'em on and keep just a step ahead of them. That's the sort of girl who nabs the matrimonial prizes this season—who really sees life and *lives!* The rest of you have to put up with jobs—and spinsterhood!"

"I don't like to hear you talk like that, Barbara," her mother reproved, her eyes troubled.

"She doesn't mean it, Mother," Susan said, apparently unmoved and not in the least shocked as her younger sister intended she should be. "She thinks it's smart to talk like that—to listen and repeat all the rot some of her new friends consider a sign of sophistication. Don't mind her."

"Like fun I don't mean it," Barbara said hotly. "I mean every word of it and if I land a job it will be a

63

mere stepping stone to greater social advantages. I'll find a way. I'll never let myself get into a rut and simply stagnate like you have, Sue Trent. I have ambitions to get somewhere—be someone."

Dick who had been silent for some time now laughed derisively.

"Gosh, Barb!" he jeered with brotherly frankness. "You certainly hate yourself, don't you? Beware, young lady! Beware the cropper you've got coming to you as sure as shooting. And I think the less you have to do with that Ruoff man the better off you'll be."

Susan looked up sharply. Barbara had suddenly gone white, but she didn't reply to her brother's pointed remark.

"Ruoff?" Susan asked. "Who is he?"

Barbara bit her lip. Color returned to her face. "You mind your own business, Dick Trent!" she muttered and got to her feet. In a flash she was out of the room and they heard her running up the stairs.

"What did you mean, Dick?" Susan asked. "Just who is this Ruoff and what do you know about him?"

"From all reports he's a wolf and he likes his gals young. Just now he's rushing Barb—the poor goon——"

"But who is he—not Sonia Mousorsky's ex-husband, Dick. Not him!" Susan cried. "Why, he's an old man—in his forties, at least."

"That's the guy. Sleek and handsome as a movie hero—or villain. He's Mrs. Halsey's brother or cousin—some relation. His wife was a sculptress, wasn't she?" At his sister's nod he went on: "I wish you'd tell me how in tunket Barb gets herself mixed up with that sort of trash. She certainly should know better."

Mrs. Trent shook her head in bewilderment and Susan said uneasily: "I don't know. I honestly don't know."

After dinner Dick sat down in his father's small study with his books and Susan helped her mother clear the table and wash the dishes. They were to have waffles for breakfast because Barbara loved them so. Mrs. Trent assembled the necessary ingredients murmuring that she hoped Barbara would get up in time to breakfast with the family. Neither one heard the front door open or close or a car drive away from the house. Susan hung up the last dish towel and turned to hear her mother ask:

"What is it Barbara plans on doing, Susan? Do you know?"

Susan shook her head. "I'm sure I haven't the least idea. If she succeeds in finding something that really interests her it will no doubt be the making of her. I hope it will be soon. The longer she puts it off the harder it will be for her."

"Barby's smart, Susan," her mother said almost defensively. "She can do just about anything she has a mind to."

Susan said nothing more. She went into the living room where she stood for some time listening to the wind and the rain. What a night! And yet there was something about it that appealed to her—that called to some long suppressed turbulence in her nature. She shrugged impatiently and went into the hall. She could hear her mother still moving about in the kitchen and went upstairs.

She passed Barbara's room. The door was open but her sister was nowhere in sight. She called her name. No answer. Dick mounted the stairs in his usual rush and stopped to explain what he knew of his sister's absence.

"She's gone out, Sue," he offered. "Mom said she wasn't to go, but she went just the same. Probably off somewhere with that Ruoff. I don't like it, Sue."

"Well, she's expecting to get a job, Dick," Susan reminded him with a confidence she was far from feeling.

"Like fun she is," her brother retorted. "Why should she? You give her everything she wants. You're a goon, Sue Trent, and I don't mean maybe."

"You're a fine one to talk, you are!" Susan jeered. "Who was it slipped her money only last week for that pair of dancing slippers she wanted?" Then, more soberly, "I know we've all spoiled her; but she is so pretty— and sweet——"

"Occasionally—and that's in the past tense," Dick interrupted. "She's anything but, nowadays. Going around with that crazy bunch isn't improving her any. She's getting worse by the minute."

"Let's hope she lands a job, Dick——"

"Honestly, Sue, you're not really naive enough to swallow that bluff, are you?" her brother demanded scornfully. fully.

Mrs. Trent came up the stairs slowly, one hand sliding along the polished rail, the other holding her side. Susan hurried to meet her.

"What's the matter, Mother? A pain in your side?"

"Just a little catch. Gas, I suspect. I don't suppose I should eat stew——Is Barbara in her room?"

"Did you expect she would be?" Dick asked. "Well, she isn't—she's flew the coop." And from his room he announced: "She'll come in with the milk in the morning, Mom. How the gal stands it is a mystery to me."

"I strongly advised her against going out tonight, Susan," Mrs. Trent told her elder daughter distractedly. "She has deliberately gone contrary to my wishes. I am very much displeased." She reached the upper hall and went directly to her room in the front of the house. Susan followed.

"I'll fix you some spirits of ammonia," she said, her arm about her mother's shoulders.

"Don't bother," her mother said—"I'm all right—just run along and don't worry," and she went inside and closed the door between them.

Susan slowly retraced her steps. Life weighed heavily just now. Why did Barbara worry them all so? Tears filled her eyes as she descended the stairs to the living room.

She found the book she had begun on Sunday and sat down to read but the mood persisted. She got up and wandered about the house, then went to the hall closet and slipped into raincoat and rubbers and went out.

The worst of the storm had passed. Rain was still falling, but gently now, and she lifted her face to its cool, soothing touch, breathing deeply of the damp air and feeling the fever of unrest gradually lessen. Her nerves quieted and her heart steadied. Perhaps she was a Martha —careful and troubled about many things, so much so that the best things of all—the things that really counted —were neglected. She had no time for them.

"It *is* Susan? I wasn't sure——" said a voice and a tall young man fell into step beside her. "And without an umbrella. I can't share mine with you this time because I haven't one either. Tell me. Were you restless? Did you feel you had to come?"

"Why, yes," Susan answered, startled into abrupt truthfulness.

"Well, believe it or not, I've been calling you for the past half hour—willing you to join me in a walk in the rain. I've been haunting this vicinity so persistently that I've almost feared your neighbors would report me to the police for loitering. I'm glad you answered my call, Susan."

"O-oh!" the girl exclaimed. Then more matter-offactly: "But I often walk in the evening like this."

"Alone, and in the rain?" he persisted doubtfully.

"Sometimes—often alone—in the rain. I love it. It rests me and helps me see things in proper prospective once more. When life gets too much for me—when I get sort of tangled up in things—why, I just walk it off —my mood, I mean." She laughed apologetically. "Don't get the idea I'm habitually introspective, Alan," she said. "Only occasionally. Usually I'm the calmest most dependable creature extant."

"You don't have to tell me that, Susan," he told her. "I had a feeling you were just that." For a moment he was silent as they turned at the corner. "Is there any reason why I shouldn't put in a bid for your friendship, Susan?" he demanded at last. "Is there—are you engaged by any chance? Don't answer if you think I'm impertinent; but it seems I have to know."

"No," Susan said honestly—a bit defiantly, "I am not engaged, nor likely to be—at least not for a long, long time—if ever." It was none of this man's business; but that's the way it was.

"Thank you. I like to know where I stand," he said.

Susan stiffened. "Stand? And just where do you stand?" she demanded coolly. This young man need not think she was waiting for a chance to annex him. That, perhaps, she had even come out tonight hoping to meet him. After all, Judge Martin lived barely two blocks from Maple Avenue.

"On level ground, Susan," he answered, "free and unencumbered by claimants for your attention—I hope. I dislike trespassers, Susan, and so am particular never to err in that direction. Understand?"

Susan stopped abruptly. "I'm afraid you are taking a great deal for granted. Mr.—er—Alan," she said coldly.

He caught her hand and drew it through his arm. "Listen, Susan," he explained. "I'm not being fresh. I had no intention of frightening you or of offending. I just happened to like you the first time I saw you and I hoped we might be friends. I'm a stranger in Ashton and it's your home town. We can have fun together if you are willing. You are not really mad, are you?" he asked softly, bending to look in her face.

"Mad? Why—why, no," she answered. "I'm not mad; but I don't like—I didn't want you to think—well, I dislike flirting. There! I think it's cheap and—and shoddy. Now you know."

Alan MacDowell laughed delightedly. "You're precious! My dear girl, I've not been trying to flirt with you. I've been offering you my honest and humble friendship. So you dislike flirting! That's rich!" And he went off into another gale of laughter.

Susan tried to withdraw her hand but he held it fast. "I've got to go home," she said, feeling suddenly like a child who had been ridiculed. "No one knows I came out."

"All right. Let's go home and this time if I'm invited in I shall accept. I want to meet the parents of a girl who doesn't approve of flirting."

"There's only Mother and Dick at home," Susan told him still coolly. "Barbara had a date. My father is dead——"

"O-oh, I'm sorry. Please don't mind my teasing, Susan. Do you know, I think you need someone to tease you out of your seriousness?"

Doctor Marshall had said the same thing. Well, if they had the worries to bear that she had maybe they would be serious, too. She had come to believe that men

68

had the faculty of sloughing off anxieties and vexatious things. Or of refusing to accept responsibilities and unpleasant burdens. She wished she had been born a man. If she had been perhaps she would have more authority over Barbara.

"I nominate myself chief and sole teaser," the pleasant voice was saying, "and let me catch anyone trespassing on my preserves. Do I come in, Susan, or am I tabu for tonight?"

They had reached the Trent home on Maple Avenue and Alan MacDowell paused for a moment before mounting the shallow steps to the front porch.

"Come in, of course," the girl said, trying to match his mood of cheerfulness. "I'll call Mother and Dick— if he can leave his studies."

Mrs. Trent was gracious and Dick not too friendly. Dick had never been especially cordial to any of his sisters' callers. He didn't care for girls, either, and considered the courting male a pest and went on the theory that all young men calling on his sisters were incipient wooers and therefore undesirable.

The conversation was general for a while—the weather —business conditions, etc., and then Mrs. Trent turned to Susan and said:

"Mrs. Thompson called while you were out to tell me her two sons had enlisted—one in the Navy and the other in the Marines. She sounded as if she were proud of them—think of it, Susan. How can any mother——"

"Why shouldn't they enlist?" Dick exclaimed excitedly. "Now's the time to get the best jobs. Gosh! They're lucky!"

His mother stared in horror at her only son. Her voice shook as she cried: "Lucky! How can you say that, Dicky? And why should they enlist? We're not at war."

"Not yet," her son said, "but soon, or I'll eat my shirt."

Alan MacDowell was listening to this family discussion with an amused but interested expression on his good-looking face.

"Don't let's talk about it. Time enough when it comes," Susan said.

"That's the whole trouble with us and the other demo-

cracies," Dick cried passionately. "Forget it—don't see it
—let's hide our heads until the thing actually strikes—it
may pass us by. What a ghastly joke that's going to prove
in the end! Right now we ought to be the best prepared
nation in the world but instead we cry: 'Don't even talk
about it!' Gosh, it makes me sick!"

"But what can we do about it, Dick?" Susan reasoned.
"After all, it's the men higher up————"

"It's the people who have the say in the last analysis,
my dear sister," the boy retorted. "And the people will
speak before long, you wait and see."

"Atta boy!" Alan MacDowell applauded and Mrs.
Trent and Susan gazed at him with startled eyes in which
lurked a spark of actual dislike.

"Just the same, we don't have to talk about it right
now—tonight—do we?" Susan insisted, her eyes on her
mother's distressed face. "Surely there are heaps more
pleasant things to discuss. Get your fiddle, Dick, and let's
amuse our guest—that is, if you enjoy amateur nights,
Alan. Do you?"

"Not on the radio; but most certainly right here in
the flesh. What do you play, Susan? The piano, I suppose.
Most girls do."

"Of course; but Mother plays the piano, too, and she
will play for us tonight. You and I will provide the
audience."

"Do you sing? I feel sure you do," he went on.

"A little. I'm no Lily Pons but I can carry a tune
pretty well. What do you do—your special social accom-
plishments, I mean?"

"Well, I, too play the piano a bit and have been known
to strum the banjo in my student days. Oh, I can sing—
after a fashion. This is going to be fun. Takes me back to
my own home. Some of the neighbors would drop in and
first thing we knew everyone would be close to the piano
yelling their heads off. It was a lot of fun."

Alan proved to be a really talented pianist and it
wasn't long until he was the sole performer—the others
delighted listeners. Later they trooped to the kitchen
where they had coffee and fresh ginger cookies, the

guest devouring them with gusto, declaring he hadn't tasted anything so good since he had come east.

It was nearly midnight when he left and Susan thought she had never met anyone quite like Alan MacDowell. He was different from the young men she knew. He was probably as old fashioned as she was herself. She decided she was going to like knowing him.

CHAPTER EIGHT

JENNIFER BURTON CAME INTO the First Aid room and paused at Susan's desk. Susan sniffed appreciatively.

"How nice you smell!" she smiled. "And how gorgeous you look! I love that coat." Her hand smoothed the soft fur while the older woman laughed softly.

"You're a nice child, Susan Trent," she said. "Is your boss in?"

Susan shook her head, a puzzled look in her gray eyes. "I can't understand it, Miss Burton," she said, gazing anxiously out the window at the place where his car usually stood in defiance of the city parking rules. "He hasn't been late like this in months. Something must have happened. Perhaps he's ill——"

"You know better than that," the woman said. "Joel's never ill. You know what I think? The Howard gal kept him out too late last night and he overslept. A fine doctor's wife she'll make." Susan kept her eyes on her desk. She had a feeling Jennifer Burton was talking more to herself than to her. As if to corroborate her idea, Cyrus Whittle's secretary turned and left the room without another word. Susan sighed. Why couldn't Doctor Marshall have fallen in love with Jennifer? She was beautiful and clever and sweet and somewhere near his own age. This Lorraine Howard was young—not more than twenty-three or four —certainly too young for a man in his middle thirties and yet Joel Marshall didn't seem that old to Susan and he was such a peach! She didn't approve of Miss Howard, anyway. She was much on the order of Eve Halsey. Gay, sophisticated and demanding. But then, men were such fools where a pretty face was concerned. Her thoughts turned to her sister. Barbara had seemed somewhat subdued since that last escapade. She had gone out just as often but had come home early—that is, early for her.

The telephone shrilled on her desk and she lifted the instrument to her ear.

"Susan?" Doctor Marshall's voice sounded upset— almost angry. "I'm over here in Smithford and will be a little late getting in. Do the best you can and keep the information under your hat. Okay?"

"Of course, Doctor," Susan replied.

"Good girl!"

Susan replaced the instrument slowly. She was more puzzled than ever. She knew Miss Howard had relatives in Smithford and supposed they were both visiting there. But why hadn't he left early enough so that he could have come to the office? She felt indignation and something almost like jealousy that Lorraine Howard had the power to make him forget his obligations. She echoed Jennifer Burton's words: "A fine wife for a doctor she'll make!" Doctor Marshall ought to marry someone who understood what was expected of a doctor; one who would aid and encourage him in his work, not a woman who would sap his energy by keeping late hours and insisting on a hectic social life. She sighed, then thrust the unpleasant thoughts from her.

She had little more time for conjecture. Work crowded in upon her. This was the day for checking absentees. Cyrus Whittle was particular about that and she and the doctor had never yet given him cause for complaint. She handed out her chief's own special prescription for headaches, bound up a torn arm, gave temporary relief to young Bobby Norton whose kneecap was causing him trouble and urged him to come in again during the afternoon. She gave doses of bicarbonate to a pair of last night's banqueters and sent two would-be malingerers back to their work after teasing them into something like shame for taking up her time. She telephoned the stock room, the foundry and the main office smoothing ruffled feathers because she had found it necessary to send certain employees home for the day.

As noon approached she began to look more and more often toward the spot at the curb where the doctor's car should be parked. What was keeping him? Darn that Howard girl and all her tribe! She decided it would be well to send Tommy out for a sandwich and milk and eat her lunch right here at her desk. She hadn't been able to do a thing with the case histories or with checking absentees. Perhaps she could accomplish some of it during the noon hour. She called Tommy in his basement office, then phoned her mother she would not be home for lunch.

This done she turned to the two newcomers. One had a tiny steel splinter in his eyeball and she made an appointment for him with Doctor Willets who often handled such cases for them. The other young man was accompanying him and after they left she prepared to eat her sandwich just as the noon whistles sounded. It seemed to her the street was suddenly full of people—hurrying along like ants, some east—some west—some rushing across the street to the nearest restaurant. The building settled into midday quiet and she broke the sandwich in two but before she could lift a portion to her mouth, the door opened and a young man entered.

Susan didn't recognize him. She wondered if he was a new employee. If he was he would have to come in later when the doctor was in. However she could take care of the preliminaries. The young man was grinning and she stiffened. He was one of those, was he? All right, he wouldn't get far with her. She reached for a blank form and poised her pen ready to receive the necessary information. There was a slight snicker from the newcomer.

"This is the First Aid room, Mr.—you didn't give me your name."

The man smirked and said nothing.

"Well?" she prodded, frowning slightly.

"You're cute," he told her ingratiatingly.

"So I'm cute. The name, please? Your address, age, nationality and department. If you will please answer promptly it will be a help. I'm terribly busy——"

"Oh, just call me Jerry, darling," he said and laughed immoderately at the joke. But Susan didn't laugh.

"Is it short for Jeremiah or Gerald, Mr. Darling?" she asked coldly.

"Sa-ay, you're smart," he admired. "I can usually get 'em with that line. No, it's just plain Jerry. I'm free, white, twenty-one and heart-whole—until I barged in here. How about a date, babe? Chuck that stuff you've got there and come out for a real feed. I'm in the dough right now and'll treat you right. Can do?"

"Nationality?"

"American, of course. Couldn't you tell?"

"Occupation? In which department of the Plant are you to be employed?"

"Oh, I'm just a man-about-town, sugar. And whatever gave you the idea I wanted to work in this lousy joint? How about that date?"

Susan stood up and although she wasn't very tall she seemed to tower above the grinning young man.

"This isn't in the least amusing, Mr.—Mr. Darling, and I'll thank you to leave this room at once or I shall be forced to——"

"Just what'll you do, beautiful? We're practically alone in the building. That's why I hung around, see? So you might as well be pleasant. Come on, babe. Give me a break. See?" He pulled out a roll of bills for her inspection.

"How dared you come in here?"

He laughed. "Oh, I saw you sitting there so cute and businesslike handing out a line to a crowd of nitwits and I decided it might pay me to get a closer view. I like it. You're cute."

"You've said that several times before. I'm not in the least amused or interested and you will save yourself trouble by getting out at once." She had seen, with a feeling of intense relief, the shining car belonging to Doctor Marshall draw up at the curb. She saw him hurry up the short walk and heard the front door slam behind him. The man in the First Aid room got to his feet. His assurance left him and he took a step toward the door which opened and closed quickly before he could reach it. Doctor Marshall looked from Susan and her untouched lunch to the now embarrassed man sidling toward the door and asked sharply:

"What goes on here? Who are you and what's wrong with you?"

Susan sat down. Her knees were trembling. "This, Doctor Marshall," she explained icily, "is a person calling himself Jerry Darling who thinks I'm cute and so came inside to get a closer view. He doesn't work here and has no business here. I wish you would throw him out. He contaminates the very air of the place. He thinks he's funny but I find him definitely obnoxious." Her voice shook and Doctor Marshall opened the door into the hall and his manner was menacing as he glowered at the intruder.

"Out!" he ordered, following him outside, "and if I ever hear of your molesting this girl again I'll finish you. Understand? I ought to turn you in; but the place for you is in an asylum where they keep your kind under lock and key." The front door slammed and the irate doctor returned to find Susan and her lunch had disappeared.

In his private room he slipped into a white coat. He wondered just what this was all about, anyway. Heaven knew he had been through enough during the past twenty-four hours without finding this mess in his office. He was surprised at Susan. She was such a quiet, rather sedate—almost too sedate—girl. She had never encouraged callers here in the office. Didn't even carry on long conversations on the telephone. She was so restful—such a comfort to be with—a model nurse. Then how come this affair? He wore an angry frown when he returned to the outer room to find Susan at the telephone, a pile of absentee cards at her fingertips. He heard her say:

"Very well, Mr. Southard. I'll make a note of that and either Doctor Marshall or I will be around to see you— What? I didn't get that. Oh! Then you will be at work tomorrow morning? That's fine. Mr. Southard. I'm sure your department will be glad. Goodbye."

Before she could call the next number, Doctor Marshall spoke to her. He was still frowning although part of his anger had evaporated. "Just what is all this, Susan? Why was that yokel quite obviously making a nuisance of himself when I came in? Give, my girl, and don't spare your blushes."

"If I blushed, Doctor Marshall," Susan said with dignity, "it was with anger. I never saw the fellow before—I hope I never see him again. He said he had been standing outside watching me 'hand out a line to a lot of nitwits' is the way he put it, and barged in to get a closer view. I took his name, address, age, etc. as I always do and was prepared to have him come back when you were here. He seemed to find the entire proceedings amusing. Then he informed me he didn't work here and had no intention of working here so I ordered him to leave. He refused and dared me to try making him. He said he knew we were alone in the building. I suppose we were—at least in this part—until you came. I was never so glad to see you as I was just now. I'm not a coward, Doctor, but there was something so slimy about him that—well, I began to feel sick. That's all. What happened to you?"

"I wish I had kicked the fellow," the doctor said vindictively. "Did you say his name is Darling? A local chap?"

"I don't even know if he gave me his right name or address. He appeared to find it just a lark. O-oh!" the girl cried in disgust. "I was so mad——"

The doctor smiled and said soothingly: "Forget it. I doubt if he will bother you again. What happened during my absence? Anything special?"

Susan gave him a detailed report of the morning's work. She felt sure he had no intention of explaining his absence and didn't ask again.

"Oh, I nearly forgot," she said suddenly. "Miss Burton came in early and asked for you. She didn't say what she wanted and I didn't ask. Shall I see if she is in her office?"

The doctor frowned again. He looked at his watch, then reached for the telephone on his own desk. As he waited for the connection to be made his hands shuffled the letters piled neatly before him and his eyes scanned each one before he tossed it aside. At last he jiggled the bar on the bracket until the girl at the switchboard said somewhat peevishly:

"Miss Burton doesn't answer, Doctor Marshall. Shall I keep on trying? I don't think she has returned from lunch. It's only a little after twelve-thirty."

"I know the time," the doctor snapped. "Just as soon as Miss Burton comes in have her call me." He slammed the instrument down and glared at the unopened letter in his hand. Susan had noticed that envelope but inasmuch as it was marked "personal" in heavily underscored letters she had not opened it.

"Who brought this, Susan?" he demanded truculently.

77

Susan had succeeded in cutting short the undeserved vacation of a third employee and was feeling better. Now she looked up from her desk to encounter the irate glance of her chief. "Why—why, the postman, I suppose," she answered. "It was with the rest of the mail."

"The stamp isn't cancelled and I bet a dollar it's another of those damned anonymous letters. If this keeps up I shall turn the whole thing over to the police."

"It may not be," Susan argued. "Why don't you open it and see? The others were all very crudely printed. This is written—quite distinctive writing at that."

"Then you noticed it? Here, you open it, Susan."

Susan laughed at him. "Fraidy-cat!" she jeered and took the envelope from his extended hand. She took out the single sheet of paper and her eye ran down the page to the signature: "A friend."

"I guess you're right, Doctor," she said. "Shall I read it aloud? It isn't too bad this time." She smiled impishly. "In fact I think the writer sort of likes you."

"Give it here. I'm saving them from now on and——" His frown deepened. "I seem to know that writing, Susan. I've seen it before somewhere."

"I wouldn't worry about it," Susan soothed. "After all, you should expect it—in your profession. Aren't doctors usually adored by their female patients? Seems to me doctors are quite often subjected to that sort of thing. Doctors and ministers. It goes with the job. Probably some pour soul adoring you in secret——"

"Shut up!" the man growled and Susan's small grin became a broad smile.

"So you can't take it?" she jeered. "One thing is certain—you got out of bed on the wrong side this morning. Here comes Jennifer Burton now. Shall I call her in? I'll run down to the drug store and buy some toothpaste."

"I'll call her myself and you'll stay right where you are, Miss Trent," the doctor said grumpily, stalking to the door.

Susan heard him say: "You wanted to see me, Jennifer? Anything wrong? Come in."

Jennifer Burton passed him in the room with her head

in the air. She paused beside Susan's desk and as the girl looked up at her she was dismayed at the bleakness in the other's eyes. Doctor Marshall drew up a chair and Miss Burton sank into it.

"It's probably nothing, Joel," she said, slipping out of her coat. "Lately I have a sort of catch in my side right here." She pressed her hand against her left side and relaxed in her chair. "I'm wondering if it is something that should be taken care of at once or if it is just nerves or indigestion. I thought before I went to my family doctor I would come in and have you check. After all, I am a Whittle employee and entitled to a periodical going over." The last was said with almost forced humor. Jennifer's dark eyes lifted briefly to the doctor's. "I don't bother you often."

"That's what we're here for," the doctor replied and Susan had a feeling he was being very guarded, almost cautious, and she wondered why. It was still barely quarter of one and too early for many employees to be back from lunch. Jennifer stood up and Doctor Marshall adjusted his stethoscope. He tested the patient's heart, lungs and so forth, and seemed a long time in doing it. Susan watched. Was something seriously wrong with Miss Burton? She looked well—her color was good, eyes clear, and altogether she appeared to be in the pink of condition. But the nurse knew from experience there were all too often secret enemies at work that kept well hidden until the damage—sometimes irreparable—was done. Doctor Marshall dropped the instrument and smiled faintly.

"Nothing wrong with your heart that I can see right now, Jennifer," he said. "Offhand I might say barring unforeseen developments you should continue to live a normal, healthy, happy life for fifty years."

Jennifer reached for her coat which the doctor held for her and turned to leave the room. Her lips were twisted in a wry smile and Susan felt a wave of sympathy for her. "Barring unforeseen developments," she repeated softly as she reached the door, then turned and smiled brightly. "Thank you, Joel," she said. "I feel relieved. I don't exactly know what I expected; but I'm glad there is nothing wrong with me—especially now."

79

She closed the door softly behind her and Susan wondered what she meant by "especially now." Doctor Marshall sat at his desk staring blankly at the anonymous letter before him. Susan went on telephoning—taking notes—sometimes sending messages or requesting the assistance of phone owners to get in touch with workers who persisted in remaining absent from their jobs. Whistles blew and Susan knew the Whittle shops were again running at top speed. The office building, too, became a beehive of activity. She frowned as she called the last number. This noon hour had been rather hectic—pregnant with drama, even tragedy if, as she surmised, Jennifer Burton was disappointed that she had failed to get what she hoped from Joel Marshall. Susan wondered what it was.

She bracketed the telephone and stood for a moment straight and slim before she hurried to her tiny private room. She felt she simply had to stretch or she would crack. She finished the bottle of milk on the dressing table and swallowed the rest of the ham sandwich. The bread was dry and they certainly were stingy with butter; but suddenly she felt famished and wished she had gone home to lunch. After all, she was entitled to an hour off in the middle of the day. She wondered if Doctor Marshall had eaten, and wiped her lips as she returned to the outer room. The doctor sat as if turned to stone. His face wore a look of doubt as he tossed the annoying note into a drawer and got up.

"I'm going out for a cup of coffee and a sandwich, Susan," he said as he slipped into his overcoat. "Can I bring you anything?"

"Yes," the girl said impulsively. "Coffee, steak, mashed potatoes and carrots with a huge green salad. Oh, yes, and a quarter of a pie—no matter what kind just so long as it's pie."

Suddenly Doctor Marshall laughed, throwing his head back and showing all his fine white teeth. He slipped out of his topcoat and flung his hat into a chair.

"Run along, Susan. I guess you're hungrier than I am. Don't hurry either. Bring me back a sandwich and a bottle of milk——"

But Susan shook her head. "I'm sorry, Doctor," she said contritely. "I was only fooling. I'm not a bit hungry—honestly. You go out and eat a decent lunch. I'll make it all up tonight. I'm sure Mother will have a grand meal for me—she always does when I miss coming home at noon." She handed him his hat and grinned. "You look better, Chief."

Doctor Marshall left and Susan watched him enter his car parked unlawfully at the curb. As he prepared to drive away he lifted a hand in salute and Susan felt a glow of pleasure. He was so wonderful—such a grand man to work with, and too darned good for Lorraine Howard. She hoped with all her heart something would occur to break that affair up. She wondered if Alan MacDowell's plans for the housing project had gone through and if she would see him again soon. She liked him.

CHAPTER NINE

IT WAS WHILE DOCTOR MARSHALL was out of the office having a late lunch that Alan MacDowell came. Susan held out her hand.

"I was thinking of you," she told him frankly. "I have been wondering how your plans were going."

"I'm afraid my dream of spending my declining years in Ashton has gone up in smoke," he said regretfully. "For some unknown reason Whittle seems to have soured on my plans. He liked them at first. Just who is this Joel Marshall Whittle seems to think is a little tin god? I never heard of him. Is he a local man? Whittle didn't say although I remember I asked him. Perhaps it's a secret. Do you know him? Ever hear of him, Susan? And just where does he get his drag with Whittle?"

"Why, Joel Marshall is a doctor, Alan. He's the Company doctor. He's my chief. I thought Mr. Whittle decided he was not to have his entire way with this housing project. At least that's what I understood. Doctor Marshall hasn't mentioned it to me—of course. What happened?"

"Well, it seems Whittle's secretary—Miss—Miss Burton, I think he said her name is—had a lot of ideas and specifications this Marshall had submitted and she thought them okay—wonderful—super-colossal—out of this world, and it seems her boss had at last reached the conclusion they were all his secretary and this Marshall chap thought them. His turn about face must have been made suddenly because only the other day when I talked with him he was definitely enthusiastic over mine. Oh, well, we have to take these things in stride. I'm going over to Marydale this afternoon to see Blaud and Dickinson who seem interested. Marydale's about twenty miles from Ashton, isn't it? Not too far to prevent my coming over occasionally. When I go back home I shall bring my car. Of course I'm sorry about the Whittle project but if I land the Marydale one my trip east won't have been in vain—from a business angle," he added and smiled into Susan's gray eyes. "From a financial standpoint, the Marydale job is much better. Blaud and Dickinson have

82

a huge plant and of course Marydale is a bigger town than Ashton. So, perhaps, all in all, it hasn't been too bad. The job here wouldn't open until spring, anyway."

Susan listened as Alan talked and suddenly felt glad that he was leaving. He could quite easily become a disturbing factor in her life and she had enough to worry her without adding more. She liked him—she felt she could, in fact, even grow fond of him, which was a little alarming. With him gone she could settle down to normal living again—or as normal as was possible under the circumstances. She walked to the door with him as he left and put her hand in his as he said goodbye. He was holding it when the street door opened and Doctor Marshall entered. Susan quickly withdrew her hand and smiled a greeting but the doctor failed to see it. With a look of surprised annoyance he went into the First Aid room and closed the door forcibly behind him. Susan pretended not to notice the interruption and said: "I think you are taking this disappointment wonderfully, Alan. Does this mean I won't see you again—before you leave?"

"I'm afraid so; but I shall be back here before I go home. May I come to see you then, Susan?" he asked. "I like your family—I like you, and I—well, may I come?"

Susan tried to keep her voice steady and merely friendly. Her heart was pounding and she felt a little quiver in her throat. "Of course," she said. "I shouldn't like it if you didn't. We enjoyed your visit, Alan," she finished impulsively. "Dick spoke of it only this morning at breakfast."

"I enjoyed it, too. It reminded me of home. Not that songfests are our only form of entertainment; but we have them often enough so they are a part of our family life." He was almost reluctant to leave and Susan began to feel a little uneasy.

"Then this is goodbye, isn't it?" she said.

He caught her hand again and held it closely for a long moment. "Indeed it is not," he told her firmly. "I'll be seeing you, darling—Susan." He turned, took a step toward the door then came back to say softly: "You are a darling, you know, Susan. And if, for any reason, I don't leave this afternoon—may I see you tonight—walk you home or —— Why can't you give me a date? Come out to dinner and see a movie or go dancing some place?"

"Why—why—I think that would be—but are you sure you ought to stay over, Alan? It won't endanger your plans?"

"I'll send word I've been unavoidably delayed," he told her ardently. "I'll be waiting at five, then. You look so cute in that uniform, Susan. You're sweet! Five, then?"

"If you like," the girl said and watched with mixed feelings as he opened the door and reluctantly withdrew.

Her cheeks were flushed when she entered the hospital room a moment later and Doctor Marshall turned to her, the frown still marring his usually pleasant face.

"So-o? And how long has this been going on, Miss Trent?" he demanded. "I understood you were heart-whole—completely unattached—you told me yourself you weren't in the least interested in men and here I find you holding hands with this—this embryo architect from who-knows where while he makes calf's eyes at you. I'm surprised at you, Susan. So he's a gay Lothario as well as—I almost said an architect, but of course that would be exaggerating."

"You're being very silly," Susan said crisply, growing suddenly calm. "Alan MacDowell is a very fine young man and he's a real architect whether you like it or not. I understand he didn't get the Whittle contract after all—that Mr. Whittle suddenly changed his mind—with the help of you and his secretary."

"His ideas are too revolutionary, Susan," the doctor explained. "We want something more conservative. Our people ——"

"How does it happen you know so much about it, Doctor?" Susan wanted to know. "Don't tell me you're an architect as well as a physician and surgeon!"

"You need not be sarcastic about it, Susan," the man said. "As it happens I studied architecture before I ever went to medical school. I worked with my father who was a contractor and builder and a good one, too. Mr. Whittle approved my plans long before he ever saw this Mac-Dowell's. I advised against his coming in the first place. How long have *you* known him, Susan? And what has happened to your declaration of independence—your disinterest in men?"

"I didn't know," Susan said commenting on the first part of his explanation. "Anyway, Alan doesn't mind too much —losing this contract," she went on. "He has another lined up—a much better one—in Marydale with the Blaud and Dickinson people. The work on that will probably be started at once. Heaven only knows when this one here will begin to materialize."

"Did you know him before he landed here, Susan?"

Susan shook her head. "No. I met him the day he arrived —at least I think it was his first day in Ashton. I guess we just sort of liked each other on sight. It seems now as if I had known him for a long, long time." She spoke almost dreamily while the man across the room eyed her bleakly. "We all like him, Doctor Marshall—I mean Mother and Dick and I guess Barbara does, too, though she wasn't at home the night he called. As for my declaration of independence as you call it—why should Alan change that?"

The doctor laughed shortly. "Does that mean it is none of my business, Susan? The fact of the matter is, I don't particularly care for the MacDowell chap—too sure of himself—brash——"

"He isn't at all—brash, I mean, and as for his being sure of himself, why shouldn't he be?" Susan flared.

"Oh, no reason at all, my dear. I didn't mean to hurt your feelings if—you are *already* fond of the fellow."

"How is it you know so much about him if you didn't meet him, Doctor Marshall? And why didn't you meet him?" Susan ignored the innuendo.

"I was late getting to the conference and met your friend in the lower hall. It was all over by that time with the decision in favor of my plans."

"Of course," Susan said acidly. "It would be."

The doctor stared at her for a long moment while the nurse tried to busy herself with the pile of case histories on her desk. Color came and went in her normally rather pale face and he noticed how very long and dark were her lashes and how beautifully arched her brows. It was queer how he disliked the thought of her being friends with MacDowell. It was really none of his business. Susan looked up suddenly and met his intent gaze. She blushed and bit her lip.

"You are not to imagine things, Doctor Marshall," she said impulsively.

"Okay." He turned away as his telephone shrilled.

For the rest of the day Susan was to wonder at her chief's unusual behavior. So many times she looked up to find his eyes on her. At last, as the afternoon wore on and they were alone for a moment, she asked:

"Is something bothering you, Doctor? Why do you look at me—like that?"

"Like what?" he asked. "I wasn't aware there was anything unusual in my regard of you, Susan; but I have been wondering just now if it would be ethical to invite you to have dinner with me tonight and—well, perhaps go dancing somewhere. How do *you* feel about it?"

It was now Susan's turn to stare. Her gray eyes were wide and dark and she looked her surprise. "But—but why?" she stammered.

The doctor laughed boyishly. "Why? Well, because I felt like asking you. Do you realize you have never been out with me in all the time we have worked together? Is it that you don't care to go or just what is the reason?"

Susan shuffled the papers on her desk and then said demurely: "Perhaps the best reason is that you have never before invited me to go out with you, Doctor Marshall. And then there's your—your Miss Howard——"

His face changed and he frowned darkly. "Let's leave her out of it, Susan. After all, I'm not married to her. I'm still my own man and if I have not invited you before it has been because—well, to put it bluntly—I have never thought of it. But I'm thinking now. How about it? Will you join me at dinner tonight?"

"I'm sorry, Doctor," she said sedately. "You are very kind, but I—I have a date——"

"Oh, of course. Stupid of me. I might have known. Forget it, Miss Trent." He left his desk and went into the surgery where he remained for some time.

Susan wondered as to why this sudden interest in her and anyway she felt that in a town like Ashton news traveled fast and the most innocent of affairs was apt to cause unfavorable comment and heaven knew she had no desire for that. The relationship here in First Aid between her and her chief had from the first been pleasantly impersonal. She didn't want to risk changing it—perhaps jeopardizing her position. She had the uncomfortable feeling that she had offended him. Why was it necessary to be so stuffy? She might have appeared more pleased. It would be fun going out with him. She almost wished she hadn't promised Alan but even if Alan hadn't invited her she knew she would have hesitated. Something would have held her back—caution, perhaps, or just her natural shyness. She looked up as he returned to his desk, his eyes on a letter in his hand. A wave of affection flooded her heart. He was such a grand person!

"Why can't you come home with me for dinner—some evening when you have no other engagement?" she said impulsively.

He grinned at her. "Now you are being kind, Susan. But I shall take you up on that—some day. Run along, my dear. You've had a hard day. I'll close up tonight. I have some letters to write anyway and they are the kind that require thought and concentration—and no disturbing elements around."

And Susan, because she was tired and more than a little upset by all that had transpired, took him at his word and left at a little before five. Alan came down the street as she left the building and she waved to him. He caught her hand and slipped it through his arm, pressing it close to his side. Susan wondered if he could feel the pounding of her foolish heart.

It was a blustery November day and twilight was already shortening its brief hour. Street lights glowed and people burrowed more deeply into collars of their heavy coats. They hurried along the as yet almost empty street with scarcely a glance at the attractive shop windows. Susan's thoughts were chaotic even while she laughed and talked with Alan MacDowell. What ailed Doctor Marshall? And what had happened between him and the Howard girl to make him speak almost harshly when she mentioned her name? She felt her pulses quicken as she recalled his look of annoyance when he saw her talking with Alan in the hall.

"Why," she told herself, "it was almost as if he were jealous." She lingered with the thought for a while, allowing a fantastic dream to take shape, then grimly blotted it out. "Don't be an idiot, Susan Trent," she chided mentally. "It wasn't you, the girl, he was thinking of, but you, the nurse—his third hand." She grinned wryly. "Don't worry, Doctor Marshall," she assured him in her thoughts. "Susan Trent, R.N., isn't at all likely to forget her place or the fact that she is a lucky girl to have a job with you, and that's the truth."

"You're a thousand miles away, Susan Trent," Alan complained aggrievedly. "Come on back to me."

"I'm sorry, Alan," she said contritely. "It's only that I'm quite apt to take my work home with me."

"Well, forget your job for a while and let's have fun. Do you belong to the country club here, Susan?"

"Not I," she laughed. "Barbara does, but I have never had either the time or the inclination. There's a fine orchestra playing at The Fernald just now and they serve wonderful food—not too expensive, either."

Alan MacDowell chuckled. "You needn't feel called upon to spare my pocketbook, Susan," he told her. "I'm quite solvent." Susan fancied he sounded a bit peeved at her solicitude.

"All right then," she said. "I'll be ready at seven—shall we say? And thank you."

She was glad that only last week her one good evening gown had come home from the cleaners'. She had always liked that special dress, possibly because it was associated with happy times. It was two years old but still not much out of date and it was vastly becoming. That particular shade of blue—the saleswoman called it larkspur and her mother insisted it was Delft—did things to her eyes, she knew, and brought out all her good points.

She dressed with unusual care but was ready when Alan arrived. "Honestly, Susan, you're a marvel!" the young man told her as he helped her into the taxi. "Right on time— not a hair out of place and looking like a million—in less than two hours! How do you do it? What a wife you will make—for some lucky guy!"

Susan laughed. Suddenly she felt young and beautiful—desirable. She knew that many eyes marked their progress as they followed their waiter across the well-filled dining room. She nodded and smiled at several people she knew and felt sure they were commenting on her escort. The dinner was all she had promised, the orchestra superb and they found that dancing together was one of the pleasures they wouldn't have missed for a king's ransom. Susan danced more than she had in years and was surprised to find she hadn't gone stale or forgotten any of the social graces she had almost ceased to remember having learned. She forgot her worries, her work and felt no fatigue even when the clock on the wall behind the orchestra pointed to midnight.

"Isn't that your doctor dancing with—yes, it's Whittle's secretary, Susan. The old duffer's some hoofer, even if I don't admire his taste in partners. She's like a grand duchess with her airs."

Susan felt a sudden anger toward Alan MacDowell. "Doctor Marshall is certainly not old, Alan," she said stiffly, "and Jennifer Burton is a darling. I think you have some of the strangest ideas."

"Aha!" the young man laughed, his arms tightening about her. "I love to tease you, darling."

But Susan was not to be mollified so easily. As they approached the other two she felt an upsurge of rebellion—or was it jealousy? She nodded, unsmiling, in answer to their recognition and was glad when the dance ended. Alan led her to the bar where they had coffee and it was there Doctor Marshall found them later.

"Won't you dance this next time with me, Susan?" he asked, ignoring her escort. Before she could answer Alan interposed.

"Susan is dancing with me tonight, Doctor Marshall," he said almost belligerently. "Her hours off duty are her own."

Doctor Marshall bowed and withdrew. Susan was angry. How dared Alan MacDowell be rude to her chief! She rose to her feet. She was surprised to feel herself trembling. Alan's face wore a look of resentment.

"The nerve of him!" he muttered. "Who does he think

he is, anyway? You may be his nurse during the day; but you're my girl tonight."

"You needn't have been rude," Susan pointed out suddenly wondering why she had ever consented to have a date with this brash young man. Her sense of fair play reminded her that Alan felt, perhaps, justified in his animosity toward her chief and Jennifer Burton. They were responsible for his failure to hold the Whittle housing contract.

"Why not?" he demanded truculently. "Haven't I him and that secretary to thank for losing the job here? Oh, let's forget it, Susan," as the orchestra called an invitation. "Don't let's lose a single minute of this number."

Susan's eyes searched the big room for a glimpse of her chief. Jennifer came close in the arms of a tall stranger and frowned as for a moment her eyes met Susan's.

"What did you do to your chief, Susan?" she asked softly. "He left looking like a thundercloud."

Alan swept her away and the girl felt her anger rising again. How dared Alan McDowell attempt to disrupt her smoothly running life?

"I think I must go home pretty soon, Alan," she told him coolly. "I'm a working girl, remember, and—"

"Not afraid of that big stiff, are you? If he so much as dares scold you tomorrow I'll—I'll—"

"Don't be silly," she interrupted sharply.

"Then what's the matter with you?"

"I told you. It's getting late and—"

"Twelve-thirty! Do you call that late?"

"It is when one gets up at six and works as hard as I do during the day. I'm sorry, but I really must go. It's been a lovely evening and I have enjoyed it a lot, but I must be getting home—"

"Okay!" Alan said resignedly. "Get your wrap and I'll flag a cab."

Susan knew he was disgruntled but somehow didn't care. Later in the cab he drew her head to his shoulder, his arm close about her.

"We'll do this often when I come back for good, darling," he told her confidently. "The trouble with you is you have let yourself get stale. You need pepping up and I'm an expert pepper-upper. You'll see."

Susan said nothing. She didn't draw away from his embrace although she was experiencing no pleasure in it. She felt, however, that she had not treated him too well and if he enjoyed the close proximity—why—it didn't hurt her, but she hoped he wouldn't attempt to kiss her—she certainly didn't want that. She lifted a hand to her mouth to pat back a yawn. His arm was withdrawn and the young man straightened. Susan sighed in relief.

"I wonder if you're really as bored as you want me to believe, Susan Trent." he demanded stiffly.

"Not bored, Alan," she told him honestly, "only very, very tired. Home never looked so good to me."

"Gosh, I'm sorry, Susan," he said as he accompanied her to the front door and opened it with the key she offered. "I was going to ask to come in for a minute but I'll let you trot off to bed." He pulled her roughly into his arms—his kiss landed on her ear as the girl tore herself free and slipped into the hall.

"Good night, Alan," she said coolly. "and thank you." She closed and locked the door and went quickly upstairs. Tired as she was, however, she saw that Barbara's door was closed which meant that her sister had come home early. She went into her own room and switched on the light. "The end of what promised to be a perfect evening," she told herself as she prepared for bed. "What ails me, anyway? Alan likes me—why can't I let myself go—be young like—like Barbara?"

Alan MacDowell was waiting for her at the corner of Maple Avenue when she and Dick reached it next morning. Evidently her rebuff had meant nothing to him, for he greeted them blithely and when Dick pedaled off, fell into step with her.

"How's my girl this morning?" he asked quizzically. "You're looking fresh as a daisy. You weren't by any chance giving me the run-around? Well, you'll find me a hard guy to brush off, my dear."

"When do you leave, Alan?" she asked.

"I could take the eight-thirty or if you are kind and will have lunch with me I'll make it two-ten instead. How about it?"

"No lunch, Allan," she told him. "This is one of the days when I have a sandwich at my desk."

"So it's to be the eight-thirty. Okay, darling. The sooner I leave the quicker I'll be back. By the way, how's that pretty sister of yours, Susan?"

"Barbara? Oh, she's fine. Why?"

"Nothing, only it would appear that the preference for old men sort of runs in the Trent family."

"Just what do you mean by that?" Susan demanded.

"Nothing, only Mrs. Martin said it was a pity she didn't stick to boys her own age. This Ruoff—"

"Ruoff again? There's absolutely nothing to that story, Alan. Barbara's is merely a friend of his sister, Mrs. Halsey, who seems very fond of her."

"Okay, okay," he said quickly. "I only reported what I heard the judge and his wife discussing."

"Gossip!" Susan cried and quickened her step. "I'm surprised at the judge. How I hate gossip!"

"You and me both," Alan assured her. "Well, here we are and I bet you're scared of that old curmudgeon. If you are, I'll come in with you."

Susan laughed without humor. "You're positively ridiculous, Alan MacDowell," she said, her eyes sparkling with something very like anger. She held out her hand there before the entrance to the Whittle offices and the young man caught it in both of his and whispered ardently:

"Kiss me for luck Susan—"

A car slid to a stop at the curb and Susan attempted to withdraw her hand but without success.

"Run along, Alan," she whispered urgently and turned to greet her chief who with a cool nod of recognition passed on up the short walk and into the building.

Alan MacDowell chuckled gleefully. "Did you catch the dirty look he handed me,! Susan I bet the old duffer's mad as a hornet fearing I'm horning in on his private domain—daring to lift my lowly eyes to his nurse. Boy, oh, boy! Will I give him high blood pressure!"

The town clock struck eight times and Susan wrenched her hand free and ran toward the door.

"Goodbye, Alan!" she called. "Be good!"

The doctor scarcely glanced up as she murmured "Good

morning!" on passing his desk and his reply was almost perfunctory. As she opened the door to her tiny dressing room she mentally vowed to put everything but her work completely out of her mind. Thank goodness, Alan was leaving town—for a while, at least.

"Suppose you take the morning shift today, Susan," the doctor said after a silence in which nothing was heard except the tapping of her typewriter as she tackled the morning mail. "You can take my car if you like and while you're about it suppose you drop in and see Ann—you remember the girl in the mailing department? She and her mother— you spoke of calling on them—being neighborly. Remember? You might do it this morning and take these books to Alec Davis."

"I have already called on the Holcombs, Doctor," Susan told him. "Mother went with me. Mrs. Holcomb is very pleasant and Mother and she got along beautifully together. She wanted to get work. I imagine they have been having quite a hard time of it. I spoke to Doctor Morland about her. I had heard they needed someone at the hospital to look after the linen and supplies. So she is working over at City and is so grateful I felt ashamed I couldn't do more for them. I'm sure she will suit even Miss Ackerman. It will give her evenings at home when Ann is there. They may have to find an apartment nearer the hospital, though— their present one is away over at the extreme end of town. But that could be managed—there are lots of empty apartments over that way—I imagine. Don't you?"

Once again Susan found the doctor's gaze somewhat disconcerting. He spoke at last almost meditatively:

"I wouldn't know." Then after a pause he went on: "I'm realizing more and more what a very exceptional girl you are, Susan. Not satisfied with doing a full day's work here in our First Aid you have to spend yourself in doing kindnesses wherever the need arises. I should very much like to meet your parents."

"There is only my mother, Doctor Marshall. My father died years ago when the others were small. But I remember him clearly. He was a wonderful father. I'm sure Mother would like knowing you."

"All right. I'll accept that invitation to dinner some evening and don't forget to make it soon. Did you enjoy your evening, Susan?"

"Well," the girl answered, "it was a change."

"Your young man doesn't like me."

"He doesn't know you, Doctor Marshall," Susan said. "If he did—"

The look he gave her brought a lump to her throat. It was at once sad and somehow pleading; but he said hastily:

"Suppose you trot along. Maybe I have disrupted your schedule; but don't try to make too many calls this morning. Mrs. Davis says Alec is much better and most of the others on your list are improving rapidly. Try to get back by eleven if you can."

Susan drove directly to the Davis home and was pleased at the marked improvement in Alec. He came to the door to meet her and while he was still much too thin and pale, his eyes were brighter and his smile came oftener.

"If I were given to gloating, I should say: 'I told you so,' " Susan said as they sat down in the pleasant living room. "How's the appetite?"

"Fair. I went for a short walk around the block yesterday," he told her. "I was pretty tired when I got home but it was worth it. Gosh, Susan, if the time ever comes when I can do a day's work without feeling limp as a rag I'll never complain of being tired again."

"I know," the nurse answered. "But remember, it will take time. You can't rush this. You've got to go slow and rest a great deal and, above all, don't worry. Keep cheerful. That sounds like a large order; but you have a long way to go and if you want to go still further, you will have to continue to be careful and obey the doctor's—and nurse's orders. Oh, Alec, I'm so happy you are better! You can't know—I'm so fond of you both. You're such a grand pair!"

"And you're something pretty special yourself, Susan Trent. I don't know what we should have done without you —and Doctor Marshall. No one could have been kinder or more considerate. You know, Lila and I were talking about you two just the other night and we both thought it seemed as if you were made for each other. You're both so swell. Gosh, Susan! Doc's got some happiness coming to him after the tough break—that girl he married—"

94

"Wh-what? What did you say, Alec? Doctor Marshall isn't married, is he?" Susan asked. Something happened to her heart. Her blood seemed to congeal.

"Pete's sake, Susan, didn't you know? Where have you been all this time? You've been working right there in the same office with him. Didn't you know he had been married —while he was still in college—before he even studied medicine? She's been in some private institution or asylum in—Smithford, I think, for years and years. But here I am gossiping like some old woman. Of course I don't suppose many people know about it but I can't understand why you didn't. It was never any secret as far as I know though, come to think of it, I never have heard anyone mention it —except Lila."

"But this Lorraine Howard, Alec?" Susan asked. "Who is she and where does she come in? I supposed she was going to marry him and—and once he appeared to like Jennifer Burton. Oh, I can't understand it. I never dreamed of such a thing."

"Well, for Pete's sake forget it. It needn't affect your relations with him. Maybe he's divorced her, although knowing him I doubt it—especially as she's sick. He's the type of man who if he makes a contract sticks to it, no matter what it costs him. A prince, that's what he is." He looked at her troubled face. "It's a darned shame!"

Susan left the Davis home with her thoughts in a turmoil. She drove slowly trying to reconcile certain events and comments to this new and unfamiliar side of her chief. She wondered if Jennifer Burton knew these things and Lorraine Howard, too. And the anonymous letters? Could they have come from someone who knew? Or even from his wife? She wondered just what was the matter with her— invalidism—insanity or perhaps just cussedness, as Alec intimated. And how could any woman once blessed with his love throw it away—do anything to forfeit it?

She visited Sylvia Bradford from the Whittle switchboard, who had been suffering from a stomach ulcer and refused to stick to the diet Doctor Marshall advised was her only salvation—her only hope of enjoying a measure of health. She demanded an operation but the doctor was just as insistent that her particular ulcer was inoperable and even went so far as to bring two specialists to prove his contention. Still Sylvia refused to listen to them. Her mother kept her on the strict regimen while she was confined to the house but just as soon as she was up and about and able to return to work or date her special admirer, she followed her own sweet will and ate anything she fancied. This last attack had been the most serious and Doctor Marshall had been concerned and somewhat disgusted at her wilfulness. Susan tried to talk some sense into her pretty, stubborn head.

"But can't you see what you are doing to yourself, Sylvia?" the nurse asked when the girl's mouth set obstinately and she refused to promise to follow instructions. "You're not only jeopardizing your health but your very life itself. Then, too, there's your position to consider. How much time have you lost this past year? I don't know exectly, but I've been here seven times so far."

"I don't ask you to come," the girl pointed out sullenly. "I wish everyone would stop pestering me. Lots of people have ulcers—if that's what it is, and nothing very terrible happens to them. I'm sick—of course I'm sick; but everyone has days when they feel rotten. I'm still young and recover quickly. I'm not worried and I don't see why any of you should be."

"Well," Susan said resignedly, "if you enjoy poor health I don't suppose anyone can do much for you. But I'm telling you something, young lady. If you don't watch your step there will come a time when you won't recover either quickly or slowly."

"You're a fine nurse," the girl pouted. "I thought nurses were supposed to use the soft pedal—be all sweetness and light—that optimism was their watchword."

"Sometimes a good stiff dose of the unvarnished truth is indicated," the nurse replied. "I suppose, then, we can look for you back on the switchboard on Monday? Good!" She stood up then turned impulsively and caught the girl's shoulders, giving here a little shake of exasperation. "My dear, why can't you be sensible?"

"Because it doesn't pay," Sylvia replied and smiled defiantly into the grave face of the girl no older than herself. "I firmly believe I'd rather have a short life and a merry one than drag on for years only half living and dying in the end without ever having tasted life. You're a sweet girl, Susan Trent, and I like you a lot; but—don't try to preach to me; for it is time and energy wasted. 'Bye, darling. See you at the Plant on Monday unless my own personal devil takes another jab at me."

Susan shook her head helplessly. What was one to do with a girl like Sylvia Bradford? The other cases she visited were less trying. The cast was about ready to come off Johnny Forsyth's leg. When she reached the house she heard the radio going at its loudest and Johnny was singing at the top of his lungs. He grinned apologetically and turned it off.

"I feel great, Miss Trent," he told her slapping the cast. "This stuff will be off in a day or two now and do you know I believe I'm going to miss it. Can you imagine that? Maybe my leg'll feel cold without it. Do you know just when Doc intends doing the job?"

"Monday, I believe," Susan told him. "You have been a model patient, Johnny. Your mother says she will miss you when you go back to work. Of course that won't be right away; but every day you'll improve and first thing we know you'll be dropping in to First Aid for a check up. I think we will have to celebrate."

"I want to get into the Navy, Miss Trent," the boy said softly, nodding toward the kitchen where his mother was putting a pie in the oven. "I haven't told her; but I'm hoping this game leg won't keep me out. Do you think it might?"

"But we aren't at war," Susan reminded him.

"No, but we darned soon will be, and I want to be among the first to enlist. I certainly don't want to wait to be drafted."

"I hate to think about it," the nurse answered. "Well, there is nothing I can do for you. You seem to be getting along famously." She turned to his smiling mother. "I wish I could send a few of our other sick folk here for you to nurse, Mrs. Forsyth. Johnny looks as if he had been on a vacation."

"I think he feels that's just what it was, Miss Trent." She lowered her voice as the door closed behind them. "And maybe that broken leg was a blessing in disguise. His

302   **97**

father doesn't think they would accept him for military service—at least not right away. He's all we have, my dear, and naturally we don't want him to go." She smiled into the girl's troubled eyes. "But don't ever let him know I ever thought of that. It would break his heart and if he has to go—why, I guess we can stand it just as other parents do."

Why did everyone talk as if war were inevitable—as if it was just a matter of days or weeks before America would be at war with Germany? She didn't like it. The thought was depressing. She turned the doctor's car and drove back to the Whittle Plant.

CHAPTER TEN

WHEN SUSAN REACHED HOME that same day she looked at the table in the hall. There was no mail. Aunt Charity hadn't answered her letter. Perhaps she was away from home—gone south for the winter. In that case even if her letter was forwarded it might be weeks before she heard. She was disappointed but concealed it when she joined her mother in the kitchen. Mrs. Trent was ladeling soup into her favorite blue tureen.

"M'm'm! That smells good!" Susan said, sniffing appreciatively. "It's cold out today. All alone, darling? Where's Barbara? Not up yet?"

"Oh, Barby got up soon after you and Dick left this morning," her mother said and from something in the tone of her voice Susan knew she was troubled.

"Has she gone out?"

"Yes. Susan, she has a job—or she calls it a job. She was quite defiant about it when she told me—as if she knew I would object."

"What sort of a job and where?" Susan asked anxiously.

"She didn't do very much explaining. It seems she is to be a sort of secretary of Mrs. Stevens-Brown, Mrs. Halsey's aunt who is staying with her just now. She said she would take care of Mrs. Halsey's correspondence too—help her with her plans for entertaining and things like that. Did you ever hear of such nonsense? Susan, my dear, I don't like it." Mrs. Trent's eyes filled with tears. "What are we going to do about it? She knows how I feel regarding Mrs. Halsey and now she will be with that woman days as well as most of the night. I'm so upset!"

Susan bit her lip. Her gray eyes sparkled with anger. Wasn't that just like Barbara? She had warned them they could like it or lump it when she decided to get a job. So this was it.

"I wish we had never urged her to go to work, Susan," Mrs. Trent went on. "It was better the way things were. At least we knew where she was part of each day. Now I shall never know a minute's peace."

"Oh, Mother!" Susan hastened to soothe. "Mrs. Halsey

isn't that bad. She isn't quite a female ogre. She's young and flighty and she's probably fond of Barbara. After all, this may be the very thing needed to break up that relationship. Yes, I'm sure this might actually work out all right, Mother. You know how Barbara hates to be bossed —simply won't take advice or suggestions from anyone. Well, she isn't going to be around Eve Halsey very long before she finds out she will have to swallow a lot of both and it isn't going to set well. I have a notion she will tire of this arrangement—and soon." She spoke with a conviction she was far from feeling; but she had to dispel that unhappy, hunted look from her mother's face.

"Do you really think so, Susan?" she asked, fearfully—hopefully.

"Of course," Susan replied. "I wouldn't say anything to Dick—or at least not unless he mentions her not being down to lunch. Here, let me take that dish for you."

The front door slammed and Dick burst into the dining room, his cheeks red from the cold. He slapped his hands together to warm them.

"Gosh, it's cold out! Seems good to be inside. Want me to take a look at the furnace, Mom?"

"Thank you, son. It's all right for now. I looked at it a few minutes ago. You might put on another shovelful of coal, though, before you go back. Sit down, both of you, and have your soup while it's still hot."

Susan was glad that Barbara's name was not mentioned. Dick was full of the latest war news and nothing could stop him from raving over America's "supineness." Susan smiled. She wondered who had used that word in describing America's neutrality. Dick liked unusual words. He turned on the radio although both Susan and her mother begged him to spare them during lunch. Hitler's blitzkrieg was storming through Russia and the announcer related the awful carnage in detail.

"Oh, for heaven's sake, Dick, turn it off!" Susan begged. "I can't stand it—at every meal. Have a heart. Listen, darling, I'll give you a small radio for your room on condition that you leave this one alone. Is it a deal?"

"Gosh, Sue!" he cried, tossing his knife and fork into the air and deftly catching them before they reached the table. "You're a peach! But not an expensive one. Promise? The little twelve-fifty ones will answer. They're okay and when I leave I can take it to camp with me—maybe."

"Hush!" his mother whispered.

"I didn't know you could buy one at that price, Dick. Will it actually work?" Susan wanted to get the talk away from war. "Where did you see them?"

"I didn't see any for sale; but down at Bert's garage they have one and Pete said that's all it cost. If you like I'll ask him to get one for me. Maybe he can get it at cost or something."

"All right. I'll give you the money and see what you can do. But if you really wanted one why didn't you buy it yourself—long ago? After all, you do have *some* money."

"I know," the boy replied. "but I'm supposed to save what I get or use it for necessities and an extra radio isn't exactly a necessity, would you say?" He smiled as he finished and Susan felt a lump in her throat. Only the other day he had given Barbara ten of his laboriously saved dollars when she wept as she showed him the worn sole in her evening slippers. And yet the two quarreled incessantly. She had often wondered about it. She didn't blame one more than the other; but it seemed as if the two never were together without fireworks. Perhaps it meant nothing; but she knew it worried her mother.

For all Dick's moods and contrariness, he was a grand youngster. Susan felt she didn't have to worry about him except that he kept hinting he wanted to enlist. She was coming more and more to the opinion that Dick was dissatisfied—that he should not be forced to study law if he didn't want to. He should be allowed to go into another line of work—even become a mechanic if he liked. While she wished, with her mother, that Dick would follow in his father's footsteps and become a lawyer, she felt it wrong to try to force him. It was her theory that one had to really enjoy his job if he was to make a success of life. Too many boys and girls were compelled to work at jobs they hated and for which they had no real aptitude. She had seen it happen right in the Whittle Plant and the personnel director was continually wrestling with such cases.

101

Susan was relieved to see that the strained look had left her mother's face and went back to work with a prayer in her heart that what she had predicted would actually happen. There were plenty of business opportunities for a girl of Barbara's charm and ability if she were only willing to search for them. And why didn't Aunt Charity answer her letter?

She was alone in the hospital room most of the afternoon and for once there was little activity so she accomplished a great deal both by bringing a large part of Forms S-47 up to date and checking over a new list of absentees. At a little before four, Lila Davis came in to have a sliver removed from a finger and stayed for a moment to visit. She was happy over her husband's improvement and grateful for all that the doctor and Susan had done for them both.

"I don't know how you do it, Susan," she said. "We are such a huge family for you to took after."

"I suppose one reason is that we both love it, Lila," Susan smiled. "I wouldn't want to do anything else and I'm sure Doctor Marshall feels the same. He could be a huge success in private practice and I'm sure he would make lots more money; but he likes this sort of thing. It's routine—a large part of it; but somehow he doesn't seem to mind that. Every employee is a real person—one he comes to know and nearly always like. He calls the most unbelievable number by their first names and they love it. He's really a marvel, Lila, and I'm sure the Whittle Plant is lucky to have him here. I have sometimes wondered just why he took this job in the first place—it isn't a large factory as factories go or especially important."

"Just at first, I guess it was because it was so near Smithford. His wife was taken there soon after the accident."

"And to think I never knew he was married," Susan said.

"Oh, I guess it was never very much of a marriage, Susan," the other told her. "Not many people know it. I don't think he ever talks about it and when it comes to that—it really isn't anyone's business. Sometime I'll tell you the story. Just now I must run."

"But how do you know so much about it, Lila?"

"My Aunt Helen lived in the town where it happened —she knew her people. Thanks for the operation, Susan. Come over to dinner some night. I'll set a date and we'll have my specialty—spaghetti and meatballs. 'Bye.'

The door closed after her and Susan sat for a moment in deep thought. There was nothing tragic about Doctor Marshall. He was never particularly gay; but he was always pleasant and seemed to have an inexhaustible supply of energy and vitality. She sighed as the door opened and a shabby, bearded man staggered in, shoving the door shut behind him. He leaned against it for a moment then lurched toward her, his hands outstretched. Susan got up. She had taken care of an occasional drunk while she was in training and wasn't afraid; but she took the precaution of putting the desk between them. No doubt the man was very drunk. She demanded coolly:

"Just what do you want? This is a hospital."

"Sure—a hos—hos—sure, I know what it is. Wasn't it in a hos—hos—wasn't I there once? I guess—you were there—such a pretty n-nurse. Help———" He slump-ed to the floor and immediately went to sleep.

Susan tried to rouse him and found that he was un-conscious—not sleeping. His pulse was slow and ragged and he was very cold. She saw that he was quite young— not much older than she was herself; but unkempt with a scraggly growth of beard on his face. His hair was long and matted with dried blood and his clothes were torn and dirty. They lay in loose folds on his body. She went to the telephone to call Tommy. She couldn't leave him here on the floor and it was very cold outside. But before she reached her desk Doctor Marshall arrived. He almost stumbled over the stranger and stared from him to Susan in astonishment.

"What—who on earth is this? Honestly, Susan Trent, lately you seem to collect the darnedest callers. The fellow's drunk. How did he get in here, anyway?"

"Walked in," Susan told him. "I know he's been drinking; but he's sick as well. Look, he must have been hurt, Doctor. There's blood in his hair and it's something more than stupor you see," as the doctor knelt on the floor beside him. "I think we should send him to City—"

"Probably the jail infirmary is the place for him. Did you look through his pockets?"

"I hadn't time. He just came in—not ten minutes ago. I was going to call Tommy to help me with him when you came."

Doctor Marshall was going through pockets in an endeavor to discover the man's identity; but they were empty. However, he pointed out that the clothes the man was wearing were obviously not his own—they were much too large. He picked up the man's long slender hand and examined it closely. It showed no signs of labor— the nails while broken and dirty were well shaped.

"I really think this is a case for the police, Susan," he said after his examination. "I believe this man has been pretty roughly handled—probably injured, robbed and doped. Call the police station while I lock this door. We don't want curious people flocking in here. Call Sergeant Neal, Susan. I can talk to him—I hope."

Sergeant Neal arrived promptly and Doctor Marshall told him his theory regarding the stranger.

"Can't do much until he wakes up, Doc," the officer said sniffing knowingly. "Why don't we just run him in and let him explain when he's slept off his spree?"

"This isn't merely a spree, Sergeant," the doctor said seriously. "The man was evidently bludgeoned—doped and robbed. There's not a scrap of anything with which he can be indentified."

"Didn't he talk when he came in? And how did he get here in the first place? An employee?"

Susan told of his coming and said she was sure he didn't work at the Whittle Plant.

"He slumped to the floor almost at once," she said. "Evidently he has recently been hospitalized. I think he should be taken to City immediately," she ended firmly.

The police officer looked from her to the doctor who agreed. "Then why did you send for me? What am I supposed to do?" the man asked gruffly.

"Find out what you can about his assailant—where his drink was doped and anything else that might help. I tell you this man is a victim, not an aggressor—a criminal.

That's why I called you, Sergeant. I know you're a blood-hound when you know of dirty work at the crossroads."

"Okay, Doc. I'll do what I can and suppose you let me be the first to talk with him when he comes to. You're the doctor. S'long."

Susan called the hospital and the stranger was taken away. He was quite unconscious and the doctor explained his supposition to the young interne who accompanied the ambulance. The young man grinned.

"It isn't possible you've been reading too many mystery tales lately, is it, Doctor?" he jeered. "My guess is the fellow went on a bender and got playfully conked on the bean by one of his frolicsome pals. But we'll take him along. City just loves catering to common drunks, you know. We haven't anything else to do."

"I'll say you'll take him along and see that he gets prompt and efficient attention. I'll just check up on his case by getting in touch with Doctor Fulton." He turned to Susan. "Call the hospital, Susan, and ask to speak to the house physician. And, Doctor—what did you say your name is?"

"I didn't say—and it's no concern of yours, anyway, Doctor," he snapped rudely. His face was red and he stalked out just as the telephone rang. As Doctor Marshall took the instrument from her, Susan said bitterly:

"I detest internes!"

The resident at City listened attentively to Doctor Marshall's explanation regarding the man being taken there and assured him that he, personally, would see his orders were carried out. Doctor Marshall turned from the telephone to say:

"You do attract the strangest people, Susan Trent. Now why should that poor chap come in here? I guess we'll have to station Tommy in the front hall to keep undesirables away."

Susan had an idea he was including Alan MacDowell in that category, but she chose to ignore the implication.

"I suppose he had nowhere to go and was lost and bewildered and—well—he just took a chance and wandered in. I'm terribly sorry for him. It's cold outside and he wasn't any too warmly dressed."

105

"I'll run over to the hospital after five and see how things line up. I can't rid myself of the feeling it's a job for the police and somehow I have a hunch the fellow is someone important. Anything happen while I was gone—aside from our friend there?"

"No. Everything was quiet this afternoon. I very nearly finished the case records—up to the P's—only a few of those and just five Q's. Another afternoon like this and I'll finish the job—to date. I called the two men from the assembly department who didn't show up for work this morning but neither one was at home—no answer. Why don't they insist upon employees' sending word if they are to be absent? Oh, I know they are supposed to, but the rule isn't enforced. It would make things a lot easier if it were made compulsory. I don't think there would be so much absenteeism, either."

"My dear girl, that subject has been threshed over and over again but nothing changes very much. As long as human nature is what it is, you will find there are people who simply will not conform. We just have to make the best of things. 'The old gentleman' feels he has the thing well in hand when he turns the checking over to us here in First Aid."

"Lila Davis came in to have a sliver taken out of her index finger. She is so happy that Alec is better. She, herself, looked almost like she used to."

"Alec still has a long way to go, Susan," the doctor said. "We'll have to find him something to do that won't tax his strength—that is, of course, when he is able to work. It's certain he will never go back to the experimental department again. Too strenuous and exacting. Perhaps 'the old gentleman' can think of something. Remind me to take it up with him later. Have you heard anything more from the Clarks?"

"No", Susan said regretfully. "I called at the house but there seemed to be no one at home. Do you think Frances will come out of this all right, Doctor? You don't think it might be permanent, do you?"

The doctor stared into space for a long moment while Susan waited anxiously. "Of course, she's young," he said at last. "It's very hard to say. Everything possible will be done for her. She will have the very best of care. Mr. Whittle was most concerned when I told him about her condition. The doctors at the sanatorium are the best in their field and I'm sure the girl couldn't be in better hands. I wondered if perhaps, the sister had called you."

"No, she hasn't and—wait a minute. I'll try to reach her by telephone." She put through the call and Mary Clark answered. Her voice was toneless and Susan felt almost sorry she had called. Doctor Marshall came to perch on a corner of her desk.

"She is just the same, Miss Trent," Miss Clark reported. "Clif and I regret we ever consented to her going. I could have taken care of her right here at home and then I would be sure——"

"Wait a minute, Miss Mary. Doctor Marshall will talk to you."

She handed him the instrument and got up and walked to a window where she watched with unseeing eyes the hurrying afternoon shoppers being buffeted by the November wind. She heard the doctor's quiet voice reassuring the unhappy woman. He had known many cases such as her sister's and many times the return to normalcy was both rapid and complete. There were sounds of weeping and he talked soothingly until the weeping stopped. He promised to drive over to see Frances at his first opportunity and would report her exact condition upon his return. It was like a comforting hand on the shoulder and Susan felt again as she had so often before that her chief was an exceptional man as well as a fine doctor and surgeon. She turned as he went back to his own desk.

"I wonder if all factories and plants are as fortunate as ours, Doctor Marshall?" she asked as she prepared to lock her desk for the night.

"How do you mean?"

"Why, have the company doctor follow up the cases and continue his interest in them even after they are out of his particular jurisdiction. Think of the doctors' bills you save them——"

"Change that pronoun to 'we,' my dear. You do as much or more than I do—that is, actual following up. I'm around, you know. I listen to your praises being sung wherever I stop. Do you know, Susan," he said quizzically, "we make a pretty good team, don't we?"

Susan laughed somewhat shakily and her eyes were very bright as she walked across the room to her own tiny sanctum. "I like working with you, Doctor Marshall," she said softly and went inside and closed the door behind her.

CHAPTER ELEVEN

As the November days shortened, the cold increased. The wind grew more bitter—the sun shone but seldom. People mourned the absence of snow, declaring that it was needed—that with plenty of snow the weather would moderate. It was too cold for November. Absenteeism at the Whittle Tool and Implement Plant increased and Susan's days were even more than usually full. Barbara had little to say about her job, but it seemed to Susan that she was quieter and she spent an occasional evening at home reading or listening to the radio. However, these evenings were usually interrupted by telephone calls, Barbara's part of the conversation being guarded and mostly monosyllabic.

Alan MacDowell returned to Ashton as he had promised he would and it happened that Barbara was at home on the evening of his first call. She looked very beautiful there by the fire in the shabby living room and Susan felt an upsurge of affection as she watched her. It was quite obvious she was attracted to the caller and for a moment Susan's heart twisted. Dick was studying, or so it was supposed, and Mrs. Trent was lying down in her room suffering from one of her sick headaches. Alan appeared to enjoy Barbara's gay banter and Susan found herself becoming more and more unnecessary as the evening wore on. Barbara glowed. She seemed to take an impish delight in monopolizing the conversation and once Susan caught her eye and knew instantly what her sister's game was. All right, Susan said to herself, if that's what they wanted there was nothing she could do about it. She had no desire to adopt the rôle of rival and didn't intend staying there to be ignored.

"I'll run up and see if Mother wants anything," she said when Barbara brought out a box of snapshots. No one appeared to hear her. The pictures were all of Barbara and her friends and while they were examining, exclaiming and laughing over them, Susan left the room and slowly mounted the stairs. Her mother was sleeping quietly and Susan went into her own room there to stand before her mirror and stare at the girl reflected there.

No, she wasn't beautiful—not in the least beautiful. Oh, she had rather fine eyes, nice hair, a clear, healthy complexion and perfect teeth. But she lacked her sister's vivacity—her charm—her "come hither" that was so essential to popularity. She was merely attractive—wholesome, where Barbara was breathtaking. She honestly felt one couldn't blame Alan, but his evident and complete defection hurt.

She heard the sound of radio music. One of Barbara's favorite orchestras was playing. Why was it her sister never thought of anyone but herself? She didn't care if she roused her mother as long as she was enjoying herself. Susan turned from the mirror and slipped down the stairs. She stood for a moment watching them dancing and forced a smile as the music stopped.

"Bravo!" she cried softly and clapped her hands. Alan turned to her.

"I say, Susan, if we are to see that picture we ought to get started. Or are you too tired? Perhaps you feel you shouldn't leave your mother as long as she is ill."

"Why, he seems actually embarrassed," Susan told herself. "Fancy Alan MacDowell embarrassed!" Perhaps he suddenly realized that it was she he was supposed to be calling on. He hadn't said anything about the movies. She had hoped for a repetition of that other evening; but of course Barbara had spoiled that plan. Well, if he wanted to go to the movies she supposed she could go. Barbara was at home, and Dick. Mother was sleeping.

"I'll get my things," she said and moved into the hall. She heard Barbara laugh and then give an exaggerated sigh.

"I hear it's a swell picture, Alan," she said, not lowering her voice in the least so that it was quite audible to Susan. "I love every picture Gary Cooper's in. I hope to get to see this one while it's here."

"Why not come with us, then?" the young man said and Susan in the hall thought she read relief in his voice.

That settled it. Let Barbara go with him if he wanted her. She would stay at home. She met her sister in the doorway and drew back as Barbara said blithely:

"You're sweet to ask me, Alan. Sure I won't be in the way?" Her blue eyes challenged Susan standing just outside the door. "I've always thought three was a crowd but—— What's the matter, Sue?"

"Not a thing," Susan told her levelly. "You two run along. I'm rather tired and anyway Mother may need me —if she wakens."

Alan was searching through the box of snapshots when she reentered the room. No doubt hunting for one of Barbara's pictures to take with him. He appeared startled when he saw her and slipped something hastily into his pocket.

"But—but you're not ready!" he exclaimed as she sat down on the piano bench, her fingers drifting idly over the keys. His voice was almost aggrieved. "What's the matter, Susan? Don't you want to go? I thought——" He paused as Barbara returned in hat and coat, pulling on her gloves.

"Not tonight, Alan," Susan said coolly. "You and Barbara run along."

"Don't be a goon, Sue," Barbara laughed, linking her arm in Alan's "I'll walk ahead if you prefer. I have no desire to spoil your plans." She winked roguishly at the young man. "Sue gets these spells sometimes," she said. "Don't notice her. She's peeved at her naughty little sister. Cheer up, darling," she pouted. "I'll take good care of him. Come on, Alan. Let's leave her to her sulks. 'Bye, Mar-tha!"

Alan stood for a moment as if uncertain what to do. His gaze shifted from one to the other. Susan refused to meet his eyes, her own were full of tears of rage and humiliation. She began to play softly and heard the street door close. A car started but she played on. The tears didn't fall. She took care of that and, when Dick came into the room a few minutes later, she greeted him with a smile of affection. He glanced around the room.

"Where's Alan?" he asked curiously. "Didn't he stay? And where's Barb?" His fair face flushed and his blue eyes, so like Barbara's, flashed scornfully. "So she pulled another fast one, did she? And you let her get away with it, I'm disgusted with you, Sue Trent. She refused some fellow—said she had a date. I heard her talking on the phone a while ago and so she had to make good and you're the goat. Why don't you show some spunk?"

111

"That's enough, Dick," Susan said coldly. "Alan wanted to go to the movies and I didn't want to leave Mother as long as she didn't feel well——No," she said defiantly, "I'll not lie to you, Dick. I resented Barbara. She seemed determined to dazzle Alan and succeeded perfectly. I doubt if he knew I was even in the room. If Barbara wants him—she can have him. Now forget it. After all, we scarcely know the man."

"You make me sick, Sue Trent," the boy muttered as he went back to the study. And Susan repeated his statement.

"And you make *me* sick, Susan Trent. 'Martha,' she called me and maybe I am a Martha; but just the same, I'll not play second fiddle to her. If Alan MacDowell prefers Barbara, let him have her—but he can't have me too. Not even as a friend. I'm just not having any, thank you." She supposed Barbara was "getting even" with her —showing her up. She had never forgiven her for the lecture she had bestowed on the occasion of her—she hoped—worst indiscretion. Well, Susan was not going to give her the satisfaction of knowing she had hurt her. It would give her too much pleasure. After all, she had merely liked Alan MacDowell—sometimes not even that. It was only the other day that she had told herself she was glad he was not settling in Ashton. Well, then. She turned down the lights, saw that the fire was banked for the night, advised Dick not to study too long and went up to her room. She would take a warm bath and go to bed early.

She was still awake when Barbara and Alan returned from the movies. She heard Barbara's soft laughter and later knew they were in the kitchen. The tantalizing odor of coffee and toast reached her. She heard Dick leave his room and go downstairs and felt impelled to call to him; but changed her mind. Smothered laughter followed and the clatter of dishes. The smell of frying bacon was added to the rest and Susan began to feel hungry; but pride prevented her joining the trio.

It was some time before she heard the car leave the driveway and Barbara, none too quietly, pass her door.

Dick, however, came stealthily into her room. He was carrying a glass of steaming milk and two pieces of toast under a napkin.

"Here you are, sis," he whispered. "I know you're awake. Who could sleep in all that racket? It's a wonder it didn't wake Mom. It's all hot so have it right away. I'm going to bed. You can leave the things on the stand there and take 'em down in the morning. We had coffee, toast and I scrambled some eggs and cooked a little bacon. That Barb snitched most of it, though. Alan kept looking at the door—hoping you'd come down, too, I bet a dollar. Don't be a nut and let Barb double-cross you. Take a leaf out of her book and beat her at her own game. Not but what I think you're well rid of him or any other fellow who comes spooning around you. 'Night, Sue."

Susan's eyes were bright with tears as Dick closed the door and shuffled back to his own room. She felt that this young brother of hers had wisdom and sympathy far beyond his years. They adored each other and lately Dick had constituted himself her champion against her sister's subtle but barbed warfare. She couldn't help a feeling of humiliation that he found it necessary and made a secret vow to defend her rights in the future. After all, she had seniority on her side and the fact remained that she was a nurse with a permanent position and it was her salary that really kept them all in comparative comfort. Why should she cringe at Barbara's jibes—at her air of superiority—her imperious manner of taking what she wanted as if it were her perfect right to do so? Susan sat up in bed.

"From now on," she told herself firmly, "I become a dominant character. I shall take what belongs to me and hold it against drought and high water—and Barbara." A wry smile curved for a moment the lips that were in danger of becoming much too grim for a girl of her years and as she slipped beneath the blankets she murmured: "And I don't mean Alan MacDowell either, at least not entirely. He's just another disappointment. What's the matter with me, anyway?" As there was no answer forthcoming, she snuggled lower in her bed and after a moment fell asleep.

113

The Trent family was late arising next morning. Mrs. Trent knocked on Susan's door and at the girl's startled acknowledgment said:

"It's after seven, Susan. I overslept this morning and it seems as if everyone else did, too. Better get up at once.

Susan was out of bed and halfway to the bathroom before her mother was downstairs. She had to hurry. She expected a heavy schedule today with a dozen or more calls to make. She hoped Doctor Marshall would suggest her taking the morning for calls—she made so much better time in the morning. People were all busy and didn't want to visit so she never had to spend much time anywhere but could check her visits off with clocklike regularity. She supposed that was why the doctor preferred mornings. He wasn't much of a visitor—liked to keep these routine calls strictly professional. Well, it was different with him. She was naturally a friendly soul. She had come to know most of the employees of the Plant and to like nearly all of them and their families. They were nice to her—seemed to like having her drop in. They would show her a new baby or a new pet. They would ask her advice about their furnishings, their hats and even their budgets. The foreigners were especially eager for her help and she felt, somehow, they had a right to it.

She went down to the kitchen where breakfast was usually served these cold mornings and sat down opposite her mother. Dick raced down the stairs, dashed into the room and flung himself into his chair. He grinned at them both, his blue eyes full of mischief.

"What, no bacon or eggs this morning? How come?"

His mother raised accusing eyes to his. "Don't you ever get filled up, Dick?" she demanded. "I never dreamed there would be nothing for breakfast this morning. And you might at least have scraped the pans."

"What makes you think I'm the guilty party, Mom?" he asked innocently. "You have two other offsprings, remember."

"We can eliminate them both. I know Susan would have cleaned up and Barbara would not have cooked either bacon or eggs. She doesn't especially care for them."

"Like fun she doesn't," Dick exclaimed. "She ate most of 'em last night after Alan and I cooked 'em. What an appetite the gal has!"

"Just the same——" Mrs. Trent began, when her eyes turned to Susan. "And you, dear? Where were you during this wild orgy?"

"I was tired, Mother," Susan replied, spreading butter on a piece of toast. "I went to bed early——"

"Leaving Alan?"

"Oh, he and Barbara went to the movies."

"I see."

Nothing more was said on the subject and Dick made a breakfast of toast and marmalade and coffee into which he poured most of the cream. Later he walked, as usual, with Susan to the corner where they parted and he pedaled off toward Judge Martin's office.

Susan's head lifted to the crisp fall morning. She loved autumn; even after the leaves were down and the bare trees stood etched against the intense blue of the sky, she gloried in their beauty. To her they were a daily lesson in faith and hope. Winter would come as it must to everyone; but spring followed as surely as day followed night. After the chill and bitterness—the dreariness and disappointments, came warmth and sweetness—gladness and fulfilment. Somehow last night's wretchedness seemed trivial in the light of this new day. Someone had said, and she liked to remember it, that for every sorrow and loss there is compensating happiness and gain. It has helped her through many a trying situation.

These thoughts raced through her mind as she strode along in the crisp November, still meager, sunshine. Perhaps later the day would be golden and almost warm; but now the sun was still close to the eastern horizon just touching the tips of trees and church spires with gold. She didn't notice a car draw up beside her or see the young man who opened the door invitingly. It wasn't until he spoke her name that she turned her head. Then her pulses quickened—she knew a mixture of pleasure and chagrin and she stood for a moment uncertain what

to do. He didn't leave the car but watched her doubtfully—almost fearfully as if expecting a snub.

"Feeling better, Susan?" he asked tentatively, his hand
still on the open door. "Won't you get in and ride the
rest of the way? I had hoped to get to your house before
you started, but I overslept."

Susan slipped beside him. "So did we—all of us.
Barbara isn't up yet—or wasn't when we left." She tried
to speak casually as if last night's *contretemps* hadn't
happened.

"I wish you had come with us, Susan," he said. "It
was a good picture but we—I missed you. After all, it
was you I wanted to see, Susan. Why did you brush me
off?"

"But I didn't," she denied, all of the evening's bitterness flooding back. "When I said I would go with you,
I thought Barbara was going to stay at home so that if
Mother—— No," she said, her eyes for a brief moment
meeting his honestly, "I thought you preferred Barbara—
you seemed to. I felt I would be just—— Oh, I don't
know what I thought, Alan. I just didn't feel like going.
That's all."

He started the car, his eyes on the road ahead. Susan
threw a side glance at his puzzled face. He probably
thought she was a jealous cat—begrudging her lovely
young sister an evening's enjoyment. She heard him give
vent to an exaggerated sigh.

"How long are you going to be here?" she asked,
wondering at his unnatural silence. She felt she had made
last night's affair very clear.

"I had planned to stay a day or two but perhaps it
would be better if I left this afternoon. After all, I don't
want to make a nuisance of myself. Would you like me to
stay, Susan, or shall I go on home? I'm bringing my car
back with me. The judge loaned me his—told me to use
it while I'm here this time. We could go over to Marydale
tonight—and I could show you the development where
Blaud and Dickson are to erect their houses. · What do
you say? Am I forgiven for—well, for pulling a boner—
if that's what I did?"

"Oh, Alan, I'm so ashamed," Susan said. "Please don't

116

blame yourself. But honestly I'm not usually so temperamental and—well, unpleasant. Do forget it. Of course we shall enjoy having you stay on for a few days if you can and I shall love seeing the Marydale plans. I'll be looking for you after dinner tonight."

"But I had planned to be here with the judge's car to take you to lunch this noon. You *do* eat, don't you?'

"I'm sorry, Alan," she said. "But this is another one of those days when I snatch a bite at my desk. I usually take the doctor's car and dash all over the city making hurried calls on various patients. If I have the morning trick I don't know when I can have lunch and if the doctor chooses the morning and I take the afternoon, I don't know just when I shall be able to get away from the office. So you see? Better give me a rain check if you like. I'm afraid today is out—definitely."

'Okay," the young man said resignedly and the little imp of perversity that seemed to ride her so often since his advent whispered that he was only trying to make amends for last night and for a moment she felt like flippantly suggesting that he ask Barbara to lunch with him—just to show him something or other—she didn't know exactly what; but she bit her lip and got out of the car. She turned to wave as she opened the door to the new wing of the Tool and Implement Plant and felt decidedly let down when she saw the car was already fast disappearing down the street. Well, it served her right if he was sore. She certainly hadn't acted especially cordial.

After all, she was first in the office. Doctor Marshall was late again. She changed quickly into uniform and was going over her list of convalescents when she saw the familiar car park beside the curb just outside the office. Doctor Marshall came briskly up the short walk and the front door banged. He had never learned to close that door quietly.

"Well, well, good morning, Susan," he said with more cordiality that he had been showing lately. He stripped his gloves from his hands and shed hat and overcoat. From the looks of things he intended taking the morning trick. Susan frowned slightly and reached for his list.

117

He came to stand behind her. "All set, Susan?" he asked, and reached to take the list from her. "H'm'm," he mused, scanning the names. "It would seem that several of these should be entirely out of the woods by this time. Call Keimele and see what he thinks about the Winthrop —Jim Winthrop case. They promised to call Keimele and, if they did, Doc certainly didn't report to me."

Doctor Keimele had evidently just come into his office which from what his nurse said was full to capacity. But he reported that Jim Winthrop had been sent to City Hospital—last night. Pneumonia. Temperature 104.2. They hadn't called him until then and he had got busy at once. He wanted to know why in heck Marshall hadn't hospitalized the man before. Mrs. Winthrop had told him her husband had been ill for weeks. Was Doc there and could he talk to him? Susan passed the phone over to her chief. She heard most of the conversation. Neither doctor made any effort to lower his voice and she heard Keimele demand the reason for the delay.

"But Jim had no fever when I saw him two days ago, Doc, and his wife flatly refused to allow him to be moved to the hospital. I felt he needed a thorough going over— x-rays, metabolism and so on. She contended he was simply putting on a show—that he did it quite often. Aside from his prolonged lethargy—she called it laziness—I could find nothing much wrong with the man," Doctor Marshall insisted. "He's on the absent list much too often. Doc, and there has been talk of letting him out. But I'll take care of that end of it. Want me to run over to City and look him over, or will you handle it from now on?"

From the sounds at the other end of the line, Susan knew Doctor Keimele was gladly turning the case over to them Susan knew her chief was in for a time with the patient's wife who would no doubt blame him for the whole thing.

"Take it and welcome, Doc." Susan heard Keimele roar. "Also, take my advice and keep his *frau* away— chloroform her if you can't do anything else. Makes me glad I'm single, old man——You, too? Better hesitate a long time before putting your head ino the noose."

Both doctors laughed and Doctor Keimele shouted, "S'long, Doc. Good luck!"

Doctor Marshall was grinning broadly as he replaced the telephone and Susan smiled in sympathy. Evidently her chief's marital status was unknown to his colleague. Now the doctor slipped the list into his pocket and picked up his overcoat.

"I'll try to be back by noon, Susan," he told her pulling on his gloves. "It depends largely on what I find at the hospital. What a female that Winthrop dame is! Have you met her?" and at Susan's shake of the head he said firmly: "I hope you never will. She's a caution. Well, be good and do the best you can, and for Heaven's sake, don't attract any more undesirables." There was a decided edge to his voice and Susan knew he was thinking of Alan MacDowell.

He had given her that same advice ever since the fellow calling himself Jerry Darling had crashed First Aid and more impressively after poor Barry Nash had wandered in and dropped at her feet. Young Nash had been through a bout with pneumonia and for days lain in a state of utter collapse. When he rallied and could tell who he was and relate his experiences, as much as he could recall, even hard-boiled Sergeant Neal was outraged and spread a net for his assailants so successfully that two of them were waiting trial right now and the Nash family—THE NASH FAMILY—Susan thought of them in capitals, for they were prominent in the middle west—had flown to his bedside.

Barry was still in City Hospital convalescing rapidly and was to be taken south as soon as he could travel. He had no recollection of coming to First Aid and he was not reminded of it.

But the Whittle First Aid figured in the Nash kidnapping news just the same. 'Full credit is given the Company doctor and nurse for their prompt diagnosis of the victim's condition and the speed and efficiency with which he was transferred to the hospital. It was undoubtedly due to their suspicions of foul play that Sergeant Neal of the Ashton Police Force was induced to set his sleuths in action with the above results. However, we believe only

119

a small part of the vicious ring has been apprehended. It is the sincere hope of the entire community that the leaders will be brought to justice in the very near future."

Barry Nash's picture, together with those of his impressive family, had been in the papers and Susan saw that he was slender and good-looking—younger han she had supposed. He was still in college and had been the subject of a nation-wide search ever since his disappearance more than a month before he had staggered into this very room.

All this went through Susan's mind as she watched Doctor Marshall drive away. Suddenly she felt depressed. This was, apparently, going to be one of those mornings quite devoid of incident. Only two people came to First Aid for treatment and Susan took care of them promptly and efficiently. After all, the morning passed and Susan felt she had accomplished a good deal. The case cards were now up to date and all correspondence taken care of. She sat for a moment, hands idle, eyes on the street. Win Brighton had just come on duty at the four corners. Lights flashed red, yellow, green. Traffic halted, trembled, and roared away. The morning's promise of a clear day had soured. The sun had disappeared. The fresh breeze had reached gale velocity; it crept through the small opening of one of the broad windows and Susan shivered. Not that she was particularly cold—for some reason she felt blue. Dust swirled and eddied along Main Street and pedestians bent before the onslaught. Only this morning, with the sky cloudless and the sun tipping trees and chimneys with gold, they had jeered at the weatherman's prediction of snow flurries and sub-zero temperature, but it looked now as if he were right.

Susan left her chair and walked over to the window. She stood for a moment gazing out at the darkening sky. There they came—the first snowflakes of the season. she flung the window wide and thrust out her hand. She felt the soft gentle touch of the flakes as they fell. Well, it was late for the first snowfall. Usually Ashton had snow in October almost before the trees were bare of leaves. She closed the window and returned to her desk. She reached for her phone and called Tommy. She might as well eat her lunch now and have it over. No knowing when the doctor would return.

Snow was whipping against the window. If this kept up she knew there would be no trip to Marydale tonight. Perhaps they could have another quiet evening at home— if Barbara had a date. Susan shook her head. "None of that," she told herself firmly. 'I have always prided myself on being a girl who didn't find a potential lover or husband in every male I met. Alan MacDowell can be very pleasant. I rather like him nearly always— as a friend —but absolutely nothing more. Understand that, Susan Trent, and watch your step." She felt better after her declaration of faith and prepared to enjoy her meager luncheon.

CHAPTER TWELVE

DOCTER MARSHALL LITERALLY blew into the building soon after one o'clock. He stamped the snow from his feet and shook his hat which even during the short walk from his car to the entrance was covered with snow. He came into the First Aid muttering:

"Brrr! Who said we were in for an open winter?"

"I didn't," Susan laughed. "If this keeps up all night the roads will be blocked by morning. Listen to that wind!"

"See if you can't contact most of the people on your list by telephone, Susan," he said. "Driving is hazardous right now."

"I can walk, Doctor," Susan told him. "I don't mind a little snow."

"Do as I say," he ordered sharply, then grinned at her.

She was able to reach most of the names listed and Doctor Marshall said they could quite easily take care of the rest within a day or two. 'I'm going over to the Prospect Street Plant, Susan," he said moving on into the surgery for certain things he might need. "There's a lot of flu in this town and we don't want an epidemic of pneumonia hitting us just now. Perhaps if I can catch the victims before it gets a real hold on them we can avoid complications. I probably won't be very long. If anyone comes in showing signs of the malady, better send 'em home. I'll try to get to them tonight or early in the morning. You might tell them to drink plenty of hot liquids and get into bed—at once—and stay there. Such weather!"

Susan watched him leave the building for the second time that day. She had heard that a great many cases of influenza had been reported. Five or six stenographers and several from the accounting department were absent leaving the offices upstairs badly crippled. She had, herself, typed four letters for old Mr. Peabody who told her he couldn't get anyone upstairs to do it for him. Of course it wasn't her work and she wasn't supposed to do it; but she felt it didn't hurt her any. In fact, she· was glad to help out where she could.

Mr. Whittle came in and complained that the place was shot to pieces. He asked where the doctor was and she told him he had gone down to the Prospect Street factories to check up on colds and incipient flu victims.

"He figures an ounce of prevention is worth a pound of cure," she said and "the old gentleman" nodded his approval.

"Doc's a good man," was his comment, and left. Susan began going through the files in search of possible errors although she felt pretty sure there were none; but she had to keep busy. Outside the storm raged. The afternoon darkened so that it was necessary to turn on the lights. Snow whispered against the windows and piled up on the sills. For a mament she watched the traffic lights and Win Brighton standing in the middle of the street in his long blue coat and cap, his arms moving rhythmically as he beat them against his sides to increase circulation. Cars skidded and once she thought he would be knocked down but the car swerved just in time and the driver landed against the nearest telephone pole, there to slump weakly against the steering wheel. Traffic halted and Win Brighton ran to the driver's side. In a few minutes the car moved slowly on down the street and everything went on as before. And then came the city spreader with its load of sand and after that cars ceased to skid and traffic moved more smoothly.

Still the wind roared and now there seemed to be but few pedestrians abroad. Those few dodged in and out of shops, dashed across the snowy street, slipped and slid along the icy pavement and at last disappeared beyond her vision. She was glad she had a pair of overshoes in her dressing room—she hoped they were still wearable. She hadn't seen them since last winter. It might be fun buffeting the storm on her way home. She had always enjoyed fighting the elements, defying them to get her down. There was something exhilarating in a storm—in meeting it head on, feeling one's blood glow and know that just ahead was a warm home with its odors of wood smoke and good food. After all, what could one desire more?

This would be just the night for music; for the songfest Alan had called that other evening. Later they could have hot chocolate and sandwiches in the kitchen and he would tell them about his family and his plans for the future while her mother and Dick would listen and after a while drift off to bed leaving her and Alan to the intimacy of a dying fire and a warmly quiet house. She smiled as she drew the charming picture. She felt sure she was not and never had been the least bit in love with Alan. The thought of such a possibility actually annoyed her. She didn't want his love—she wanted his friendship —his companionship. He had jibed that she was suffering from a family—a mother complex—that she was a funny girl. Well, what of it? Probably that was quite true and what of it?

She wondered if Barbara would come home early— maybe to dinner, or if she would stay on at the Halseys'. Thinking of Barbara made her wonder about her letter to Aunt Charity. She would wait another week and if she didn't hear she would send another letter. The more she thought about her sister's being at Eve Halsey's the more she disliked it. And yet she felt sure Barbara would listen to no advice from her on the subject.

Doctor Marshall returned a little before five. Susan had received no calls from the office upstairs and no one had dropped in to the First Aid room. To her it had been one of the most boring, tiresome days she had experienced in the years of her employment at the Whittle Plant.

"How is Jim Winthrop, Doctor Marshall?" Susan asked as the doctor sat down at his desk and lit a cigarette.

"Not too bad. In his case the sulfapyridine took hold quickly and his temperature was nearly normal when I left the hospital. However, the man has some thyroid trouble just as I thought. We'll have to take care of that when he recovers."

"And his wife, Doctor?" Susan asked demurely. "Did you see her?"

"I left word she was not to be admitted—not while I was there." He looked at the nurse quizzically. "You know the old saying about the female of the species, Susan. I think Kipling had someone like Sarah Winthrop in mind when he wrote his famous poem. The nurses at City have already got her number." He chuckled. "What sort of an afternoon did you have, Miss Trent? I came in almost fearfully not knowing what I should find waiting for me."

"I think I was never so completely bored in my life, Doctor Marshall," Susan told him. "Only one person came in during the entire afternoon and that was Mr. Whittle. He complained the whole place was shot to pieces. He asked for you and I told him you had gone down to the Prospect Street Plant and he seemed pleased with your foresight."

"Dan Morse over in the pattern room called me an old fogy. He declared there was no sense in coddling a man just because he had the sniffles. He has a bad cold himself and sneezed all over the place. I ordered him to bed with hot drinks and plenty of blankets. He refused to go. I called his wife and she talked to him. He went home—or I took him, growling all the way. But he went to bed meek as Moses and his wife almost kissed me when we came downstairs after tucking him in. The man had a temperature of 103. Think of all the people he infected. I read the whole darned room a lecture on how to treat a cold and treat their neighbors at the same time. I hope they listened; but I have my doubts. There are ten men sick in that one room alone."

"I believe this colder weather with plenty of snow will help, don't you?"

"Oh, they say it will and I certainly hope so. I sent more than a dozen men home from different departments and the foremen nearly mobbed me. But after I told them about Dan Morse, they drew in their horns. I guess they thought perhaps I'd do the same to them—maybe they figured I put a hex on Dan." He laughed and leaned back in his chair. "Gosh! I'm tired. Let's call it a day Susan."

"Ten to five. All right. You run along and I'll close up. I'm a little tired myself; but not from overwork," Susan said.

"I'll drive you home, Miss Trent," the doctor said and while Susan had been looking forward to walking she didn't dare refuse this time. However, she didn't go with him because Alan MacDowell came into the office a moment later and asked for her, Doctor Marshall told him she was getting ready to go home and what could he do for him.

"Not a thing, Doctor," the young man said annoyingly cheerful. "I'm waiting to drive Susan home. It's a wicked night and I have the judge's car outside. No objection to my waiting for her, have you?"

"Not the slightest," the doctor answered shortly and picked up his hat. "It was my intention to drive Miss Trent home but as long as you came expressly for that purpose, I'll leave that pleasure to you. Good night."

Susan came out just as he was leaving and was startled to see Alan standing in the middle of the room.

"O-oh!" she said, buttoning her coat. "Did, you come for me, Alan? I didn't know and I accepted the doctor's offer to drive me."

"He's gone," Alan said. "And is he the old grouch! But somehow he seems younger than I thought."

"Well, I told you he wasn't old, though of course he is older than we are. Come on then. I didn't have a very hearty lunch and feel the need of nourishment. Perhaps you would like to come to dinner tonight, Alan. Would you?"

"But your mother——"

"Mother won't mind. We always have enough and you were coming over tonight anyway. If it will make you feel better I'll call Mother right now so she can set another place at table."

"Well ——" Alan agreed. "But if she hesitates the least bit you let me know. It will be all right."

"She won't," Susan promised and she didn't. Susan turned from the telephone and reached for the light switch. The room was thrown into soft gloom. Her hand encountered Alan's and he drew her into his arms.

"You're sweet, Susan," he whispered there in the friendly dimness and his kiss was hard and, to Susan, devastating. She drew away from him, her hand to her trembling lips.

"Oh, no, Alan. Not that! I—I——"

The young man laughed. "Come on, you silly," he cried. "A kiss isn't necessarily compromising. Don't act so stricken."

Susan clenched her hands and swallowed hard. He

opened the door and she went out into the brightly lighted hall then turned to lock the door. "I know it isn't," she told him shakily; "but just the same you must never do it again. I—I hate that sort of thing."

"I don't believe it," he laughed as he hurried her down the snowy walk to the judge's car. "And don't tell me you've never been kissed before."

"I've never made a practice of it," Susan told him primly. "I think it's cheap."

Alan laughed again, this time somewhat ruefully. "How old are you, Susan Trent?" he asked. "No, let me guess. I don't believe you can be much older than I am."

For some reason Susan was annoyed. "I'm not quite twenty-four," she said stiffly. "I don't know how old you are—I don't particularly care. Do I look older?"

"Now you're peeved at me. I'm just a tactless idiot. It's because you're so serious, Susan. I'm twenty-six, myself, and old enough to know better than to ask a girl's age. I'm sorry ——"

"Anyway, it doesn't really matter, does it?" Susan asked.

"Of course not. Gosh, this is some night! I see where we don't go over to Marydale and I think I'll take the judge's car home and walk back to your house. I don't think he has ever left it out in the weather since he bought it—at least five years ago."

He let her out at her door and drove off down the street. The snow was already deep on their sidewalk and Susan wondered if Dick was at home and why he hadn't cleared it. She went into the hall, slipped out of her outdoor things and called to her mother in the kitchen. "I'll run upstairs and get into something else and be right down to help," she said. "Alan will be here in a few minutes. He took the judge's car back."

She heard Dick whistling as he went around to the back door where he left his bicycle and a few minutes later heard the scraping of the shovel against the stone walk. She was glad he was clearing away the snow without being told. She unfastened the belt of her street dress, fluffed up her hair and was dusting her nose with a bit of powder when she saw the letter leaning against a cold cream jar. It was typewritten and bore a New York postmark. For a moment she had thought it might be from **Aunt Charity**. She slipped a nail-file beneath the flap and pulled out a single sheet of paper also typewritten. The signature at the bottom was Charity Trent.

Susan scanned the few lines. Miss Trent had been in New York for two weeks of shopping and relaxation and would arrive at her brother's house within the next day or two. She hoped her niece whose picture had accompanied Susan's letter was as sensible as she was pretty. If so perhaps arrangements could be made that would prove agreeable to everyone. Until then, she remained, Faithfully, Charity Trent.

Not a warm letter or particularly friendly; but Susan was both relieved and anxious. She would have to tell her mother what she had done and they would have to make preparations for her coming. She hoped she had done right and that Barbara would go—for a visit if nothing more. But the news would have to wait until after dinner—until after Alan had left. She slipped into a favorite sheer wool frock of warm russet. It was young and very becoming. So Alan thought she looked as if she might be older than he— twenty-seven or eight, perhaps. She smiled ruefully. This was one of the time she didn't care for Alan MacDowell. She hurried down stairs.

"Barbara not home yet?" she asked her mother.

She phoned that she probably would stay at the Halseys' for dinner as there were certain things she wanted to finish. But she promised to be home early tonight—and she said *early.*"

Susan didn't take much stock in her sister's promise. She knew time meant nothing to Barbara and any time before sunup was early to her. Dick finished the walks and came in with Alan, leaving the snow shovel on the front porch.

"Holy mackerel, what a night!" he exclaimed as he tossed cap and Mackinaw toward the hatrack where they, miraculously, stuck. Alan was more particular with his overcoat and hat although the result was no better. They went into the living room and Dick put a match to the fire already laid in the grate. "Something smells good, doesn't it?" he said as the fragrant aroma of coffee and roast meat crept to them. "I'm hungry as a hunter. How about you, Alan?"

"Well, I can always eat," he replied, "and tonight is no exception."

"Do you know, we ate our breakfast last night, Alan?" Dick told him. "All the bacon and every last egg in the house—so we breakfasted this morning on toast and marmalade. Mom wasn't too pleased although she didn't scold. Mom never scolds when we clean out the icebox."

"You're lucky. Molly, our hired girl, used to threaten to skin us alive when we had one of our raids. She left us flat on more than one occasion although she always came back. Does your mother do all the cooking?"

"Sure. Why not? Mom's a swell cook—none better— and anyway, we're poor people."

"I didn't mean it that way. So are we. But you have sisters. Don't they help?"

"Sure. Sue does. Barb never has. But you know how it is with girls, Alan," he said determined not to be disloyal to his sister even though he was sore at her. "Barb's popular —she's never at home for more than a minute or two at a time. Doesn't have time to help. Mom says she doesn't need it— that she can manage everything by herself and she seems to—with what help Sue and I give her. We're not social butterflies, you see."

"Barbara is beautiful, isn't she?" was all he said and Dick's look was almost pitying as he agreed.

"The poor boob!" he said to himself.

During dinner the storm abated somewhat and while the wind continued its wild fury the snow had almost ceased when, the dishes out of the way, they gathered in the living room for another evening of music. But something was missing and Susan tried to think what it could be. Perhaps it was only that a repetition was always apt to be a little flat—never quite reaching the perfection of the première. And when while it was still quite early Alan rose to leave, Susan felt relief. She was glad he was going. She wanted to talk to her mother. Barbara hadn't come home and Mrs. Trent began to worry.

"I shall call up the Halsey house and see if she has left," she said when Alan had gone." Barbara promised she would be home early and here it is nearly eleven."

"Only eleven? Why that's early in Barbara's lexicon, Mom," Dick explained. "The mere shank of the evening so to speak. If you phone she will be mad as hops. Better not."

Mrs. Trent went into the kitchen to make a few sandwiches for her younger daughter when she should come in, and poured milk into a pan so that it could be heated in a few minutes. She would fix hot chocolate for her and see that she was thoroughly warm before she went to bed. Barbara was so careless about her health.

"You two run on to bed," she told Susan and Dick. "I shall wait up for Barby. She should be along most any time now."

"Nonsense, Mother," Susan objected. "You go on up and I'll wait for her. I know you're tired. I'm not in the least sleepy, anyway, and perhaps I can finish my library book. But why wait up tonight, Mother?" she asked. "She hates it and we haven't for a long time now."

"She said she would be home early—promised me," Mrs. Trent worried.

"Well, I'll wait for her," Susan said matter-of-factly. She had completely forgotten Aunt Charity's letter.

After the others had gone upstairs, Susan settled herself before the still growing fire and picked up her story where she had left off on Sunday. The warmth of the room, the deep continuous roar of the wind outside and the quiet of the house lulled her into forgetfulness. The ringing of the telephone roused her. She couldn't have slept very long for it was not yet one o'clock. Her left foot had gone to sleep but she hobbled into the hall and picked up the telephone. Probably Barbara had been persuaded by Mrs. Halsey to spend the night there.

"Is this the Trent residence?" a woman's voice asked and Susan's heart turned to ice. Something must have happened to Barbara. She said quickly:

"Yes—yes. This is Susan Trent. What is it? What has happened?"

"Plenty. That precious sister of yours has eloped."

"Eloped! Nonsense. How could she? I can't believe that ——"

"You'd better believe it. She ran away with Nigel—Nigel Ruoff. She thinks he's in love with her. She's crazy."

"But where did they go? Who is this speaking?" Susan demanded.

"I haven't the faintest idea where they went and—well, I'm a woman."

"Can't you give me any inform ——" A click reached her. The line was dead.

Susan stared at the silent instrument for a dazed moment then slowly bracketed it. What could she do? Where could she go? Mother! Mother must not know. She ran upstairs to Dick's room and tried to rouse him. It was hard work. He was a sound sleeper but at last he sensed her agitation.

"Get dressed, Dick, and come on downstairs. I have to go out and I want you to be here just in case ——"

"In case what, Sue? Barbara?"

"She was detained or stuck somewhere by the storm and I'm going after her."

"I bet she's off with that Ruoff wolf," her brother muttered disgustedly. "How are you going after her, Sue? You haven't a car and I bet you can't get a taxi at this hour." But Susan was halfway down the stairs. Doctor Marshall had told her to call him in any emergency. Tonight she was taking him at his word. She dialed his number. It was some minutes before he answered but he seemed to be wide awake and said instantly:

"Why, Susan! What has happened?"

Susan explained something of their predicament and he promised to be at her home as soon as he could get there.

"You can tell me the rest when I see you, Susan. Chin up, my girl. We'll bring the erring child home."

But Susan wasn't too confident. She dialed the Halsey number and when a weary male voice answered demanded to know where Miss Trent was. The man, evidently the butler, informed her he hadn't the least idea. She had gone out with Mr. Ruoff early in the evening. No, Mr. Ruoff had not returned—neither of them had returned.

"Let me speak to Mrs. Halsey, please," Susan said.

"But—but—the time — Mrs. Halsey has retired."

"At one o'clock? I don't believe it; but I don't care if she has. You get Mrs. Halsey—at once. Do you hear? Or would you prefer I call the police and have them ——"

"Oh, no. No. You must not do that. I shall see what I can do." He left the line open and Susan waited tense and angry. At last a receiver clicked and a smooth, soft voice said:

"This is Eve Halsey. Albert has said you wanted to speak to me. Well?"

"This is Susan Trent, Mrs. Halsey. I want to know where my sister is."

"Barbara?" An obvious yawn and a murmured apology reached Susan and she cried:

"Of course, Barbara. Where did your brother or cousin or whatever he is take her? You had better tell me quickly or ——"

"Well, really, Miss Trent, I'm not your sister's guardian. I don't know ——"

"Then I shall get in touch with the police and I mean it."

"That's telling her, Sue," applauded Dick at the foot of the stairs just as a car swept up to the porch and Doctor Marshall ran up the steps to the door which Dick opened for him.

"No. No, don't be foolish. Wait," came from the Halsey end of the line and Susan heard someone call:

"Tell her to try Joe's Lodge and Café—Nigel usually takes his sweeties there."

It wasn't very clear but Susan somehow felt the information might be correct especially when Mrs Halsey cried angrily:

"Shut up!"

Susan dropped the instrument, shrugged into her coat, pulled on hat and overshoes and caught the doctor's hand, urging him to hurry. The telephone was still sputtering where Susan had dropped it and Dick picked it up.

"I hope they give you the works for this—you and that cousin of yours deserve it." Dick made his voice as menacing as possible. "I'd like to be a mouse and see how she takes that one," he muttered to himself as he bracketed the instrument. He found an apple on the kitchen table, put another chunk of wood on the fire and prepared to wait in comfort. He wasn't particularly worried. Barb had often been out much later than this. Barb was smart —nothing very bad was apt to happen to her. But she ought to have her ears pinned back for getting the family all worked up over her escapades. The thing that puzzled him was why Sue should be in such a stew about it. He bet it was something to do with that Ruoff wolf. He stammered as he tried to speak that combination even in his mind and with his mouth full of apple.

CHAPTER THIRTEEN

SUSAN felt that if she lived for a hundred years she would never forget that drive over the suddenly treacherous highway on that stormy November night. Doctor Marshall's car was powerful and negotiated the deepst and most hazardous drifts with more or less ease but fear and dread rode her like some evil spirit and she sat silent and tense as they fought their way over each mile of the journey. It was long after two by the clock on the instrument panel when they approached Smithford and veered off along a country road to the place known as Joe's Lodge and Café. Doctor Marshall knew where to go and his mouth was grim as he plowed through the snow for the next half mile. Susan's hands were clenched tightly in her lap. Should they find Barbara there?

"Please God let her be all right—please God—please God!" she prayed over and over.

Light glowed ahead and the doctor asked:

"Would you like me to go in alone, Susan? I know Ruoff by sight and can handle him."

"No—oh, no. I'll go—but would you mind coming with me? I have never been here before and ——"

"Of course I shall come with you. I wouldn't think of your going alone. We won't do anything dramatic—just go in and ask for something to eat—and drink, while we look around."

Doctor Marshall opened the door and ushered Susan inside. Not many people were in evidence. The foyer was a bit gaudy but quite attractive with its palms and shadowy corners and the night clerk dozed behind his desk. He perked up as the doctor stopped and said casually:

"Bad night out. I know it's late but could we get something to eat—and perhaps a place to thaw out before we go on?"

"Sure," the clerk told him eying them both with something like curiosity. If he recognized the doctor he made no comment "Just go inside there and I'm sure you will be taken care of."

The doctor led Susan into the bright glare of the huge bar and dining room. There were, perhaps, two dozen people there and at once he saw Nigel Ruoff seated at a distant corner table. He was quite alone. A waiter approached and led them to a table near the door and after the doctor had ordered coffee and sandwiches he pointed out the man they sought.

"But where's Barbara?" Susan asked, fearfully. "What has he done with her?"

Nigel Ruoff seemed to be occupied with a pack of cards, shuffling and reshuffling them before he spread them out on the table before him. No one appeared to take any notice of him and the waiter who filled his glass from time to time hovered solicitously but was never too close.

Doctor Marshall looked thoughtful as if figuring something out and then reached into his pocket and brought out a metal disk which he gave to Susan. It was the medal given him recently by the Whittle Plant in recognition of his efficient service. Susan thought it looked like a policeman's badge. She examined it closely and looked up at him with a question in her gray eyes.

"Take this and go out to the desk clerk and ask what room the girl who came with Mr. Ruoff is occupying. If he acts difficult let him see that medal but not too closely. Tell him the girl is a minor and there is danger of the place getting into trouble. You want to avoid scandal and if it can be done quietly you will not bring charges. But, on the other hand——"

"I know," Susan said, getting to her feet. She was white and frightened but most of all she was angry. "Keep that —that creature here," she whispered.

"Leave it to me," the doctor told her, "and if there is trouble—call. I'll be right there."

Susan walked out of the dining room and over to the desk where the clerk still dozed.

"I want to know where the girl is who came with Mr. Ruoff," she said coldly.

The man behind the desk stared at her for a moment as if he thought she had lost her mind. "I'm not giving out any information regarding our guests," he told her flatly. "It's against orders."

"I insist upon knowing," Susan said still coolly although her knees were shaking. "You will save yourself and the

135

proprietor of this place trouble by doing as I ask." She opened her hand containing the medal and he stared for a moment while Susan said: "That girl is a minor and you face serious charges by allowing her to remain here. We traced them to this place and we mean to take her away quietly by ourselves, if possible, or with the aid of the police——"

"She's in a private dining room upstairs," the clerk whispered. She didn't wait but ran up the stairs and along a dimly lighted corridor that seemed miles in length. At last she found the room she wanted and knocked firmly. A muffled voice cried:

"Go away! You can't come in here. Please—please go away. I'll scream if you don't." She was sobbing wildly.

"Barbara!" Susan called. "It's I—Susan. Open the door."

There was the sound of scurrying feet and the door opened a crack—then was flung wide and Barbara threw herself into her sister's arms. Susan drew her inside and closed the door.

"Get your wraps, darling, and let's go home. We have all been terribly worried."

"How—who—where is *he?*"

"He's down in the bar playing a game of some sort and having plenty to drink. Hurry. Let's get out of this place as soon as possible."

"But how? The storm? There are no buses running at this hour."

"Doctor Marshall brought me here and is waiting to take us home," Susan explained. Barbara was shaking as with a chill and Susan helped her with her coat—the lovely fur coat they had given her last Christmas—and crushed the soft hat down on the tousled head. They went into the hall to meet the desk clerk and an irate proprietor. Susan was no longer frightened. She was merely terribly angry.

"Are you the owner of this place?" she demanded when the big man attempted to bar their way.

"And if I am?" he said brusquely. "What do you mean by barging in here and disturbing a guest? Who are you and what authority——"

"You'll find out and have a chance to explain a good

many things to a jury, Mr.—Mr.—Joe, is it? You and a certain Nigel Ruoff. Let us pass."

But the big man held his ground—for a moment. Susan, her arm tight around her younger sister, gave a cry of pure rage, and in the quiet of that dim corridor it sounded loud and a little terrifying. Doctor Marshall mounted the stairs two at a time and Susan felt a glow of admiration as she watched him thrust both men aside and say quietly:

"Wait in the car. I won't be a minute after I settle with these two. Hurry."

And Susan hurried Barbara down the stairs and out through the front door, along the snowy sidewalk and into the doctor's car. It was but a moment until the doctor joined them. The three were silent until they were back on the state road. It was then that a car approached from the rear, it's glaring headlights blinding them, and with its horn blaring a warning crowded them into the deep snow that was piled alongside the highway.

"And that, my friends," the doctor muttered, "was Ruoff. He'll break his worthless neck one of these days and small loss at that."

"I didn't know," Barbara moaned against Susan's shoulder.

"Of course you didn't," her sister comforted. The doctor, however, said nothing but his silence was pregnant with unspoken disapproval. Susan felt it and wondered if Barbara did, too. The car turned into Maple Avenue and it was with intense relief and gratitude that she saw the lights of home in the distance. The clock on the instrument panel showed quarter to four.

Susan hoped Dick hadn't let the fire go out in the living room. She would have the doctor give Barbara a sedative and she would tuck her into her bed herself. Only then would she feel sure she was safe. There were to be no recriminations or censure tonight. Susan was far too thankful it had ended as well as it had.

"Come in for a minute, Doctor Marshall," Susan whispered as the car stopped. Dick stood in the open door. "Give her something to quiet her and make her sleep, will you? I'll put her to bed and then we can have the coffee we

137

missed—or I can cook something. After all, it is almost morning."

In the living room the doctor opened his pocket case and handed her two small white tablets. "I'll wait down here until you come back," he said. "That fire looks good. What became of the boy?"

"Dick? I'm glad he disappeared. It made it easier for Barbara."

The doctor said nothing. Susan left him and saw that her sister was in bed and covered warmly, that her window was open, and that her light was out before she returned to the living room. Barbara had been unusually quiet and docile. Susan was sure she had suffered the scare of her life and devoutly hoped she had learned her lesson.

The house was very quiet. She crept downstairs and stood for a moment in the doorway. Doctor Marshall sat relaxed in a deep chair, his head thrown back against the worn upholstery. His eyes were closed and Susan saw the lines of weariness etched deeply in his face. She ran back to the kitchen and found Dick making chocolate. He had a plate of sandwiches on a tray and cups lined up on the table. The percolator was bubbling merrily and Susan flung an affectionate arm about the boy's shoulders and gave him a sisterly hug.

"You're a darling, Dicky," she said. "It's a shame to keep you up all night. Why don't you go to bed now and get what sleep you can?"

"How about some of this for Barb? Do you suppose she'd eat it?"

"No. Doctor Marshall gave her a sedative and, Dick—let's forget tonight, shall we? I think Barbara is through with the Halsey crowd as of now. Anyway, Aunt Charity is coming in a day or two and I imagine she will want to take Barbara back home with her—for a visit. It will do her the world of good and help her forget—some things."

"Gosh!" the boy cried. "Mom didn't tell me Aunt——"

"Mother doesn't know it—yet. I didn't have a chance to tell her last night. The coffee's ready. Will you take some in to Doctor Marshall, Dicky?" She put the sandwiches on the tray with a cup of steaming coffee and Dick left the room. Susan pressed a hand to her tired eyes. She opened the back door letting the wind blow into the warm room. She heard her brother and the doctor talking. Dick returned. He complained about the open door and closed and locked it.

"Don't you want some coffee, too, Sue," he asked, "or would you prefer chocolate? I could cook some bacon and eggs if you want your breakfast—it's almost morning."

"Not just now, Dick," Susan said and went into the living room. Doctor Marshall stood with his back to the fire, his cup in one hand and a sandwich in the other.

"Whoever made these sandwiches certainly knows how," he told her, biting into the one in his hand with relish. "This is a man's sandwich, Susan. I'll have another and then I must run. Don't try to get down to the office early, Susan. I'll manage." He wiped his lips and fingers on the napkin that covered the tray and waved aside Susan's apologies for failure to provide him with one. She went into the hall with him and watched him shrug into his overcoat.

"I can never thank you enough for what you have done tonight, Doctor Marshall," she said, her voice husky with feeling. "I don't know what I should have done——"

"Forget it, Susan. I'm glad I was able to help you." He patted her shoulder. Susan's eyes were bright with tears and suddenly she was in his arms—her head pressed against his heart. She stood for a long moment, her face buried in his rough coat while great shuddering sobs shook her slight body. The man held her close, his arms comforting, his cheek against her hair. "Darling—darling!" he murmured —or did she dream it?

"There, there, Susan," he murmured. "Everything is going to be all right. I have a notion your worries are over in that quarter."

Susan lifted a flushed and apologetic face. "For-forgive me," she gulped. "I—I don't often let go like this." She drew away. "I—I'm terribly ashamed."

"No need to be," he said almost brusquely. "Suppose I give *you* a sedative?"

But Susan shook her head. "Dick and I are going to have breakfast in a few minutes. Smell it? Will you stay and have some?" she asked impulsively.

"Thanks, my dear. I think I'll run along. I have learned

to make an hour or two of sleep do the work of ten. Better do as I suggest and stay home tomorrow—morning, anyway. I'll get along—somehow." He smiled in his own endearing way and opened the door. For once he closed it softly behind him. Susan heard the car leave the driveway and went down the hall to the kitchen where Dick was frying strips of bacon. Four brown eggs stood on the table and bread was already in the toaster which was clicking rhythmically. With a long-handled fork in his hand, Dick was turning the bacon in the skillet. Susan sat down at the table and watched him. He was growing very tall. Probably would be over six feet. She wished he wasn't so thin.

"Some girl is going to be very lucky one of these days, Dicky Trent," she said affectionately, "when she marries you."

"Aw gee!" the boy muttered, his fair face flushing. "Scouts have to be able to cook. We'd probably starve if we didn't—sometimes. You can pour the coffee, Sue. The bacon's done and it doesn't take long to fry the eggs. You could get down a jar of marmalade if you like. We might as well make a meal of it while we're about it."

He removed the bacon from the pan and poured the eggs into the hot fat covering them at once. There was much sputtering and steaming and Dick cautiously raised the lid for a split second from time to time until he pronounced them done and lifted them triumphantly to the platter on which the bacon lay in wait.

"How's that?" he asked and Susan assured him it couldn't have been more perfect if she had done it herself. Brother and sister sat facing each other at the kitchen table and after a while Dick asked:

"Tell me what happened, Sue. Where was Barb? And what did you do to that Ruoff wolf?" He grinned as he said the last two words aloud. "Try saying Ruoff wolf fast, Sue," he suggested.

"I never want to say them either fast or slow, Dick, and I feel sure Barbara won't either. Nothing had happened, fortunately. They were stuck over near Smithford—the storm, no doubt—but *we* got through all right. We left the man there and brought Barbara back with us—she was frightened and terribly sorry, Dick. That's why I want you to forget it." Susan spoke earnestly and Dick was impressed but he had to know more.

"Was he sore, Sue? How did you get her away?"

Susan thought fast. "She was as eager to come with us as we were to have her," she told him hoping his curiosity was satisfied. "As far as I know the man made no effort to stop her. His car passed us as we were coming back so I guess it wasn't stuck too badly. This bacon is delicious, Dick. More toast, darling?"

"I guess I will have another piece. Do you know, Sue, I sort of enjoyed tonight—after I was really awake, I mean—sitting in there by the fire with the storm outside and the house so warm and quiet. I wasn't really very worried about Barb. She's cute. She always lands on her feet. But I was darned glad when you came back, just the same. Mom slept through it all. Going to tell her?"

"Good heavens, no, Dick! You be careful not to drop even a hint."

"What excuse will you give for our having breakfast at four o'clock instead of seven?" he wanted to know. "She'll ask and wonder."

"I don't think so. The storm was bad—you were awake and so was I. I heard you in the kitchen and went to see what you were doing and both of us being hungry we decided to eat breakfast. That's the explanation and we'll stick to it. We'll tell no lies even though we won't tell the whole truth. I doubt if she will puzzle much over it. Anyway, she's going to be so excited over Aunt Charity's coming that I doubt if she will give it a thought. I want to tell Barbara before I leave for the office—if I can I want her to be prepared."

"What's she like, Sue—Aunt Charity?" Dick asked. "Do you remember her at all?"

"Not very distinctly. I never saw her but that once—when Father died, you know. I was only seven. She seemed like a great lady to me at that time. I remember she wore a silk dress and a hat covered with feathers. She had a wonderful fur coat, too. At least it looked wonderful to me. She was a lot older than Father, you know, and they didn't see a great deal of each other. She was an exceptionally clever business woman and is quite wealthy. I understand. Somehow, I have never cared for her—she repelled me at that time and I have never gotten over it. But of course that is silly because she is our nearest relative just as we are hers. We must try to make her visit pleasant and I hope she and Barbara will take to each other."

"You're an optimist, Sue," the boy said, grinning at her. "It's quite possible, you know, that Barb will refuse to go with her and that the old lady will want to take me home with her."

"Don't speak of her as 'the old lady,' Dick. She isn't very old. Still in her fifties, I imagine. And we couldn't let you go, darling. You are the only man we have. We couldn't get along without you."

Dick's face was suddenly older than seventeen. "You may have to before you think," he told her and Susan's heart froze.

"The war?" she whispered fearfully. "Oh, Dicky, you wouldn't enlist?"

"I'd much rather enlist than be drafted," he said defiantly. "And I'll be eighteen in two weeks, remember, and subject to the draft."

"But we're not at war."

"You keep saying that, Sue, with the whole world bursting into flames? Do you think we should sit back and let that maniac run wild over the entire world? What sort of people are we anyway? Gosh, Sue, it makes my blood boil when I hear people say—'It's none of our business. Europe's always squabbling—let her squabble.' This is more than a squabble. This is wholesale slaughter—massacre! We've got to get into it and put a stop to this sort of thing once and forever. They muffed it last time—we won't this. Mark my words." Dick's blue eyes flashed and his voice was intense and terribly sincere.

Susan's heart caught as she watched him. He was so young—so dear. She tried to shrug off this new anxiety. "Well, we aren't at war—yet, darling," she said trying to speak confidently. "Better wait until we are. Why, if worse comes to worst I may have to go myself. Nurses will be needed, you know, and it may be they would draft me."

Dick looked at her cautiously. Was she trying to sidetrack him?

142

"Let's build up the fire in the living room, Sue," he suggested. "Maybe I'll take a little snooze. You're not going to wash these dishes, are you?" and at his sister's nod he said resignedly: "Oh, well, I'll help then."

At six o'clock Susan slipped upstairs to look in at Barbara. The girl was awake and she met her sister's cheerful greeting with a choked:

"Oh, Sue. I've been such a little fool! How can you stand me?"

"Forget it, darling," Susan said gently. "We're not ever going to refer to it again. I have some news for you. Aunt Charity is coming to visit us."

Instead of being delighted, Barbara still looked forlorn. She sat up in bed and Susan handed her the robe she had flung on a chair the night before. "When is she coming?" the girl demanded.

"She may be delayed on account of the storm but her letter said in a day or two. Perhaps we shall get a wire or phone message this morning."

Barbara slipped into mules and turned to leave the room. "I'll take a quick one this morning, Sue, and be down to breakfast in a jiffy. I suppose it means cleaning the house from top to bottom."

"It does not," Susan said firmly. "You can clean the guest room and help Mother plan the meals but that's all. She will have to take us as she finds us."

Barbara lingered for a moment and then asked: "What struck her, Sue? She has never been here—well, not since I remember."

"I wrote her," Susan said feeling it better to explain. "I felt that a change would be good for you and——"

"Would cure me of being such a fool, I suppose." The girl spoke bitterly and Susan knew a feeling of deep sympathy.

"Partly that, darling," she said, honestly. "And if Aunt Charity invites you to go home with her for a while I hope you will go. You will have forgotten this—this unhappy mess when you come back. You will meet new people and see a completely different phase of life that should help a lot. You don't think I was being officious, do you, Barbara?"

"Not more so than usual," the girl replied and Susan was sure she spoke without malice.

"I'm sorry if you feel that way, Barbara," she said. "It was only that I wanted to help—to protect—guard you from things that might hurt you."

Barbara swung around. Her blue eyes were dark with misery and her face white. "Did it ever occur to you that I might prefer to fight my own battles, Susan? That this constant supervision might irk me? No, you were my big sister—a trained nurse. You knew of the evil in the world and I—I at nineteen living in the twentieth century was supposed to be pure and innocent as an unborn baby. I know the facts of life, my dear sister, quite as well and perhaps better than you do."

Susan was aghast, shocked and a little angry. "Then if you know so much why on earth did you go off with that Ruoff wolf?" Suddenly she laughed, her mirth rippling through the still quiet house and bringing Dick upstairs on a run and her mother's head from her pillow. Barbara stared at her as if she thought she had lost her mind.

"I just happened to think of something Dick said," Susan gulped, wiping her eyes. "He asked me to say Ruoff wolf fast. It is a tongue twister, isn't it?"

"What's so funny?" the boy asked from the hall.

"Nothing in particular," Barbara told him. "Sue just had a brain storm, that's all."

Dick went on to his own room and Barbara turned to her sister and asked if Dick knew. Sue shook her head.

"He thinks you were stuck in a snowdrift out in the country and we rescued you. I didn't think it necessary to hurt him or Mother either."

With a little cry of relief and shame Barbara threw herself into Susan's arms. "I'm an ungrateful brat, Sue," she whispered contritely. "You have always been so good to me —too good, that's been the trouble. Forgive me—please— please forgive me!"

And Susan, because she loved this beautiful, wilful sister of hers, held her close and assured her of full forgiveness. They kissed and Susan went down the hall to her mother's room. She explained about Aunt Charity's coming visit and felt certain of the excitement and pleasure her mother would

144

enjoy preparing for that visit. Nothing was said about Barbara and Susan volunteered no information. Mrs. Trent didn't even notice how the contents of the refrigerator had shrunk and Dick and Susan managed a fairly decent second breakfast. They were out of the house and down the street before Dick broke into one of his roars of laughter. Susan joined him with spirits suddenly light. After a night of fear and heartache and in spite of the wild November weather, a new day dawned—a bright new day. She went on to the Whittle First Aid with an eagerness that had been absent for a long time.

CHAPTER FOURTEEN

As SUSAN APPROACHED THE Whittle Plant she saw the factory carryall standing before the entrance where Doctor Marshall usually parked his car. Her steps quickened. Something must have happened at one of the Prospect Street factories. She went inside to find the hall full of men and Tommy just ready to open the door into the First Aid room. He looked up as she entered and stepped back.

"I'm glad you're here, Miss Trent," he said in relief. "Doc ain't come in yet. But you can take care o' these people. I'll stick around just in case you need any help."

Susan ushered the dozen or more men into the big hospital room and excused herself while she changed into uniform.

"What happened?" she asked as she assembled gauze, antiseptics and adhesive. "The doctor will be here in a few minutes but no doubt I can handle some of the minor injuries. Now tell me."

"Just a simple explosion," someone said sarcastically. "Just one of those lousy saboteurs you read about and never expect to come in contact with."

Susan lifted her head and stared at the speaker. "How do you know? Was anyone seriously hurt?"

"They took five to the hospital—Weiman among 'em. Prob'ly two of 'em will die though not Weiman—oh, no, not him. You couldn't kill that blasted Heinie!"

There were growls from some of the others and orders to "pipe down!"

"Then that's where the doctor is now," Susan said positively. She worked fast and efficiently and tried to fix in her mind the name of each one she treated so she could keep his record straight and up to date. One young man, Jerry Knowlton, had a bad shoulder and after she had dressed it she suggested his going over to City for an examination. But the man protested that he would be all right. His shoulder didn't hurt too much. He had perfect confidence in the way she had handled it and intended going back to work. Several of the others had already gone out to the factory conveyance there to smoke and compare notes. Susan advised against young Knowlton's return to work but failed to convince him she was right and he joined the others in the carryall. The last two had third degree burns that were more painful than serious and she quickly disposed of them and sent them away grateful and far more comfortable. She stood at a window and watched the big car leave the curb. Hands waved and faces smiled at her and she felt an upsurge of happiness that she had been able to help them.

She sorted out the cards from the file and began jotting down what information she could recall, wondering about the five who were at City and the two who would probably die. One was Karl—Karl something—why, it was Weiman! The name rang a bell in Susan's memory. He was the man who wanted a job in Assembly or Precision. The one Doctor Marshall had been dubious about. He had been transferred to the machine shop. The doctor had frowned when he heard it. Karl Weiman. She found his card and sat staring at it for a long moment. Suddenly she shivered. The men seemed to dislike him. Was it because he was a foreigner? But he wasn't. He was born in America or so his card stated. It was his parents who were foreign. But she knew that antagonism against all Germans—all foreigners—had been growing, during these last few weeks and months.

Mr. Whittle came into the room and drew a chair up to her desk. "Give me all the information you have regarding Karl Weiman, Susan," he said. "I have his shop record. I want whatever you have on him. We are getting ready for a Federal investigation of this explosion." He took the card Susan offered and the folder she found in the private file. "Doc not back yet? Expect he's going to be kept busy over at City most of the morning." Cyrus Whittle's face looked haggard. Susan knew he felt this affair keenly. She was tempted to tell him about Weiman's visit to the First Aid several weeks ago and his wish to be transferred to one of the other departments. But she decided Doctor Marshall was the one to talk about that.

"He—Weiman was injured, wasn't he? Seriously?"

"They didn't say how serious," Mr. Whittle told her, "but the men are very bitter toward him. Blame him for the whole catastrophe. I wasn't aware there had been any trouble in the foundry—personal animosity—real hostility down there. He was transferred over to Bill Andrews only because the work was lighter—or that's the story. This Weiman's a citizen. Just because his parents happen to be Austrian doesn't necessarily mean he's an enemy. But the men don't like him—call him a Heinie. I heard 'em. I was over there just now and they're all for handing him over to the police. But for the life of me I can't see what actual proof they have."

Susan felt that he was merely thinking aloud and remained silent. Somehow she wondered if the other employees knew more than they were willing to state. Mr. Whittle left without saying anything more and Susan settled down to work again. Her telephone rang and her mother reported that Doctor Marshall had called right after she and Dick had left the house. He wanted to know if she would go to the office after all. What did he mean?

"I was supposed to have the morning off, Mother," Susan said. "But I felt in my bones I should come down and it's a good thing I did. It has been a busy morning and I'm afraid I won't be able to come home for lunch this noon. The doctor is at the hospital. There was an explosion down in the machine shop this morning and I'm terribly busy. Did you tell the doctor I had already gone to the office, Mother?"

"Yes, and he said: 'I might have known she would.' Charity hasn't arrived yet but we are expecting her and we have planned a very nice luncheon. I do wish you could manage to get home, Susan."

"I'm afraid I can't, darling; but I'll be home soon after five, I hope. 'Bye."

Susan had been subconsciously refusing to give thought to the few moments she had stood in the hall of her home this morning, her head resting on Doctor Marshall's shoulder, his arms close about her and his cheek against her hair. She had refused to remember his tender voice whispering: "Darling—darling!" But now the scene rushed back to her and she blushed to the roots of her hair. She had not repulsed him. In fact it had all seemed quite natural as if she belonged there.

"But—but he's married!" she reminded herself. "He

143

has a wife! Oh, how could he—how could *you*, Susan Trent?"

A feeling of guilt and remorse sent her into her tiny sanctum where she stared unseeing at the revealing face reflected in the mirror above the dressing table.

"A fine one you are," she scourged herself. "Being so shocked at Barbara. At least Ruoff is divorced and Doctor Marshall——" What did she actually know of the doctor's marital status? Nothing at all. She covered her face with her hands. Depression seized her and a deep sadness. Was she falling in love with her chief? And what good would that do her? She had prided herself on her irreproachable behavior—her complete impersonality ,toward doctor or patient. She had felt herself safe—immune from sentimental entanglements. She bit her lip and tried to think back over the years she had worked beside him—his efficient third hand. There had been nothing in all that time to warrant her thinking—fearing that she entertained for him anything more than an affectionate regard—the esteem of a nurse for her chief. That was absolutely all—it must be and she wasn't going to be silly and imagine a lot of impossible complications. He had merely acted as any sympathetic family physician and older friend—nothing more. She had gone to pieces there before him and he had acted without thought. She would remember it that way and forget the "darling—darling." It meant nothing at all.

She heard the door open and returned to the outer room. She felt calmer and completely herself again. Jennifer Burton stood beside the doctor's desk and smiled as the nurse approached.

"The doctor still at City, Susan?" she asked and walked over to the window where she stood with her back to the room. She brushed her left hand across her thick white hair and Susan saw the blazing diamond on the third finger. She caught her breath.

"Wh-what goes on, Miss Burton?" she demanded, joining her at the window. "When did this happen and who's the lucky man?" She picked up the slim white hand of Cyrus Whittle's secretary and gazed admiringly at the gleaming ring. "He must be a millionaire—at least. Happy, darling?"

"Very happy, Susan," the woman said quietly. "But he's by no means a millionaire and never will be. He's far too kind and generous for that. Haven't you guessed, my dear? I'm sure most of the others have."

"Guessed?" Susan asked, her heart turning to ice. Was it the doctor? He used to admire this tall, lovely woman before Lorraine Howard sidetracked him. Had he returned to her? But he was already married!

"Where have your eyes been, Susan Trent?" Miss Burton laughed and pinched the girl's chin. "Why, he's been courting me for years and I—well, I was contented just to work beside him—be his closest friend and confidant—and —well, darling, he needs someone to take care of him. He needs me and—I think I need him, too."

That didn't sound like Doctor Marshall. "Do you mean ——I don't understand," Susan stammered.

Jennifer Burton caught the girl in her arms and held her in a close embrace while over her head she explained quietly—too quietly Susan felt—that she was going to marry Cyrus Whittle before the new year. She loved him sincerely and wanted nothing better than to devote the rest of her life to making him happy.

"Oh, Jennifer!" Susan breathed convulsively and whether it was in relief that it wasn't Joel Marshall or in astonishment that it was "the old gentleman" she couldn't have told. But she recovered and went on quickly and sincerely: "He's a prince, Jennifer Burton. and I—I know you are going to be terribly happy. I'm so glad for you darling. So very glad!"

Then calm, serene blue eyes of the woman gazed into Susan's for a long revealing moment before she smiled and said softly. "Cy *is* a prince, Susan—a different kind of a prince from the one I used to dream of; but the right sort of a prince for me. I'm leaving work on the first, Susan. I shall miss this place—especially, I shall miss you. Come see me."

"Is this official? I mean has the engagement been announced or are you keeping it quite until after you leave?"

"Oh, no. We aren't children, you know. We don't care who knows it now. I wanted to tell you myself ——

150

Now I must run, but I'll see you again. 'Bye"

The door closed behind her and Susan stared out the window at the bleak, wind-swept street. Perhaps she had been wrong all this time and Jennifer Burton had never been in love with Doctor Marshall. Perhaps she had imagined it all, but she had seen the strange, unhappy look in her eyes on the day she had come for an examination. Cyrus Whittle was a fine man—not so old either—and she hoped with all her heart that they would find happiness in uniting their two lonely lives.

She called Tommy and asked him to bring her a lunch and the janitor stopped in for a little chat before he left. He was full of news, most of which Susan had already heard. He was all for tarring and feathering Karl Weiman. Ashton had no use for such as he.

"But are they sure he is guilty, Tommy?" the girl asked. "After all, it might have been an accident, you know We have had accidents before—when there was no war in prospect. If he is guilty, how is it he was injured? Wouldn't he have saved his own hide?"

"Not necessar'ly, Miss Trent," Tommy insisted.
"Them Heinies'll stop at nothin'. They been trained to think it's an honor to die fer that Hitler. No, Miss Trent, they won't never think nothin' o' dyin' or gettin' killed if *he* tells 'em to do his dirty work. He's a traitor—that Weiman is—an' I hope they give 'im the works. Hang 'im at least."

Susan smiled and shook her finger at him. "Don't be so bloodthirsty, Tommy. It's a good thing the explosion was no worse and was confined to the machine shop."

"An' no thanks to him," Tommy grunted. Then as if by magic his face cleared. A broad grin spread over his thin face that never seemed to be quite clean. "I s'pose you heard about the weddin' we're goin' to have here, Miss Trent?"

"You mean, Mr. Whittle and his secretary? Yes, I heard about it and I think it's wonderful, don't you?"

"Sure. He's a gentleman an' she's what I call a lady—always the same wherever you meet her an' always speaks no matter where she sees me. If I'm dressed up she ain't no pleasanter 'n if I'm wearin' greasy overalls. I like Miss Burton an' she'll make 'the old gentleman' a fine wife."

"Tommy," Susan asked curiously, "why does everyone call Mr. Whittle 'the old gentleman'? He isn't old."

"I know it. I worked here when his father was 'the old gentleman' an' I heard they called *his* father that, too. I guess it sort o' goes with the job. Sort o' becuz he's head o' the concern—sort of. They started callin' this one 'the young gentleman' while his father was alive, but it didn't take hold, so they called 'im 'son' until his old man passed on an' then he was 'the old gentleman' even when he was less'n forty. Queer, sort of, ain't it, how a name'll stick? What you want I should bring you fer lunch, Miss Trent?" he asked glancing at his huge wrist watch. "Gotta git back on the job. Can't stand here gassin' all day—though I like it fine," he finished gallantly.

"Oh, bring me a chicken sandwich and a pint of milk, Tommy." She handed him the money and watched him cross the street to the nearest lunch room. He didn't enter there this time, however, but moved on down the street to one farther along. Why was that, she wondered idly. When he returned with the bag containing his purchases she asked him and he was very explicit.

"Gotta sassy girl in Chet's," he explained. "She's new an' I don't like her. Ain't nothin' but men in Shaw's place an' they treat me right. I bet you'll find they put butter on the sanwidge, Miss Trent," he told her. "I called 'em down in the other place fer skimpin' on the butter an' she bawled me out. Well, she's lost 'em some danged good customers 'cuz I told the bunch here an' they will trail over to Shaw's now. S'long, Miss Trent. If you ever need me, just sing out." It was his parting advice each time he left her and Susan felt she could depend on him in most emergencies.

Two girls from the accounting department strolled in just as she was about to start her lunch. It was nearly twelve and she thought she might hear from the doctor during the noon hour and wanted to be free for any instructions he might give her.

"Gosh, Sue," Hilda Somers cried as soon as she was inside the room, "did you see Miss Burton's ring? Isn't that a sparkler, though? I bet it set 'the old gentleman' back a pretty penny."

"Well, he's got it," the other said with something like malice in her voice. Susan stared at her for a moment. Was it possible she was jealous or angry at the news? "Well, he has," she reiterated, catching the nurse's curious gaze. She was an attractive girl—tall and buxom. Susan recalled that she had been doing special work for Mr. Whittle and that the office manager had found it necessary to deflate her ego because of it. She was young—not more than twenty-five or six. Surely—But the girl went on spitefully: "Jen Burton's been trying hard enough to land him. What does he see in her, anway? She's old."

"Oh, but she isn't," Hilda contradicted. "It isn't age that's made her hair white. Is it, Sue?"

Susan shook her head. "No. Her hair has been white since she was in her teens. It's a family—heritage, I almost said. I love it."

"That's an old gag, Susan Trent," Sybil Grant insisted. "I've never yet heard a gray-haired woman acknowledge she was old enough for it. Phooey! I'll eat my shirt if Jen Burton will ever see fifty again."

"Then start nibbling, Syb," Hilda advised, "because I happen to know she's only around forty and after all Mr. Whittle must be in his fifties. I think it's swell. I'm all for it because I adore them both."

"You would!" Sybil muttered.

"Don't notice her, Sue. Her head hasn't returned to normal since 'the old gentleman' gave her a special job and she's sore because Harold hasn't got around to getting her a ring—yet, if he ever intends to." She laughed teasingly and Susan was astonished at the look of hate in the other girl's eyes although she managed a grin. They were supposed to be pals, Susan wondered.

"Perhaps he'll give *you* one," she said pointedly and Hilda blushed and shook her head.

"That's your trouble, Syb," she told her without malice. "You're so darned jealous of any girl Hal's even the least bit pleasant to. You're too possessive. No man likes to feel he's in chains—before he gets ready to welcome them. I've told you and I've told you but you simply won't listen. First thing you know—"

"You!" Sybil interrupted angrily. "You know so much

about men why don't you get one of your own instead of trying to grab mine?"

"Girls, for heaven's sake—" began Susan but Hilda laughed and gave her friend a little shake.

"Don't be a goon, Syb. I don't want your precious Harold—wouldn't take him as a gift." She winked at Susan and went on: "Sue will think you're nuts. Come on, I'm meeting Mom and Jacky at the Cafeteria for lunch this noon and have got to hurry. I'll be seeing you after lunch, Sue— and without the lady Jeremiah—I hope. S'long."

The door closed after the two and Susan picked up her neglected sandwich and broke it. It was just as Tommy had said. There was butter on it and plenty of white meat. She wondered why Hilda and Sybil had dropped in to see her. Of course she had always known that the First Aid was a sort of clearing house for mental and spiritual as well as physical ailments but just what was the matter with Hilda Somers? She appeared to be all right. Before she could raise the sandwich to her mouth, Mr. Whittle came in almost bashfully. Susan put down the portion of sandwich and held out her hand.

"Congratulations, Mr. Whittle!" she cried, "and I do mean congratulations. Jennifer is a grand girl and I'm sure you are going to be very, very happy. I don't know when I have heard more thrilling news."

The man beamed on her and pressed the hand she extended in both of his. "Sort of put the explosion and saboteur gossip into the background, hasn't it, Susan?" he chuckled. "A good thing, too. Buzz-buzz-buzz—and black hostile faces. Jen's and my news sort of perked 'em up. now we see smiles and everyone's on his job again. Yes, my dear, I'm a lucky man and no one knows it better than I do. What she can see in an old duffer like me—"

"Hush!" Susan cried. "I don't think Jennifer would like hearing you call her future husband names, Mr. Whittle. And you are anything but an old duffer. We all think you are the finest man in the world--the kindest, most thoughtful and the fairest. There! Does that give you any idea of your standing in the community, Mr. Whittle?"

The man laughed. His eyes were very bright. "I think you must have a bit of Irish blood in your veins," he said a little huskily, "but I like to hear you say things like that. It makes me very proud. Have you heard anything from Doc?"

"Not a word; but he will probably call during the noon hour or will be here this afternoon. You don't know anything more—about the accident, I mean?"

"Only that the five hospitalized seem to be holding their own. If it's humanly possible to save them, Doc will do it. Federal men are down at the Prospect Street factory going over the place with a fine tooth comb. They'll find out if it's sabotage or just another accident. Either is bad enough but I hope to heaven it's the last. This war, Susan! Where will it end?"

"Does anyone know?" the girl asked.

"I suppose not. There's my George with the car—always prompt. Can I bring you back anything, Susan? Have you enough lunch? Can't be having you sick, my dear."

The door closed once more and Susan reached for her sandwich and hastily took a bite as if in fear she would be prevented again. The milk was cold and she sipped it slowly and wished she had asked Tommy to bring hot coffee instead. The telephone shrilled and she swallowed with some difficulty. Even then her voice must have sounded thick for the doctor said, "I bet you're eating lunch, Susan. I'm sorry."

"It's quite all right," she told him. "How is everything?"

"Not too good. Weiman is the one we're most worried about. He doesn't respond too well; but we're hoping. The others will probably come along all right. How have things been with you? Anything you couldn't handle?"

"Not so far. I tried to get Jerry Knowlton—you remember him?—I tried to get him to come over to City for an examination; but he refused. I did what I could and he professed himself satisfied. But I wish you could have seen him."

"Just what are you worried about? What was his trouble? I can't seem to remember—there were so many."

"His shoulder. It looked almost like a gunshot wound—something went right through his shoulder, gouging out a chunk of flesh. I bathed it thoroughly and dressed it with sulfaminol and bound it up. He refused to wear a sling and apparently his arm muscles were not affected—at least not at that time. Later they will probably stiffen considerably. But he insisted he was going back to work. What could I do? I hope his foreman sent him home."

"Probably did—if he couldn't work. Don't worry, Susan. He'll be all right. Anything else?"

For a moment Susan didn't answer. The engagement was uppermost in her mind just then and she blurted it out before she realized the time might be inauspicious.

"Yes," she said quickly, "although this hasn't anything to do with the explosion—not that one anyway. Can you stand a shock, Doctor?"

"I can stand anything. Out with it. It isn't—not—"

"Yes. Then you guessed? I was stupid. I didn't. Isn't it wonderful, Doctor Marshall? He was just in here and—he's such a dear— I'm pretty excited— And the ring, Doctor—wait 'til you see it!"

"Is that all?" The doctor's voice was brusque and Susan felt rebuffed. She was sorry she had mentioned it at this time. It was quite apparent to her that he did care for Jennifer Burton. But he was married!

"Shall you be back here today, Doctor?" she asked crisply, determined to match his mood.

"I hardly think so—unless, of course, something comes up that you can't handle. You might get in touch with those on the sick list. I'll call you later and you can report as to their progress. I think, perhaps, I can be of greater assistance right here at City. Most of the flu cases here are our own people, but I'll try to get to the others—the most serious—sometime this evening. It will no doubt relieve the minds of their families to know that. Goodbye."

As Susan again picked up the remainder of her sandwich her thoughts veered away from Doctor Marshall and his mood to Alan MacDowell. She wondered if he had gone home. He had appeared somewhat distrait last evening as if he had many things on his mind. What a contradictory, unpredictable man he was! The memory of his kiss here in the office discomfited her. It was such an unwarranted thing to do and she hadn't liked it one bit. It had completely put him beyond the pale as far as she was concerned. She had been quite prepared to like him at first and later she had tried to overlook some of his, to her, unattractive traits; but

156

she knew now that she wouldn't care in the least if she never saw him again. What was the matter with her? Why should she be so critical—so squeamish?

She wondered if, perhaps, he had fallen for Barbara—that it was because of her absence last evening that his visit had been so flat—so disappointing. It might easily be, but she felt certain her sister had no real interest in him and yet how could she be sure? What a ninny she was to spend her time in conjecture! And anyway Barbara would go home with Aunt Charity and probably stay on indefinitely or until she grew tired of it. Perhaps then she might even find something to interest her—a job, maybe. She devoutly hoped so.

It was Barbara who telephoned just after Doctor Marshall came into the office at quarter of five that afternoon. He looked tired—almost haggard—and his greeting of Susan was almost unfriendly. Susan, who had been waiting for his telephone call, passed over the list of absentees against which she had noted each one's condition as reported by the family. His eye ran down the page and he slipped it into his pocket without comment.

"How is Karl Weiman now, Doctor?" Susan asked tentatively.

"No change."

"Have you heard if the Federal men discovered anything important?"

"No. Oh, Whittle said something about there being no signs of sabotage as far as they had gone—"

"He will be happy about that," Susan said. "He was terribly concerned—that's why he and Jennifer announced their engagement to sort of ease the situation—at least, that's what I understood. I seemd sort of odd—'

"Great Scott, Susan," the doctor interrupted testily. "That engagement has been pending for months. Why was there any need of making a public announcement? Everyone knew it—"

"Well, *I* *didn't* know it,' Susan snapped. 'When Miss Burton came in here this morning and I saw her ring I—why, I thought it was you"—she paused for a moment a little frightened at what she had said but went firmly on—"she was engaged to."

157

For a moment the doctor had nothing to say. "Why on earth should you think a crazy thing like that, Susan Trent?" he demanded. "I admire Jennifer just as I admire Lorraine Howard—that doesn't mean I want to marry either of them. One can admire a fine picture or statue or public building or even a view without wanting to own it. I suppose being in love yourself makes you infect everyone you see with the same virus. I suppose now you'll be laving us."

"Leaving? Why should I and what makes you think I— I'm in love, Doctor Marshall?" Susan was puzzled.

It was then that Barbara telephoned to say Aunt Charity had arrived and was anxious to see Susan. When would she be home? Couldn't she get a ride with someone or catch a bus? Barbara sounded excited.

"I'm sorry, Barbara," she said. "Im afraid I may be a little late. You see the doctor has just come in and there are quite a few reports and matters to straighten out. Don't worry darling. I'll be along soon."

"You don't have to stay, Susan," the doctor said, still stiffly. "And I might as well tell you now that I don't think it would be a very good thing for you to continue working here after you are married."

Susan stared at him as if she feared he had lost his mind. "What—I don't know what you're talking about. I have no intention of leaving—unless you—what ever gave you the idea I was getting married or that I was even in love? I'm not and that answers both questions."

A sudden smile lightened the austerity of the doctor's face. "Either you're crazy or I am," he said "What was all that talk of someone 'such a dear' being in the office and you being so all-fired happy about it?"

"Mr. Whittle came in—after Jennifer had told me about their engagement and I congratulated him. And he *is* a dear, Doctor Marshall, and I̶ am happy for both of them. They're grand people!"

"O-oh!" was all the doctor said and after a moment he suggested driving her home. The whistles blew as Susan was changing into street clothes and while Doctor Marshall put out the lights and locked the door, she left the building and went down the short walk to where his car was parked beside the curb. It wasn't until then that she remembered about Hilda Somers. She had said she would be in to see her after lunch. She hadn't come.

CHAPTER FIFTEEN

THERE WAS LITTLE CONVERSATION during the short drive from the office to Susan's home in Maple Avenue. Both the doctor and nurse were tired. It had been a hectic day and Susan looked forward to dinner and a quiet evening at home. She sighed contentedly.

"I suppose in spite of your being dog-tired you'll be going out with that pseudo-architect," the doctor muttered as the car turned into Maple Avenue. "I thought he had gone. What's he hanging around here for?"

"Aunt Charity Trent is here, Doctor Marshall," Susan told him, ignoring his ill temper.

"Oh, she is? And who may she be?"

"My father's sister. I hope she is taking Barbara home with her for a while. It will help her forget last night—"

"Good heavens, Susan!" he exclaimed as he slowed up on nearing her home. "Do you want her to forget? Seems to me the memory of that close shave should remain a lesson to her all the rest of her life. Haven't you yet learned that your sisterly concern and coddling aren't good for her? Don't try to salve that affair, my dear. The girl needed a lesson and—"

"I know she did; but recriminations and scolding aren't going to help right now," Susan said. "You can't reach Barbara that way. She just hardens. No, I'm trying to act as if it never happened—"

"We-ll," the man murmured, "you're her sister and should know how to handle her; but I'm all for using a firm hand—"

Susan laughed jeeringly. "You and your firm hand! Why, you're the gentlest, most sympathetic person I know and you wouldn't hurt a fly if you could avoid it. You see, I know you, too."

The doctor looked sheepish for a moment and laughed as he drew up at the curb. A young man was running along the sidewalk and paused beside them. It was Alan Mac-Dowell. The doctor swore under his breath and neglected to reply to Susan's thanks and good night. His car sped down the street and Alan stared after it.

"Wasn't that your doctor, Susan?" he asked. "I somehow

thought it was you in that car. I was coming to meet you and walk you home. Didn't you leave sort of early?"

"Five. Barbara called and wanted me to come straight home as we have company, so the doctor offered to drive me—"

"I think the man likes you, Susan," Alan teased.

"I hope he does," the girl answered, "because I like him, too. He's a grand man to work with."

"Nothing more?"

"Won't you come in, Alan?" Susan asked, refusing to answer what she felt was none of his business. "When are you leaving Ashton?"

The young man laughed ruefully. "Here's your hat. What's your hurry?" he said. "I should like to come in for a moment if I may, Susan," he said. "I should like to say goodbye to the others."

Susan moved toward the steps and they entered the house together. Barbara rushed to meet her sister. Her eyes were shining and her whole face radiant. Susan heard Alan catch his breath then draw back as Barbara stared at him in surprise in which lurked a shade of annoyance.

"O-oh!" she said not too cordially. "Hello, Alan. Come into the living room and meet Aunt Charity Trent. How did you get home so quickly, Sue?"

"Doctor Marshall drove me. Come along, Alan," she said and led the way into the living room where an imposing, white-haired woman sat knitting beside the roaring fire. She looked up and smiled as the three entered.

"Susan, my dear!" she exclaimed with what the girl felt was sort of belated enthusiasm. "How good to see you again! Come kiss me at once."

Susan obediently did as she was bidden. She felt no affection for this woman who had preferred to remain a stranger all these years.

"This can't be Richard—no, of course not. Richard is still a child."

Barbara giggled. "Better not let him hear you say that, Aunty," she warned. "No, Aunt Charity, this is a friend of Susan's. Alan MacDowell—Miss Trent

Alan took the smooth white hand the visitor extended and said:

302   161

"I merely stopped in to say goodbye to you all." He looked at Barbara but she turned to the door.

"I'll call Mother," she said and hurried away. Alan's eyes followed her and Aunt Charity watched him disapprovingly.

"And what do you do, young man?" she demanded. "And where are you going? Don't you live here?"

"I'm an architect, Miss Trent, and I'm going home to Illinois for Thanksgiving and then I expect to spend the next few months or a year in Marydale which is some twenty miles east of Ashton." He turned as Mrs. Trent came into the room. Barbara was not with her.

"So you are leaving us, Alan?" Mrs. Trent said, offering her hand. "It has been pleasant knowing you," she went on, "and I hope whenever you are in Ashton you will drop in to see us."

Susan accompanied him to the front door. She, too, held out her hand and saw that his gaze was over her shoulder toward the kitchen. Why had Barbara disappeared?

"Goodbye, Alan," she said, "and good luck!"

The door burst open and Dick catapulted into the hall, shedding cap and Mackinaw in one swift movement, "Hi, Alan!" he greeted the man standing somewhat uncertainly beside Susan. "Coming or going?"

"Just leaving, Dick, and I want to say goodbye. You've all been swell to me. If you ever come over to Marydale, look me up." Still Barbara didn't appear and Dick looked from his sister to Alan curiously.

"Tell Barbara Alan is leaving, Dick," Susan said, "and then come back to the living room. Aunt Charity is here."

Dick went down the hall toward the kitchen, shouting: "Barb—oh, Barb!' Evidently she wasn't in the kitchen and he repeated the performance at the back stairs. There was no answer. He returned to report he couldn't find her and Alan's face fell. Susan felt sorry for him.

"I'll tell her goodbye for you, Alan," she told him kindly. "She is very excited at the prospect of visiting Aunt Charity. Please forgive her."

Even after that he was some time taking his departure but at last the door closed behind him and Susan breathed a sigh of relief. Barbara came out of the study.

"Do you think that was kind, Barbara?" Susan asked her.

"Kind? He's your friend, not mine," she pointed out. "And don't remind me of the date I forced upon him—back when I was a crazy fool, Sue, I'm trying to live that down. I'm not at all proud of my old self, darling; but—" Tears filled the blue eyes and she gave her sister a hug. Dick's expression was skeptical and Susan hastened to squelch any chance of an argument.

"Come in and meet Aunt Charity, Dick," she said, taking his arm and drawing him with her into the living room. Barbara trailed along.

"And this is my son, Richard," Mrs. Trent announced proudly.

"Hi, Aunt Charity," was the boy's greeting, bending his tall height to take her hand. She drew him closer and lifted her face as if expecting him to kiss her, but the boy drew back. Barbara giggled.

"Dick's a woman hater, Aunty," she explained and Dick glared at her.

"Aw, I am not!" he growled.

"What a fine family you have, Margaret," Aunt Charity said almost enviously. "It's a pity we haven't kept in closer touch all these years. I suppose you are still in school, Richard?" she asked although the entire situation had been explained to her. "And college? I suppose you will attend Hamilton as your father did?"

Dick said nothing. His mother murmured that she must see the dinner and Susan said she should go up and change into another frock .Only Barbara seemed completely at ease. Dick escaped after Susan and the two mounted the stairs together.

"Gosh, Sue!" the boy complained when they separated at his door, "I bet she'll make me go to Prep or have a regular tutor. Darn it, why doesn't she mind her own business? I won't do it."

Susan shook her head at him. "Forget it, Dick. She wants Barbara. I don't think she'll bother much about the rest of us."

"Well, I hope not," Dick said and disappeared into his own room only to whisper loudly from the half-open door:

"I hope she doesn't intend spending Thanksgiving with us, Sue."

Susan hoped not either. She still didn't particularly like her Aunt Charity and marveled at Barbara's enthusiasm. Perhaps, though, she would improve on acquaintance. She dressed quickly and went down the back stairs to the kitchen where her mother was finishing preparations for dinner.

"We're having dinner at the usual time, Susan," Mrs. Trent said. "Barbara urged me to wait until seven; but you had practically no lunch and I explained to Charity that you must be hungry. Anyway, we are plain people and she might as well realize it first as last. I don't intend putting on airs—"

"Now you're shouting, Mom," Dick applauded as he crept in to stand close to the table and snitch a piece of celery which he munched loudly. "Let's be ourselves—if she doesn't like it let her lump it and beat it for home."

"Now, Dick, she's a guest and we must all try to make her visit pleasant. After all, she's your father's sister and Susan invited her."

"I'll hold that against you 'til my dying day, Susan Trent," he grinned reaching for a cheese straw.

"Stop it, Dick!" his mother cried. "You'll spoil your dinner and we are having a rolled roast of veal with your favorite stuffing."

"And can't I smell it, though," the boy assured her. "But having company spoils it for me. I can't eat all I want to."

Barbara came down the hall and demanded to know why everyone had deserted them. She caught hold of Dick's arm to drag him with her. "You've got to come, Dick. She'll think it queer if everyone stays out here. I explained that Susan always helps Mom with the meals but you don't, you big lug! Come on and be nice to her. She's really a darling —when you get to know her."

Dick went reluctantly and Susan heard her mother sigh. For all Barbara's repentance she was still a thoughtless, spoiled child. Perhaps visiting Aunt Charity would be the best thing for her, for Susan had an idea her worthy aunt had ideas of her own. She might not be too easy to live with.

164

The dinner was delicious as the Trent dinners always were. Aunt Charity seemed to enjoy it and Dick, while somewhat subdued, managed to make an excellent meal. Susan and her mother washed and dried the dishes. Dick disappeared into his father's old study. Aunt Charity complained of being tired after her trip and Barbara accompanied her to the guest room and remained for most of the evening. Susan and her mother spent a quiet evening before the fire in the living room quite as if the wealthy Miss Charity Trent were not spending a few days as a guest in their home.

"You don't like her much, do you Mother?" Susan asked, watching the busy fingers wielding the shining knitting needles. Mrs. Trent was knitting socks for the Red Cross and prided herself on holding the record for the Ashton Chapter.

"Why—why, Susan!" she stammered.

"Well, I don't either," the girl said frankly. "I never did."

"She is different from us, my dear," her mother excused. "Really, I don't actually dislike her. I just don't feel that I know her—I never did. She never cared for me even as long ago as when your father and I were married. I was very young and she felt I was not a fit wife for her brother. Then, again, she never quite forgave me for refusing to give you to her. My dear," the flashing needles were still and the knitting dropped to her lap, "what should I have done—what should we all have done without you, Susan?"

"I wouldn't have gone with her, darling," Susan said. "I had a will of my own even then. She seems to have completely captivated Barbara, hasn't she? Aren't you glad, Mother? It will no doubt do her the world of good and somehow I have a hunch Barbara will appreciate you and her home a great deal more after she's been with Aunt Charity a while. Don't worry. I asked for it and we must look upon it as providential—it will wean her away from that Eve Halsey crowd. By the way, did Barbara go over there this morning?"

"No," her mother said, picking up her knitting. "Barbara told me she had quit that job. She was fed up with the whole crowd. Those were her words, Susan, and it was certainly a big relief to me. It was just as you predicted, my dear. She found out what Eve Halsey was really like. At least I suppose that was it. Anyway, she has left them and I am very thankful."

It was after ten when Barbara came downstairs. Her mother rolled up her work. Susan raked aside the ashes in the grate and turned out the lights. Dick had gone to bed with a glass of milk and a plate of cookies.

"I'm going home with her, darlings," Barbara told them ecstatically. "Isn't it thrilling? She's going to take me to New York after Thanksgiving and we'll see some good shows and do a lot of shopping and oh! I'm so excited I don't expect to sleep a wink tonight." The telephone rang and Susan saw her sister flush, then pale. "You answer it, Sue. If it's for me, tell him—them I've gone to bed. I won't talk to anyone—not anyone at all," and she fled down the hall to the kitchen.

Susan told the woman on the line that her sister could not talk to her. She recognized Eve Halsey's voice and went on coolly:

"Barbara will not be coming to you any more, Mrs. Halsey. Good night!" She replaced the instrument in its bracket and turned to her mother. "That's that," she said thankfully. "I think I shall have a glass of hot milk. Won't you join me?"

But her mother shook her head. "I'm tired, my dear, and think I shall go right up. Don't be long."

Susan went into the kitchen where she and Barbara drank their milk and laughed and talked companionably as they hadn't in months. Later they went upstairs together and Susan gave her sister an affectionate hug as they parted for the night. Her heart was light and she fell asleep as soon as her head touched her pillow.

The roaring of the wind wakened her before her alarm sounded next morning. Somewhere a loose shutter was banging intermittently and she sat up and turned on the light beside her bed. The curtains at both windows billowed wraithlike into the room and the shades flopped and buckled with every fresh gust of wind. She reached for her robe on the foot of the bed, slipped into mules and scurried across

166

the room to shut both windows. Her clock said five-thirty. Outside it was inky—not a star to be seen; even the street lights appeared to be out. Back in bed she snuggled down beneath the blankets for a few minutes, then raised her head to listen. Someone was up. Her teeth chattered as again she slipped into robe and slippers and opened her door. A light was on in the hall but not a door was open. She went to the head of the stairs. There was a light in the kitchen. She bet her mother was already up. She ran downstairs to find her mother fully dressed mixing waffle batter.

"For heaven's sake, Mother," she scolded, "why on earth are you up at this hour? It isn't six yet."

"I couldn't sleep, Susan," her mother explained. "So, when I heard the clock strike five I thought I might as well get up. Charity warned me that she was an early riser."

"Oh, she did, did she? Then I'd better get Barbara up and Dick. I'll run up and dress and be down in a jiffy. I'm sorry, darling; but it will soon be over. She won't stay long, I'm sure."

"And then Barby will be gone, too." There were tears in her mother's eyes and Susan was remorseful.

"And safe from Eve Halsey's influence, don't forget," she reminded her.

"But she has already broken with them, Susan," her mother pointed out. "That worry is over."

"Is it?" Susan asked. "You don't know that crowd, Mother, and I'm afraid you don't know Barbara, either. She is not contended here at home and you know it. This visit will help, I'm sure. Now for heaven's sake don't try to stop her going—let her see we are glad she is to have the opportunity."

"*You* didn't want it," her mother reminded her and Susan felt she was almost angry. She went upstairs and once again she wondered if it was always wise to try to protect those one loved from facing facts—from looking realities in the face—recognizing ugliness and evil as they actually exist. Perhaps if her mother knew what she did, she would be only too eager for this visit.

She roused Dick to see to the furnace and Barbara to get her bath out of the way before Aunt Charity should need the bathroom. She dressed with her usual efficient haste and

167

went down to set the table in the dining room and help her mother where she could. They breakfasted at six-thirty because that was Aunt Charity's usual hour and Barbara surprisingly, helped with the dishes so that Susan could have a little visit with their guest before leaving for the office.

The visit, however, wasn't too successful. Susan resented criticism of her mother's management and what her aunt called Dick's lack of ambition. Miss Trent admired Barbara and wanted to do things for her—"give her a taste of life as it should be lived." Susan bit her lip and held her quick temper in leash. Her aunt asked innumerable questions about her work at the Whittle Plant and about Alan MacDowell. She wanted to know what he was to Barbara, if anything, and to her. Susan told her coolly that he was a mere pleasant acquaintance. That he meant absolutely nothing to either of them and that it wasn't at all likely they would see much of him in the future.

The visitor appeared satisfied with her explanation and when Dick announced it was twenty of eight and they "had better scram," Susan knew a vast relief. She slipped into outdoor wraps and the two left, hurrying out into the cold, blustery November morning, thankful to be away from the inquisitive, domineering aunt whom Susan had invited to be their guest.

"Gosh, Sue," Dick cried as they bent before the gale, "I hope she doesn't stay long! I get prickles down my spine when she talks to me."

"Fraidy-cat!" his sister jeered. "I don't think she will stay long. I heard her complaining to Barbara that she liked her own things about her and that Dorcas brought her a cup of tea at exactly six every morning."

"So English, don't yuh know!" Dick scoffed. "Well, she didn't get any tea this morning and I doubt if she will pass out because of the omission. Barb's welcome to her with all her money. But we'll miss Barb, won't we, Sue?"

"Of course, but I don't imagine she will stay long—not more than a few weeks. I wish, though, she were going to be home for Thanksgiving. It will be the first time we have not all been together on a holiday."

"Aunt Charity is expecting us there for Thanksgiving.

Sue. I heard her trying to talk Mom into it. I have a notion Mom doesn't want to go."

"No," Susan said. "I doubt if she will. We'll have our own turkey and stay right here in our own home. I couldn't go, anyway. We are far too busy. It would mean a part of Wednesday and Thursday and Friday morning even if we came right home. No, even if the rest of you went, I couldn't."

"Good!" the boy said as he left her at the corner. "See you at lunch, Sue."

And Susan walked on toward the Whittle Plant, her step light and her heart less troubled than it had been in many months. Somehow she had an idea things were going to work out all right. She saw Doctor Marshall's car at the curb and quickened her pace. Hilda Somers came down the street to meet her and the two fell into step.

"I want to see you about something, Sue," Hilda said, linking her arm in that of the nurse. "I want to enter training at City Hospital in February. Do you think I can?"

"I don't know why not," Susan said. "You're a high school graduate and over eighteen, aren't you? As far as I know you're perfectly well. Why don't you send for an application? That's the best way to find out."

"Oh, I think they would accept me alright," Hilda said. "But I'm wondering if I can stand it—if—well, I'm a little squeamish—about blood, Sue, and people dying and—well, doing all the intimate things a nurse is expected to do. How did you get by?"

"Well," Susan answered slowly, "it's hard work. Don't let anyone ever tell you it isn't. There are times when things go against the grain—when you're nauseated at the sights and sounds and smells—when patients are ornery and cantankerous and you wish you dared shake some sense into their heads—when your feet hurt and your head and back ache and you long for home and mother and a good cry; but, Hilda, that passes. You watch a surgeon perform a miracle—a doctor put new life into the hopeless, perhaps dying—you aid in bringing new lives into the world and give help and comfort to those appointed to die. You are a part of it all—a trained nurse! It's a hard life, Hilda; but a glorious one. I love

it! I wouldn't do anything else. It gives you something—
a strength of character— an understanding of human frailty
a sympathy and courage that no other training can—
unless it's that of the doctor or surgeon. Maybe I'm pre-
judiced, Hilda; but I think you will make a fine nurse
and if there is anything I can do to help you—you know
I'll be only too happy to do it. Have you spoken to Mr.
Hammond about leaving?"

"No. I don't want to leave until I'm sure I'll be accepted. I have a pretty good job here and I may not be so
lucky again. Please don't say anything about it, Sue. I just
wanted to hear what you thought of the idea. Thanks a
lot. I'm going to send for that application this very day."

She opened the door and followed Susan into the hall
where they separated, Hilda running up the stairs to the
main offices. It was just eight o'clock as Susan walked
into the First Aid room. Doctor Marshall was at his desk
and answered her blithe greeting without lifting his eyes
from the paper he held in his hand. Susan went on into
her dressing room wondering if, perhaps, it was another
anonymous letter.

CHAPTER SIXTEEN

THE DOCTER STILL SAT AT HIS DESK when Susan returned to the room and as she passed him she heard him sigh as if in exasperation.

"Is it another one, Doctor?" she asked as she drew out her chair. She had in her hand the bottle of formaldehyde taken from the surgery cupboard. Tommy had asked for it last evening as she and Doctor Marshall were leaving the building. She saw that the bottle was nearly full and moved it to the extreme edge of her desk. Their supply was getting low and she would have to put in an order for more. "I should think whoever is sending those letters would grow tired especially when you take no notice of them. Is this one bad?"

"She's dragging you into it now, Susan," he said gruffly.

"Me? Why me? And how do you know it's a she—a woman who sends them?"

"Not sends them necessarily; but writes them. Because I know the woman. That's why," he muttered.

"You do?" Susan exclaimed in astonishment. "Then—"

"Here. Read it yourself." He passed the note to her. "I don't know how she knew about our being at Joe's Lodge though," he added as Susan began to read.

> "You been sticking your neck out much too often, Doctor Marshall," the note read. "Joe's Lodge is plenty unhealthy for you and the dame. Better keep your trap shut in the future or it will be shut for you—and permanently."

It was unsigned.

"Why, it's threatening, Doctor Marshall," Susan said. "What does it mean?" She examined it again. "It's different from the others somehow."

"That's just it. I must have stumbled on something, but what? And what had she to do with it? How did she know we were at Joe's Lodge?"

"I don't understand it," Susan said. She was puzzled.

This note was different. The others warned him against women—any woman; but this one warned against—what?

Doctor Marshall got to his feet and walked to the window where he stood with his back to the room.

"It's a long story, Susan, and not a pretty one," he began when the door opened and two men entered. Both were strangers and Susan saw that one, the shorter one, wore a black patch over his left eye. Doctor Marshall swung around.

"Good morning," he said casually. "What can I do for you?"

"We'll tell you, Doctor," the taller of the two said smoothly, "and—who knows—perhaps we can do something for you."

"Yes?" the doctor questioned. "In what way?"

The newcomers turned to stare at Susan and the taller one nodded to the other. "Watch the dame, Chuck," he said out of one corner of his mouth and the man with the patch turned to examine Susan with interest.

"What is all this?" the doctor demanded truculently. Susan felt goose-pimply and got to her feet. She stood leaning on her desk near the telephone. It would be a simple matter to knock it over if necessary. Something about these men frightened her. There was a sinister gleam in the tall man's eye and he kept one hand in the pocket of his overcoat. She had seen something like this in the movies. She wondered if it was a holdup. But why?

The tall man moved back and turned the key in the lock. It was then that Susan knocked the telephone off her desk, breaking the fall with her knee so there was no sound as it fell. It dangled there close beside her, completely hidden by her white starched skirt. She heard Ida say "Yes?" and again "Yes?" then silence. The shorter man stared at her suspiciously. Susan's gaze was blank even if her knees shook.

"What is all this?" the doctor asked again, his voice unnaturally loud and strident. He had seen Susan's maneuver. The tall man replied, his hand moving threateningly in the pocket of his coat:

"You'll soon know, Doctor Marshall. We want some information from you and then you're going on a nice, interesting trip—you and the dame. First—hand over those letters and make it pronto. See?"

"You're either drunk or crazy," the doctor shouted. "Get out of here—both of you. You'll find I don't scare easily." He reached for his telephone and the shorter man sprang toward him. Susan screamed.

It was only a moment later that she heard the sound of running feet. Someone turned the handle of the door, then hammered on the heavy panels.

"What's up, Doctor—Susan? What's going on in there? Let us in," Cyrus Whittle shouted.

"Keep still!" the tall man hissed.

Susan thought she must be dreaming. This couldn't possibly be happening to her in First Aid in broad daylight. Doctor Marshall stood quietly beside his desk. Now the man with the patch was pointing a gun directly at her while the taller covered the doctor. Suddenly the telephone on the doctor's desk shrilled. Nobody moved. Now there was more and louder pounding on the door, anxious voices and the sound of many feet. The tall man slipped silently to a window and opened it wide, his gun never wavering.

"Be quick, Chuck," he hissed and again Susan knew a feeling of unreality. "I'll take care of these. Out you go. Join you in a minute after I finish with this—this bird." The short man straddled the window sill, pausing long enough to pull his cap low over his eyes.

The pounding on the door became more insistent; but it was of heavy oak and showed no evidence of giving.

"Open this door!" someone shouted. And another and heavier voice demanded: "Open in the name of the law!" It was then the man with the patch disappeared through the window and the taller one, gun in hand, sprang toward the doctor who suddenly crouched as if to make a running tackle. Too frightened and angry to scream, Susan's hand reached out for something to throw. Her fingers touched the bottle of formaldehyde. She threw it with all her might directly at the intruder's head where it landed a glancing blow then crashed against the steel cabinet behind him, smashing into fragments and deluging him with the powerful disinfectant. He let out a shriek of agony and rage and the doctor, coughing and sputtering and weeping

173

from the fumes, was upon him. Just then the lock on the door gave way and a dozen or more men fell into the room among them the traffic cop from the four corners. Doctor Marshall now had the gun and stood over the stranger who appeared to be completely out. Susan collapsed in her chair. It had all happened in a matter of seconds.

"Get the other one!" the doctor wept, mopping his streaming eyes. "He can't be far off. Probably has a car out there some place."

The officer had handcuffs on the intruder and although he, too, was weeping, managed to maintain a look of calm efficiency. Two bookkeepers from upstairs had rushed outdoors. Cyrus Whittle had already called the police station. The tall man was coming to, sputtering and weeping, coughing and cursing, while the policeman grinned down at him, apparently enjoying himself.

"You use pretty strong perfume, brother," he accused the prostrate man and sneezed loudly. The intruder shook his head as if to rid himself of the terrible fumes. His eyes were red and swollen shut. His hair was wet, and his shoulders. Susan felt a spasm of pity. She reached for a towel and went toward him. The officer held her back.

"It won't kill him, Nurse," he said grimly, "more's the pity."

The culprit screamed a string of oaths. The officer's hand silenced him.

"Shut up, you!" he ordered. "Now you're going for a nice ride," as a siren sounded. "Up you go, and no funny business." But the man refused to get to his feet and it took the combined efforts of four members of Ashton's police force to take him out to the patrol car.

"I wonder if they caught the other one," Susan asked.

"My dear child, you should go home at once," Cyrus Whittle said solicitously. "This has been a severe shock."

Susan shook her head. "I'll be all right when we get this room aired," she told him. "It all seems unreal to me, Mr. Whittle. Why should anyone want to hurt us—the doctor and me? What have we ever done——"

Doctor Marshall, who had been nursing his bruised knuckles, turned from the open window where he had been trying to get his breath. He grinned down at her.

174

"Of course it had to be something like formaldehyde you threw at him, Susan."

"It was the first thing my fingers touched. I thought he was going to kill you, Doctor Marshall. I was scared and I was mad, I guess. I didn't know what to do."

"You did plenty, my dear," he told her. "Look, Mr. Whittle. She knocked the telephone from its bracket so our girls at the switchboard heard everything that went on. Our Susan's a clever girl as well as a great pitcher. Gosh, Susan," he went on quizzically, "you look as if you had been on a week's spree and heaven knows how I look."

"Worse," Susan told him.

"How about shutting up shop and both going home for the day?" "the old gentleman" suggested.

"This will pass off in an hour or two," the doctor said. "Better put on your coat, though, Susan. It's darned cold here and we've got to keep these windows open. Oh, Tommy!" as the janitor appeared in the hall with mop and pail, "you're psychic." Tommy grinned. He didn't know what it meant but if Doc said it, it must be all right.

Susan slipped on her coat and closing the office door went out into the hall and sat on the stairs. It was there a reporter found her and began asking innumerable questions. Susan referred him to the doctor who remained at his desk. The young man opened the door and stepped back as if pushed by a violent hand.

"Whew!" he cried and hastily shut the door. Susan laughed. The reporter didn't. "Say, it's enough to strangle a fellow. Is that what you tossed at the guy? Why couldn't you have used something less malodorous?" Doctor Marshall came into the hall.

"Did you want to see me?" he asked still rubbing his knuckles. Susan feared he might have injured his hands—his clever, surgeon's hands that meant so much to them all.

"I'm from the *Ashton Sentinel* and want the story of what happened here this morning. Mind answering a few questions?"

"I scarcely know myself," the doctor said. "It all happened so quickly and so unexpectedly. These two men barged in here and threatened us, Miss Trent very cleverly dropped the telephone so that the line was open and the switchboard girls heard the commotion and took steps. When our reinforcements arrived they found the door locked. One of the men went through the window, the other prepared to rush me; but again our plucky nurse here tossed a bottle of formaldehyde in his direction, scored a direct hit and the intruder passed out. That's the story, brother, and you can fill in the details. I'm sure neither Miss Trent nor I want to think any more about it."

"But why? Why should they try to harm you two—perhaps murder you? There must be a motive, Doctor," the man insisted.

Doctor Marshall shrugged. "That's for the police to find out. Your guess is as good as mine. I'm a doctor—not a detective, my friend."

"Your hands—they look pretty well battered, Doctor," the man persisted. "Mean to say you just stood there and let Miss Trent handle the situation? I don't believe it."

The doctor laughed. "Oh, I threw him off balance and landed a right hook on his jaw that sent him to sleep; but it was after Susan tossed that bomb." He chuckled and stared at his hands.

"Do they hurt terribly, Doctor?" Susan asked.

"Oh, no," he replied nonchalantly. "They'll be all right—probably sooner than our visitor's jaw. The other chap was lucky. I wonder if they caught him. Have you heard?"

"Oh, yes, they got him all right. Not the cops, though. Two fellows from the bookkeeping department nabbed him just around the corner from here. I wonder if I could talk to them."

"I wouldn't know. Suppose you go see Mr. Whittle. Right up these stairs——"

"You wouldn't be trying to give me a bum steer?" the reporter wanted to know. "I've been enjoying myself right here." His eyes gazed admiringly at Susan.

Tommy came out of the big First Aid room and grinned as he saw the young man with the notebook on his knee.

"It's all okay now, Doc," he said. "I scrubbed 'er good." His gaze at Susan was worshipful and the girl smiled and shook her head.

"You don't want to belive all you hear, Tommy," she

told him and got to her feet. "We'll have to send for your formaldehyde now. We're down to our last quart and intend hoarding that. But you'll have it by this afternoon —tomorrow at latest. I'll order it at once."

"Okay, Miss Trent," the janitor said and departed with his mop and pail. The reporter went up the stairs almost reluctantly, and Susan and the doctor returned to their desks. Almost at once people dropped in for treatment of minor ills, and the morning passed without either again mentioning the anonymous letter. Susan went home to lunch and found Barbara feverishly packing for her approaching visit. She had helped herself to the best of her sister's belongings and Susan made no objections. She was far too upset over the morning's excitement to mind anything so trivial. It was at luncheon that her mother noticed her red eyelids and commented on them.

"Do you suppose you should have glasses, Susan?" she asked worriedly.

"Oh, no," the girl replied. "Somehow a bottle of formaldehyde got broken and nearly smothered us. It's all right now, however, and my eyes will be better by evening."

"I can't understand how you are contented to work under such conditions, Susan," Aunt Charity murmured, helping herself liberally to the salad and cold chicken. "It doesn't seem to me an especially refined career for a girl of your breeding."

Susan smiled. "I'm probably a throwback, Aunt Charity," she replied, "I love my work."

"She has a very good position, Charity," Mrs. Trent said.

Susan noticed her brother watching her and hoped he hadn't heard of the morning's fracas or if he had that he would not mention it here at home. They were scarcely out of the house after lunch, however, when the boy began asking questions. Susan tried to make light of it; but she knew he was worried.

"How do you know this is the end of it, Sue?" he asked.

"End of what, darling?"

"How do you know they won't try again—to get the

doctor and you? I don't know why the papers had to ring you two into that Nash affair anyway. Probably the gang are sore because of the investigations. Gosh, Sue—I wish they hadn't. You be careful—don't——"

"All right, Dick. I'll be careful. I won't accept rides from strangers or even talk to people I don't know. Not that I ever did; but I'll promise not to if it will make you happier."

"You can joke about it if you want to but just the same there are some pretty tough hombres in the world."

Susan laughed. "This isn't the wild and woolly west, darling," she pointed out. "I never saw either of these men before. Run along, Dicky, and don't worry about me."

"Gee, Sue," her brother said admiringly, "you're smart. I'm darned proud of you—so is Judge Martin. He said he was coming over to tell you so."

The day was cold and blustery with frequent flurries of snow. It stung her face and hurt her red, swollen eyelids. She walked fast and reached the office before one o'clock. The doctor looked as if he had not moved since she left at noon. A pile of letters was before him and he was frowning somberly as he contemplated them.

"I'd turn these over to the police if it weren't that she has implicated you in that last note," he said as she returned from changing into uniform.

"Not by name, Doctor," Susan reminded him.

"But I'm not in the habit of going to Joe's Lodge and the police will want to know just why I went this time. Does it seem possible it was only night before last, Susan?"

"And that will bring Barbara into it."

"It would and we can't have that. And yet, if Joe's mixed up in some shady business—something sinister—the police should know it."

"Why the police? Why not the FBI, Doctor Marshall?" Susan suggested. "I don't think I should mind if they knew. Everything you tell them is definitely hush-hush. This is a job for them, anyway, it seems to me. There is more to this than meets the eye. Why not call them? Some of them must be here now. They haven't finished their investigation of that explosion. I've been thinking

178

about those letters and I don't think a woman's responsible. She may have been a tool; but——"

The doctor looked at her admiringly. "Our minds work alike, Susan," he said. "That's just what I shall do. Get "the old gentleman" on the phone and ask him to send the two Federal men down here when they come in. If we're interrupted we can always go into the surgery."

If Susan wondered why the doctor didn't call himself, she made no comment but did as he asked. As it happened the Federal men were in Cyrus Whittle's office when she called and "the old gentleman" promised to send them down at once. They came, two solid, impressive looking gentlemen in ordinary business suits, who looked like anything but detectives. It seemed they were just about to make an appointment with the doctor for a little private investigation regarding the Nash case. Doctor Marshall laid all his cards together with the pile of anonymous letters on the table. It was then Susan heard the story of his youthful marriage that was not a marriage at all. Of the accident that crippled, in mind and body, the woman he thought was his wife and killed the man who was her lawful husband. He told of the financial debacle that caused her father's suicide immediately afterward and of the years he had paid for the woman's care in a Smithford sanatorium.

"Quixotic, I grant you; but I had once thought I was madly in love with her—and she had no one else—or so I thought; but lately, I have been wondering." He spoke quietly, almost somberly.

He displayed the letters and told how the writing of one was like that of the woman he had married. When they reached the last letter they asked questions and it was then that Susan took a part. She explained how her young sister had been working for Mrs. Halsey and how Mrs. Halsey's brother or cousin, she wasn't sure which he was, a Nigel Ruoff, was bringing Barbara home two nights ago and instead had taken her to Joe's Lodge and Café. It was a stormy night and she had become worried at her sister's absence and then some woman telephoned to say that Barbara had eloped with this Ruoff. Of course Susan hadn't believed that; but became alarmed and called the Halsey house where Mrs. Halsey professed to know nothing about it and someone in the background had said Ruoff had probably taken her to Joe's Lodge as that was where he took "all his sweeties"—those were the words.

Susan told how she had called Doctor Marshall and they drove there under difficulties as the roads were slippery and almost impassable in places. She didn't know Ruoff by sight but the doctor did and she went in to the clerk and demanded the number of the room that had been assigned to her sister. When the clerk refused to give her the information she had given him a glimpse of a medal the doctor had handed her for that purpose. It looked official and did the trick. She ran up the stairs and found her sister hysterical. As they were going down the stairs the clerk and Joe—she thought it must have been he—tried to stop them and she had cried out and Doctor Marshall came upstairs and hustled them away. That was the whole story exactly as it had happened. She hoped Barbara's name would not have to be mentioned but something should be done about that place.

"Something will be done, Miss Trent," one of the men told her. He had been taking rapid shorthand notes and reached for the doctor's telephone. He talked softly and rapidly for a moment and the two stood up and one of them said:

"You have given us much valuable information. We'll see you both again." They went out and a few minutes later Susan saw a car draw up before the building and the two men got in. Behind it were two other cars and Susan cried.

"Doctor Marshall! They're full of policemen! Do you suppose they are going to raid that place—Joe's Lodge?"

The doctor seemed not to hear. His face was worn and his eyelids were still red and swollen. "I can't figure out how Carlotta is mixed up in this, Susan," he muttered.

"Perhaps she isn't," Susan said, for want of something to say.

"Yet it's her writing on that one note. I could swear to it. And she was always jealous of my friends—not that she has any right, of course, but she probably fears that if I marry she will be cut adrift. But I have taken care of that. Poor Carlotta!" He sighed and Susan felt an upsurge of rebellion. Why should he feel so sorry for her? Why should this woman spoil his life? She was less than nothing to him—had not the slightest claim on him—and yet her evil influence was like a miasma, some noxious spell, upon him.

"What is she like—this pseudo wife of yours, Doctor?" Susan asked angrily. "Is she so compelling that you can't break away from her?"

The doctor stared at her for a moment then said almost with astonishment: "I haven't seen her in a dozen years, Susan. She refuses to see me and I haven't insisted. I have nothing but pity for her—poor, misguided, unhappy creature that she is."

"Why do you let it worry you, Doctor Marshall?" Susan demanded impatiently. "Sometimes I think you're far too easy—too soft-hearted. People impose on you—like—like this Carlotta. Why do you let them?" She wished she could jar this man—rouse him to the realization that he was being used—made a monkey of by a bitter, unscrupulous woman.

The shadows of the November day deepened and Susan switched on the lights. Outside snow was coming down in earnest and wind swirled it into eddies before it hit the ground. Win Brighton stood at the four corners as was his custom at this time of day and directed traffic. The shops all along Main Street glowed with light. Even the headlights on some cars were turned on. It was four o'clock. One hour to go. She stood at the window and watched the storm for a long moment.

"Of course you know I'm in love with you, Susan," the girl thought she heard the doctor say and swung around to stare at him in disbelief. His eyes were on his hands resting on the desk. He was gazing at them critically and Susan knew she must have been dreaming. She eyed him warily as she sat down.

"Don't you?" the quiet voice asked.

"I beg—— Wh-what did you say? I'm afraid I don't understand," the girl stammered.

"I said I was in love with you," he repeated, not looking at her. "Perhaps this is neither the time nor the place to mention it; but I felt I wanted you to know."

"But—but——" Susan began.

"I am a dozen years older than you, Susan," he went on.

"Oh, stop it—stop it!" she cried and ran to him. "Is it a tragedy for you to love me? Is it?" she demanded.

His head lifted. "Yes," he said sadly. "Can't you see that it is?"

. "Why?" Susan asked truculently. "If it is, then I'm a part of it, because I love you. There!" she cried. "We might as well have a good one while we're about it, only I don't feel the least bit tragic. Doctor Marshall. I feel—" Tears choked her and she fled into her tiny private room and slammed the door.

She didn't know how much later it was that she heard the ringing of the telephone. Her watch said four-thirty. She listened but could hear little. Doctor Marshall called to her. He must be standing close to her door.

"I'm going over to the police station, Susan, and won't be back tonight. Be sensible, my darling," he went on in a lower tone. "I love you."

Susan beat her hands together in exasperation. "You dear, stupid idiot!" she stormed as she heard the office door slam behind him. "You darling, blind imbecile! What am I going to do with you?" But from the glow in her gray eyes and the radiance of her smile it was apparent she was confident of the efficacy of the proposed treatment.

CHAPTER SEVENTEEN

THE TRENT HOME ON MAPLE AVENUE was silent. The house was dark with the exception of one room—the big living room, where a bright fire glowed in the grate and a softly shaded lamp illumined one corner. On the hearth-rug before the fire, Susan Trent sat, her eyes dreamily fixed on the burning logs. Barbara and their guest had gone to bed long ago. Barbara and Aunt Charity were leaving on the seven-forty-five train in the morning. Mrs. Trent was tired and a little sad. Dick, fortified with the usual apple and plate of cookies, had somewhat reluctantly followed his mother upstairs. Susan had begged him to keep his curiosity in check until after their guest had gone. He had confiscated the evening *Sentinel* as soon as the boy brought it and at Susan's suggestion had whisked it out of sight. In the excitement of Barbara's preparations for leaving, no one missed it. He and Susan had answered what telephone calls had come and as far as Susan knew the others were entirely unaware of what had happened that day in the First Aid room at Whittle's.

Now she sat with her head back against the davenport and reviewed the day's hectic events. The *Sentinel* had given no explanation of the attempted attack, merely mentioning the fact that an investigation was in progress. She heard the hall clock boom eleven times and yawned sleepily. She really should go to bed even if she didn't sleep. Tomorrow was another day and probably would be as hectic as usual, though she hoped not in exactly the same way. She tried not to think of Doctor Marshall's declaration. Perhaps he was sorry he had made it. What did he mean by asking her to be sensible? Was she ever anything else? Sometimes she wished she weren't—that she were frivolous and foolish like other girls.

A car slid up to the curb and stopped, but she heard nothing until someone knocked not too loudly on the front door. Her heart missed a beat. She sprang erect and stood for a moment irresolute. Suppose it was another of that gang of hijackers. She switched on the porch light and opened the door a crack then swung it wide.

"I know it's late, Susan," the doctor said apologetically. "But I couldn't wait—I had to see you tonight. So many things have happened—such wonderful things, my darling." He opened his arms and Susan, unhesitatingly, went into them and for a long ecstatic moment there was no sound except the crackling of the fire in the living-room grate. Eons, or perhaps it was only minutes, passed and the dropping apart of a log in the fireplace separated them. Doctor Marshall shed his overcoat and followed Susan into the room where he drew her to a seat beside him on the davenport.

"Now tell me everything," Susan said leaning her head comfortably against his shoulder, quite as if she had been doing it for years.

He kissed her hungrily and sighed in sheer content. "It is almost unbelievable, darling," he began. "First of all, Carlotta has been dead for ten years."

Susan sat up abruptly. "Then who—what——"

"And Ruoff is or was her husband supposed to have been killed in that railroad crash some sixteen years ago. I know it all sounds fantastic, but that's how it is. Ruoff owns the sanatorium in Smithford where Carlotta went after the accident—he bought it from the original owners just before she died. It all began—that is, our part of it—with our insistence that young Nash was the victim of an assault and putting the police on the case. They got two of the gang and immediately you and I were tagged for extinction."

"But why did they kidnap a college student, Doctor? What possible use could he be to them?" Susan asked.

"Someone pulled a boner there," the doctor went on. "They took the wrong Nash. It was Gregory Nash, a Princeton senior, son of the famous scientist, Hannibal Nash, they wanted. It seems Greg and his father have been working on a formula that is of great interest to our government, and, incidentally, to others as well. The FBI suspected this and have been praying for a break. Well, Susan, we gave it to them. You see, this Ruoff owns Joe's Lodge and Café and is the American brains of a huge international narcotic, bootleg and smuggling ring that deals in everything evil from opium to unlawful immigration. The FBI have been after him for years and are jubilant they have at last caught up with him. And by the way, his name isn't Nigel Ruoff, but Conrad Schiller—wanted on three continents."

"Then Barbara——" Susan whispered shudderingly.

"Barbara was lucky, Susan," he said. "Thank God it was such a beastly night! It prevented him or his henchmen from completing their diabolical job of whisking her away."

"And Eve Halsey?"

"She has acted as a front for years but just how seriously she is involved I don't know. It seems that Joe's place is or was a hideout for a lot of Ruoff's rotten pals, Susan. The police have suspected evil doings there for years but have never been able to put their finger on anything definite. It took our innocent entry into the place to bring it into the open." He sighed again and relaxed against her shoulder.

"But he was the husband of the famous sculptress—Sonia Mousorsky, too. She divorced him, didn't she?"

"He got around—that bird," the doctor said grimly. "Perhaps he married other women—he's the type they fall for."

"And he has been exploiting you for years. That accounts for those letters—to keep you from forgetting your assumed obligations. But haven't you seen her—this Carlotta—in all that time?"

Doctor Marshall shook his head. "I tried to once—just at first; but she immediately became violent and the nurse in charge advised against future attempts. I had thought I might help her, you see, but—well—it was a relief to me. All feeling for her had vanished—I couldn't even hate her. It was as if she never had been."

"And those men wanted the letters—but just why——" Susan asked.

"Incriminating evidence—dynamite—apt to explode quite unexpectedly and with devastating results. They were taking no chances."

"I'm so mad, Doctor Marshall," Susan cried. "I could—I wish it had been Ruoff who got that dose of formaldehyde!"

"He'll get a dose of something far worse, my dear,"

the doctor told her. "One of the men informed me there are some pretty serious charges against him—not the least of which is murder. They are trying to trace some connection between Karl Weiman and that gang and it wouldn't surprise me to hear he's a part of it. Your eyes are like stars, Susan. Have you thought of me—thought of what I said to you, darling?"

Susan shook her head. "Of course not," she retorted. "Why should I? You were so terribly tragic—so unhappy about the whole thing that of course I simply put it all down to the fact that what had happened had made you slightly delirious."

His arms held her close against his heart and his cheek was pressed to hers as he rocked her back and forth as he might a child. Susan murmured softly: "What ever became of Lorraine Howard, Doctor? How I detested that woman! You were infatuated with her, weren't you?" she accused and attempted to draw away from him, but he refused to let her go and she settled back. "Well, are you going to explain that?"

"There is nothing to explain, Susan," he told her seriously. "Lorraine is a very beautiful girl but I never really liked her. There was something she lacked—something that you have and that no other woman in the whole world possesses."

"Not even Carlotta?" Susan asked and held her breath.

"That was all very long ago, my darling," he murmured against her lips. "I was a callow youth not yet twenty. She was older, beautiful and sophisticated. I hadn't a chance—not that I'm blaming her entirely and yet——-"

"There you go," Susan cried indignantly, pulling back from his arms and staring up at him with angry gray eyes. "Making excuses for her. She was a bad woman, Doctor, and you ought to know it. She deceived you from the very first and how can you sit there and condone her actions?"

"I love you when you scold me—when you try to defend me, darling," he murmured. "I love your protective manner—I have missed so much—so many years." His face saddened. "I wish I were no older than you, Susan.

Twelve years is too great a disparity between us. I must seem pretty ancient to you."

"Nonsense!" Susan said sturdily. "I have never cared, particularly, for boys, Doctor Marshall. Somehow they bore me."

"Do they? Did that architect—what's his name—MacDowell bore you, Susan? I was insanely jealous of the fellow——"

Susan laughed and patted his hand which now looked much better than it had earlier. "I don't think I was ever really in love before, Doctor," she said gravely. "Oh, there was a time I *wanted* to be in love—I guess every girl goes through that stage; but after I came to the First Aid, I, somehow, lost interest in boys—you see, I was closely associated with a man—a real man—and I mean that, darling. I think I have loved you for years—even if I wasn't aware of it."

There was a long blissful silence and the hall clock boomed twelve times. Susan lifted her head.

"Hungry, darling?"

"At a time like this?" he teased. "Have you no romance in your make-up, Susan Trent?"

"Well, are you?"

"Oh, I could eat a bite or so if you insist," he laughed. "Want any help?"

They went to the kitchen where Susan made chocolate and the doctor sliced cold chicken and bread and put them together with lettuce and mayonnaise.

"Do you know, Susan, I didn't have any dinner today. Somehow we were so busy and so interested that it was late when we left the station. Then I had to go to the hospital to look at three of our pneumonia patients so that I forgot all about eating.'

"Is this enough, Doctor?" Susan asked. "I could make coffee and open a can of homemade soup."

"I would like the coffee, darling, if it isn't too much trouble; but the sandwiches are fine."

Susan put a teaspoonful of instant coffee into a cup and poured hot water over it and he eyed her with delight. "Clever gal! I've heard of that stuff but never happened to have any of it. Cream and two lumps of sugar, my

187

dear. Swell!" he applauded as he tasted it. "I think we should keep some of this at the office, don't you?"

"We use this when we're in a hurry," Susan explained.

Doctor Marshall set down his cup. "When will you marry me, Susan?" he asked ardently. "Let it be soon, darling."

Susan stared at him in consternation. "Marry you—— Why—I—I—can't marry you, Doctor Marshall," she said, her eyes enormous in her suddenly white face.

The man turned to her in amazement. "What? What do you mean? Why can't you marry me?" His hands fell on her shoulders and he gave her a little shake. "What do you mean, you can't marry me?"

"I can't marry anyone," she murmured. "I have heavy obligations. Three people are dependent on me— Mother —Barbara and Dick." She turned her head away from his searching eyes and tried to shrug off his hands; instead he drew her into his arms.

"You foolish girl," he murmured adoringly against her hair. "Don't you realize that from now on your people will be my people? It is going to be my sacred privilege to carry all your burdens and obligations. I have no family of my own. My father died several years ago and my mother when I was a mere lad. Don't you know that I shall adore belonging to a family? Even if you insist we live right here in your home—I shall agree—that's how mad I am about you, Susan Trent. Oh, Susan—Susan——" he whispered and found her lips.

"I am not a wealthy man, darling," he said after a moment, "but there will be plenty for us all—even college for Dick, if he wants it. I sort of have an idea," he went on seriously, "I may be of help to that young brother of yours. After all, he is getting to be a young man and he needs an older man to help and advise him. We're going to be friends, Susan, you'll see. Now let's set the date. We don't have to wait for a lot of folderols, do we?"

"If you mean a wedding, Doctor——"

He interrupted her with the order that he was no longer her chief and she should learn to call him Joel. Would she do that? An audition, please.

"Just the same, Doc—Joel," she began, when he stopped her further argument in the way that had become surprisingly delightful to them both. Susan drew away and shook her head at him. "All right, Joel," she told him, "you asked for it. If you feel like saddling yourself with my family—— Oh, darling! You're so sweet!" she cried and buried her face in his breast.

It was some time later that the decision was reached to lay the whole plan before Susan's mother and let her decide everything. Susan felt sure it would please her.

Susan stood in the open door and watched him drive away. She was in a daze of happiness. It was all so wonderful—so unbelievable! Automatically she put out the lights and mounted slowly to her room. She prepared for bed in a dream and knelt in a wordless prayer of love and gratitude. She expected to spend the remainder of the night planning for a future as the wife of Joel Marshall, her adored chief. But suddenly she heard the unwelcome sound of her alarm and sat up in exasperation. It simply could not be morning yet. Why, she hadn't even closed her eyes! It was exactly six o'clock. She smelled coffee and bacon and something else that might be hot rolls. She found robe and slippers and slipped down the hall to the bathroom. Fortunately it was empty and she showered quickly and was back in her room before she heard her brother's warning whistle as he left his room.

It was early when Barbara and Aunt Charity left for the station, Dick accompanying them. There were tears from Mrs. Trent and a few from Barbara but on the whole everything went off better than Susan had feared. By the time her sister returned the Ruoff incident would have been forgotten—or so she hoped. The two on the front porch looked after the departing taxi and Susan slipped her arm through that of her mother.

"I'm sure she will have a lovely visit," she predicted, "and come home in a more contented frame of mind."

"I hope so—I shall miss her, Susan. She has been like her old sweet self these past few days. Charity doesn't deserve her——" She wiped her eyes and followed Susan back to the dining room where the girl poured fresh coffee into their cups and sat down opposite. She was determined to tell her mother her news. It might help soften her grief.

"I have something to tell you, Mother," she said, almost shyly. Her mother raised her head and looked at her.

"You—you sound different and you look different, Susan!" she said in surprise. "Why, you're lovely this morning! You were always nice-looking, Susan; but now you are positively radiant! What is it?"

"I'm in love, Mother—Doctor Marshall loves me. He wants me to marry him. Do you mind?"

"Why—why—I don't know, Susan," her mother said doubtfully. "I don't know him—except quite casually. When did all this happen and why haven't you told me he was paying you attention?"

"I didn't know it myself until yesterday, darling," Susan laughed. "It was last night we—were sure——"

"Last night? I don't understand."

He called after you were in bed. There is a long story leading up to all this, darling, but I haven't time to tell you now. Dick hid last night's *Sentinel* in the desk in the library. After I have gone suppose you get the paper and read about what happened yesterday morning at the First Aid. I'll be home for lunch at noon and will explain everything then. In the meantime, think over what I have just told you—about Joel and your elder daughter. I'm so excited I don't see how I can ever settle down to business this morning; but I must not be late just because I'm going to marry the chief." She laughed softly.

"But, Susan," her mother demurred, "how are we going to get along without you?"

"We thought perhaps we could live right here with you. But Joel is coming tonight to—well, to get acquainted and talk things over. Oh, Mother, you're going to love him! He's so sweet!"

Mrs. Trent looked bewildered for a moment, then said brightly: "Invite him for dinner, Susan. What does he like particularly—in the way of food, I mean?"

Susan's smile was one of relief. She felt sure her mother was now safely past the crisis. She would be too busy to miss Barbara much. She was leaving the house when Dick ran up the front walk. "Gosh, Sue, I thought maybe you had gone," he cried. "Why did you shove that job off on me? I want to hear all about what happened yesterday—don't leave out a single detail. Did you tell Mom?"

"Yes, I told her," his sister said. "Oh, not that! I told her something else. If you're going along with me now I'll tell you my piece of news first."

It was characteristic of Dick to object to his sister's thought of marrying, but he admired Doctor Marshall—he was a swell guy. He had been fine about Barbara and if Susan had to marry someone he supposed it might as well be the doctor. This was a concession coming from Dick and Susan was relieved. She added details to the *Sentinel* story.

The day was dark—November was living up to its reputation; but to the girl in the blue coat and hat hurrying along on winged feet it was summer, warm and sunny. Her heart skipped a beat as she saw the familiar car at the curb in front of the Whittle building and, unconsciously, her pace quickened. The two Federal men were in the office when she entered it a few minutes later and Doctor Marshall's greeting was, of necessity, almost perfunctory. Susan experienced a letdown feeling. "I shall be at the Police Station for a while this morning," he said as she passed his desk. "I have made a list—look it over, and perhaps there is something you can add to it. I shall probably be back here by noon. If not I'll phone you. Right?"

"Right," Susan said and went on into her dressing room. She heard the outer door open and close and came out in time to watch the doctor's car, with the three men in it, leave the curb. It was then she opened the folded paper the doctor had given her. It contained just one sentence written a dozen or more times. "I love you!" She was smiling happily when the first patient opened the office door. Her day's work had begun.

THE END

www.ingramcontent.com/pod-product-compliance
Lightning Source LLC
Chambersburg PA
CBHW020636180626
46816CB00003B/988